THE HUNTING DARK

Also by Lynn Hightower

The Enlightenment Project novels

THE ENLIGHTENMENT PROJECT *

Novels

HIGH WATER
THE PIPER *
EVEN IN DARKNESS *
THE BEAUTIFUL RISK *

The Sonora Blair series

EYESHOT
FLASHPOINT
NO GOOD DEED
THE DEBT COLLECTOR

The David Silver series

ALIEN BLUES
ALIEN EYES
ALIEN HEAT
ALIEN RITES

The Lena Padgett series

SATAN'S LAMBS
FORTUNES OF THE DEAD
WHEN SECRETS DIE

**available from Severn House*

THE HUNTING DARK

Lynn Hightower

SEVERN
HOUSE

First world edition published in Great Britain and the USA in 2024
by Severn House, an imprint of Canongate Books Ltd,
14 High Street, Edinburgh EH1 1TE.

Trade paperback edition first published in Great Britain and the USA in 2024
by Severn House, an imprint of Canongate Books Ltd.

severnhouse.com

British Library Cataloguing-in-Publication Data
A CIP catalogue record for this title is available from the British Library.

ISBN-13: 978-1-4483-0995-5 (cased)
ISBN-13: 978-1-4483-1572-7 (trade paper)
ISBN-13: 978-1-4483-0996-2 (e-book)

Typeset by Palimpsest Book Production Ltd., Falkirk,
Stirlingshire, Scotland.

Praise for Lynn Hightower

"Readers will compulsively turn pages to see how it all ends"
Publishers Weekly Starred Review of *The Enlightenment Project*

"Lynn Hightower is a brave, bold writer – and this spooky, suspenseful masterpiece could be her best yet. Super-recommended!"
Lee Child on *The Enlightenment Project*

"Superb"
Publishers Weekly Starred Review of *The Enlightenment Project*

"This taut psychological page-turner has a gripping, tightly woven plot and is jam-packed with head-spinning twists and an overwhelming sense of menace that will keep readers riveted"
Booklist on *Even in Darkness*

"Psychologically compelling"
Kirkus Reviews on *Even in Darkness*

"Fast pacing, a strong and sympathetic main character, and a genuinely frightening supernatural being keep the pages turning in this ghostly thriller"
Booklist on *The Piper*

"A stand-alone nightmare that will keep you awake till the last page and maybe even afterward"
Kirkus Reviews on *The Piper*

About the author

Lynn Hightower is the internationally bestselling author of numerous thrillers including the Sonora Blair and Lena Padget detective series. She has previously won the Shamus Award for Best First Private Eye novel and a WH Smith Fresh Talent Award. Lynn lives in Kentucky, in a small Victorian cottage with a writing parlor.

www.lynnhightower.com

FOR ROBERT

Acknowledgements

Great appreciation to my agent, Matt Bialer, and everyone at Severn House Publishers, most especially my brilliant editor, Rachel Slatter; Martin Brown, Senior Brand Manager; and Michelle Duff, Sales Director. To the brilliant and creative Marla Carlton and Axel Muench of Specto Design. To Carl Moses, LCSW, for insights on catatonia and traumatic fear in children, to Jenn Moses for cheering me on, and Patrice Rayssac for spitball sessions in French. To my valiant German Shepherd, Leah, who kept me safe while writing this book.

And to the resilient and brave individuals who were willing to tell me the story of their experiences with things inexplicable and malevolent.

The United Nations has called forced mental health treatment a human rights abuse.

Entre deux eaux . . . *Walking between two worlds.*

This story is inspired by true events. The place where this happened is real. The location is disguised, and you will not be able to find it by reading this book.

Darkness calls to darkness, and there are no mistakes in the universe. That is the danger of a place such as this, a place that calls to you when you are vulnerable. The house, the land around it, the trees and the woods that circle it – there is a definitive line of demarcation, isolating it from the rest of the world. Take that as a warning. Because squirrels, snakes, birds . . . *life*. It stays on the other side. So should you.

Go there, and you will slowly notice you are not alone. And whatever it is that is there has nothing to do with life . . . *as we know it*. And whatever this is . . . *it is conscious*.

An experienced exorcist will tell you that 80 percent of their work involves the dark infestation of a house. This is not about a haunting or the presence of ghosts. This is about ridding a home of a cluster of dark spiritual entities whose goal is to drive the inhabitants of the house to suicide, psychosis and malevolent acts.

It starts small. Like a ripple in the water. Testing the surface. Aware of you. Monstrous beneath. Hiding where you cannot see.

It comes softly at first. Like it anticipates you. But is not quite ready for you to know it is there.

If it sent you a text – and it does send texts – does that surprise you? it would say . . . *Looking forward.*

If you live in a house infested with dark, unseen things . . . they watch you. *All. The. Time.*

A house is a powerful thing; it can be a lure. For people who want a home of their own. A kitchen where they can make coffee, grab breakfast, cook dinner. A private bathroom, a little bit of yard for the kids to play in, a bed to sleep beside someone they love, feeling their warmth, the way they roll up in the blankets, the way they wrap their arms around you after a very long day.

In the Amish countryside of Kentucky, between the medium-sized town of Bowling Green and the very small town of Osage, there is a house. Built in the seventies. Ranch style. Added on. The rent is cheap, *very cheap*, and it is beautiful all around that house.

There is not a basement, but there is a crawl space with random odd and disturbing things. A child's shoe, tiny. One white glove, caked with dirt – the kind of soft cotton glove a woman would wear to church, at Easter, in the sixties. No one would wear a glove like that now.

There are no rats. No mice. No spiders. Nothing *lives* in that crawl space. Nothing can.

If you are looking for privacy and quiet, this is the place. You will hear . . . nothing. Nothing *natural*. No birds singing. Deer will not range through your garden; there won't be a possum waddling through your backyard in the middle of the night. Animals are smarter than humans. This is the kind of quiet that you will love until it starts to worry you – and to make you afraid. And then you will hear things you cannot believe.

This is tornado country – storms tear through on a regular basis. And it is Bluegrass country, where the grass is lush and the farms are thriving – cattle, horses, sheep. The local Amish will keep a distance from you, and the local workmen will not come to your house. They will tell you right to your face to move, but they won't tell you why. They all say the exact same thing. *You need to get out.*

If you have a dog, the dog will run out of the house and refuse to come home, unless you leash it and drag it back. If you have a cat, it will settle outside the door of a specific bedroom in the older part of the house where you are never ever comfortable. It will stay there for hours on end. Watching. Cats are braver than you think. They protect you in ways you cannot imagine. They are hunters in their heart. Predators. And in a house like this, a predator is exactly what you need.

There are odd and mysterious geometric symbols on the wall in a child's bedroom. Red dots, circles, trapezoids, triangles and hexagons. Drawn by a child with a steady hand and an innate knowledge of geometry. Over and over again. Repeated in patterns on the walls, on the door and in a circle on the floor around the bed. There are other symbols, on the living room wall, ones you'll have seen before. Satanic symbols. When you paint over them . . . they come back. Fading back into the paint on the wall like a bad memory. Feeling like a threat. Like something that is . . . amused. Having a bit of fun. But also with the steely conviction that it will leave its mark, and it is there to stay.

Most of all, this house is sad. Terrible things can happen to the people that live there. People who come because they have no other choice. People who are falling into their own personal abyss of old traumatic wounds; people who don't realize that they have been selected – and invited in. People who are going to be hurt . . . unless they get away first.

Run.

ONE

It started with a text, anonymous. *Looking forward.*

I was in bed but unable to sleep, uneasy about something I could not quite catch hold of. My beloved was in a deep sleep beside me, nestled close, radiating warmth. She had been otherworldly lately – Moira, my beautiful wife – with that look she gets, like she is tired in her soul and fading. The kind of look that made me worry.

I moved quietly out of the bedroom, one last glance over my shoulder at Moira, who was breathing steadily but completely still, like she was deep in a place where I could not find her, like she might not choose to come back. She got that way sometimes now. She was burrowed tightly under the blankets, and her thick, dark-chocolate hair was all that I could see on the pillow.

I shut the bedroom door and went to check on the fellas, both sweetly sleeping. Vaughn and Marcus still shared a room, but we had set up bunk beds. Vaughn took the top, he was the oldest. Sometimes we hung blankets to make a fort.

Mr Timothy, Moira's green-eyed, tiger-striped cat, sat at the end of Vaughn's bed, wide awake and watching like he had been expecting me for a while. We did not speak. We rarely do.

Tash, my very good girl and the world's best dog, lay in the doorway of their room, guarding. Security system engaged. Tash was awake, and she stood up and stretched when she saw me in the hallway. She sat beside me on the top step, laying her soft white muzzle on my knee. I do my best worrying right there, sitting at the top of the staircase in my 1930s American Four Square house.

I could hear the wind in the trees. Yesterday we had heavy rain with the sun shining through. It felt tornado-ish. When you live in Kentucky, you know the feeling. It's the tornados you don't feel that get you. The ones that come in the dead of the night. People in Kentucky die in tornados – people with the kind of bosses who won't let them go home. Won't let them get safe.

The wind whipped up suddenly, blowing through the trees. It made me uneasy.

I put on a pair of reading glasses and studied the screen on my phone.

I get texts like this sometimes. Anonymous. Murky. Dark things stirring and sending a knot of dread into my stomach. I wish I could tell you that I take this kind of thing in stride, and I know it is best to ignore them.

I am a neurosurgeon. With hospital privileges in all the best places. You can google and find me on Healthgrades, Vital Signs. I have a website.

There is no website for my other practice. My sideline work – *THE ENLIGHTENMENT PROJECT Research & Protection, NGO* – brings me people in trouble, people who are desperate, people with a long, hard history of spiritual attack. People like me. They come for that *other* form of healing. Deliverance from the mysterious realm of malevolence – a place I know so very well.

I was possessed at the age of eleven, tortured by the lure of a dark entity that singled me out after my father died. I was a vulnerable child, drowning in unbearable grief. I wanted to protect my mother, who cried softly in the night when she thought I was asleep. To keep both of us safe in a world I did not trust. I wanted my father back. I wanted the power to fix things that could not be fixed.

And that is how they caught me up. Making me feel powerful. Making me feel safe. Too young to understand until too late that it would come with a terrible cost. I did not comprehend, then, why I had been selected. I did not understand until I was a surgeon with an Enlightenment research project, that I posed a considerable threat. That I had been targeted by a darkness that would try and possess the man I would become. I did not realize, as a child of eleven, how dangerous I would be.

It was my fascination with the brain, the consciousness and the unknown – my need to heal, the instinct to protect – that would set me on two converging pathways. That of a neurosurgeon, intrigued by the power of spiritual enlightenment. How it could heal my patients who suffered from brain tumors, neurogenerative diseases, inflammations of the body, of the brain. And how it could empower people under spiritual attack. People possessed. People in the hard, brutal grip of dark things no one understood. I wanted to heal them not pathologize them. I wanted to heal myself. Science I believed in. Faith I did not have. Spirituality came from my gut, and I was sure that the combination of science and spirituality was the fix.

And that is me. Always looking for the fix.

I developed The Enlightenment Project. To research a treatment that administered the gentle electrical stimulation of the spiritual neurons that flow through the brain like a symphony of strength, wisdom, healing. A network of power – always underestimated, always there. Neurologists who drove themselves mad in search of a *God spot* in the brain were missing the point. The body and the spirit compartmentalized are the body and spirit marginalized. This is the misguided arrogance of science.

The neurons of spirituality can bring good things . . . and dark things. Heal addictions and depression, fire creativity. Or unleash a dormant seed of evil, giving it life.

I had been naive when I began the project. I had not realized that the treatment brought choice, and some made the decision to welcome the abyss. The treatments gave you spiritual strength. How you used it was up to you. For a time, I backed away and shut the research down.

But it was effective and it was powerful, and the only hope for those who had serious ingrained possessions. I worked with Father Perry Cavanaugh, the exorcist who had rescued me when I was eleven, who had come to me with the fire of beliefs I did not share, and a confidence and wisdom and *belief in me*. I looked up to him. I admired him. He became the big brother who could show me the path and teach me the way. And years later, when I was caught up in the horror of my research project, with an outcome that fed the darkness or vanquished it, he was once again there when I needed him. Together we formed our enlightenment NGO, and our uneasy collision of science and faith became a rescue and healing path.

Most of our patients are weary exorcists, shamans, practitioners of Eastern medicine . . . spiritual people on the professional side, who needed cleansing and peace of heart. No religious affiliation required. And we had a small subset of patients with deeply ingrained possessions – patients wavering on which way to go, patients everyone else had given up on.

Some we helped. Some we made worse.

There is a part of me that is thrilled with being a dangerous man. I have grabbed hold of something I still do not understand but am compelled to pursue.

Inherent in science is a deep-rooted fear of anything spiritual. Even when quantum physicists admit that energy cannot be destroyed, they refuse to see what that means in terms of death. Which does not exist, because energy simply passes to another form. Consciousness has been ignored and even ridiculed in the scientific world for so many years that the obvious conclusion that consciousness is the beginning of everything and is present in all things brings on an avalanche of academic pearl clutching.

How some academics can be so uneasy about consciousness baffles me, since they are, presumably, sentient, conscious human beings like the rest of us. But science is an ideology like everything else. And in the world of psychiatry, which can no longer ignore the prevalence of people tortured by *something* no one can explain, the *Diagnostic and Statistical Manual of Mental Disorders* lists *possession.* It is hidden away under the honest but worried subheading of *research* in the category of *dissociative disorder*, which used to be called multiple personality disorder – a controversial diagnosis of a condition that many psychiatrists refuse to admit actually exists, though ignoring it doesn't mean it doesn't happen. It does.

And I do not know if this is a good thing. I do not know if it helps to pathologize people under spiritual attack. There are psychiatrists who believe in possession but do not think psychiatry offers much in the way of help. Because the one thing that does seem to be agreed on is that possession, whatever it is, does not come from within. It does not come from a damaged psyche. It is external – it comes from outside you. It *comes after* you. Psychotropic drugs aren't going to help you, and that is pretty much all they've got.

The only thing agreed upon is that people are in trouble and people need help. And you're going to be in a world of hurt if that is all the science of medicine can offer. Until they up their game, you are going to have to find help somewhere else.

And so I have the Enlightenment Protocol, though I myself will not submit. I am so often tempted and so often curious. But I am too afraid that it will overwhelm me, and that I will somehow get lost in the yin and the yang, the darkness and the light. Physicists – quantum scientists – they would call that *entanglement.* The observer and the observed become physically entwined just by the simple act of awareness. That is how possession happens. That is how it starts.

There will always be dark things in the world. Dark entities of energy, if you want to look through the filter of science. Quantum entanglement sounds intriguing, but be careful you do not get snarled up in something that is . . . *wrong*. Eighty-five percent of the universe is dark matter, and nobody knows exactly what it is. If that thrills you, then you are not thinking it through.

The screech of tires brought me to my feet – there were headlights arcing a path of light into my home through the tightly closed shutters. I heard a car door slam, a baby crying hysterically and footsteps, then pounding on my front door.

Shit. Whatever was *looking forward* was on my doorstep now.

TWO

She'd had a rough night, whoever she was. Eyes slanty, like a cat, wide and full of shock. She wore baggy jeans a size too big, a tight, long-sleeved black tee shirt, Ariat boots, scuffed and worn. Her shirt was torn at the shoulder, dust and dirt on the front of her shirt and jeans. She was young, tired, terrified.

And there was something familiar about her. I couldn't place what.

'You're Dr Archer? Noah Archer?' She looked me up and down, face going pink. She was fair skinned, hair a pure strawberry blonde, light and fine, blowing around her face in the wind. Freckles on her nose. She was out in the sun a lot. She didn't much take to a tan.

Lucky for her, I was in sweats tonight, not boxers, thick grey socks. Shirtless though. She was too young to be impressed. I grabbed my sweater off the table by the door. An old navy blue one that Moira had been wearing that afternoon. There was a new hole in the elbow. She'd been gardening. It was chill out, leaves falling. Time to get the yard ready for winter. We'd already had an early freeze.

'I'm Archer. Who are you?'

'I'm looking for my dad, and he . . . he's not answering his cell, and he *always* answers his cell when it's me calling, even though . . . even though I don't call him much. And I'm sorry, I know it's late, but he always told me that in an emergency I should come to you. But mainly I'm looking for him.'

'Who's your dad?' I looked over her shoulder. I couldn't see much more than the blinding headlights of an olive-green Fiat, like a giant Easter egg parked at a slant in the back of my driveway, engine still running. I could hear a baby screaming, shrill and wrenching and full of outrage. It worried me. 'And maybe you should go get your baby. He doesn't sound happy.'

'*She*. And she's not *my* baby. You think I'd leave an infant alone in a car with the engine running? *She* is in her mom's lap, and her little brother is right next to her, but they had a scary night.'

Scary. Interesting word choice, but I believed her. I had gotten a text.

'And my daddy is Perry Cavanaugh.'

'*Perry* Cavanaugh?'

'Are you deaf?'

'No, I'm not deaf, but if I was, that would hurt my feelings. I've known Perry since I was eleven years old – he's my best friend, and he *never once* mentioned a daughter.'

She jerked back like I'd slapped her; used a fist to rub the tears that sprang into her eyes, and her shoulders sagged. 'Since *you* were eleven? So basically you've known my dad a *really* long time.'

Mouthy this one. But so young. So scared. Trembling like she might blow over.

Tash moved out from behind my legs, and went outside to the Fiat and up on her hind legs to peer into the passenger-side window. I trotted out to the driveway, wincing at the cold seeping through my socks. I heard Moira's voice behind me – inviting the woman inside. I looked back over my shoulder. '*Moira.*'

She gave me a look. *She* was wearing boxers, mine by the way, and a big long sweater that reached her knees. Barefooted. 'Jesus, Noah, she looks just like him.'

'I don't need to come in. I just need my dad.'

The door on the Fiat opened and a little boy got out. Looked about ten, in a newish red Batman hoodie and red Converse high-tops, thick black hair and a lot of it, down to his collarbone. His mother was right behind him, a hand on his arm in case he escaped, an infant tucked on her shoulder, quieter now but still not happy with the world.

'Patrick, come here please – right now.'

'I *am* here. But I have to go to the bathroom, I told you that three times already, and I have to go *now*.' But he scooted back to his mother, and Tash followed him like she was connected by a string. He reached out, and Tash gave him a kiss.

'Sorry, Tash won't hurt him. But let me get her.'

The mother had thick black hair of her own, in a long loose ponytail that had gone sideways. She said something I couldn't hear over the wail of the baby, who twisted sideways, caught sight of me, abruptly stopped crying as she studied me then held out her arms. I gave the baby my irresistible smile, and she bucked and leaned toward me.

'I'd love to hold her, but I know you don't know me.'

'You think I'd be here if I didn't? You're Dr Noah Archer.

Neurosurgeon. Elle says you're OK. Her dad thinks the world of you. She says you're the uncle she never met.' She smiled at me, eyes brown, circled with fatigue, an endearing gap between her front teeth, and let her baby come to me.

How little she was. How warm. She grabbed a tiny handful of my sweater and nestled into my neck, sucking her fist.

'Her daddy holds her just like that. She's missing him. Oh my God, she's almost asleep.'

'I'm a baby whisperer.'

'That's not on your website.'

'It should be. Come on in the house – it's cold out here and none of you need to be in this wind.'

She leaned into the car – shut off the engine. The lights. Took the keys. Then her knees buckled and she sagged and went down fast, but I caught her and kept her on her feet. Hands full, but always a multitasker.

'I'm OK, sorry. You've got the baby. I can—'

'I've got you both. Take your time – we'll go slow. If you feel like you can't make it, tell me and I'll carry you in.'

'I got you, Mama.' Patrick went round to her other side and took her hand, and she laughed a little – and cried a little.

I gave him a nod, man to man. 'Good job, Patrick. Let's go inside and find you a bathroom.'

'I bet you got a lot of bathrooms in a house that big.'

'Three, last time I counted.'

'I can count them for you.'

'Patrick, old son, you impress me, you really do.'

THREE

Patrick had been reluctant to admit he was hungry, but when I mentioned that I liked nothing more than a middle-of-the-night ham-and-cheese sandwich, he had lit up and said for himself he'd just take the cheese. Lucky I had some Kraft American singles, because he had zero interest in the aged Swiss or Tillamook.

He had turned down my offer of a video game or television in the back room where the fellas hung out, and went like a magnet back to his mom, curled up at her feet, back against the couch while he ate his sandwich. He'd had a hard night. I tucked a blanket around him.

Everyone said yes to coffee and no to the cookies I put on the coffee table. Then things got awkward. Or more awkward.

'So,' I said. 'How can I help?'

Perry's daughter, Elle, shrugged. 'I need you to help me find my dad, but evidently he is mysteriously missing.'

'He's in Rome,' I said. 'Holding daily seminars on exorcism at the Vatican conference for the International Association of Exorcists.'

Patrick looked up at the word exorcism.

Elle shook her head. 'Not anymore he isn't. It's nine a.m. in Italy, and while you were in the kitchen, I tried yet again to track him down. Not too helpful, those Vatican dudes. This time I got a woman in an office who seemed very suspicious and didn't want to help much, but when I told her I was his daughter and there was a family emergency, she admitted that he'd evidently left Rome after two days into the seminars and canceled the rest of his presentations. She wouldn't tell me why, she didn't sound happy with him, and she said she had no idea where he was and no idea who I could ask.'

I exchanged looks with Moira. She was holding the baby, who nestled in her arms, and she looked tired and a little baby besotted. We both were.

'It's not like him to do that,' Moira said softly, giving me a marital significant look. Then she glanced over at Patrick.

'Let's talk in the kitchen, Elle,' I said.

She nodded and looked to her friend, who'd told me to call her Pammie.

'You tell him everything, I need to stay in here with the kids – they're shook. If that's all right?' Pammie looked from me to Moira.

'It's fine, of course,' Moira said.

Elle followed me into the kitchen. I caught a glimpse of Patrick reaching for the cookies, which was encouraging. If he could eat cookies and a sandwich, he was winding down from a hell of a night. I wondered what had been going on.

Elle and I perched side by side on the bar stools. I saw her noticing our swanky kitchen. Mainly the La Cornue gas range. If the house caught fire, I would get Moira, the kids and the animals out, then come back in to drag that stove to safety.

'Look, I'm really sorry to storm your castle in the middle of the night like this. The plan was to go to my dad's place, settle Pammie and the kids in for the night. And to get Dad to go back with me to that house.'

'What house? What's the crisis?'

She took a breath. 'I'm an atheist – or agnostic at best. It's how my mama raised me. But whatever is going on there . . . I can't even speculate right now. What's the word y'all use? Preternatural? It just . . . it's just happening and it's real. It's like nothing I've ever seen.'

I nodded.

'You aren't shocked?'

'No.'

'It's the kind of thing my dad is good at. My mom would be useless here, and she'd make things worse.'

'Tell me what happened.'

'What happened is I have to go back out there. *Now*.'

'Why?'

'Look, I got a call from a cop I know pretty well. Small town, OK? Andi – Officer Craig. She was doing a welfare check on one of my patients, Pammie LaRue.'

'And that would be her in the living room.'

'Yeah.'

'Why the welfare check? Who called that in?'

She gave me a knowing look, and I got the impression she liked that I knew how this kind of thing worked.

'Mental health welfare check. You get me? Because Pammie called the new crisis hotline and what she told them disturbed them so much they called the cops. She didn't know that the line isn't anonymous. That they're set up to track your location if needed. And she's got history. Suicide attempt when she was a freshman in college. So they were looking to put her under a seventy-two-hour hold and put the kids in care, if the officer felt she needed emergency intervention. Once that happens—'

I nodded. I knew. The dirty little secret. Most people trust that the helpline is confidential. It's not. Mostly they save a lot of people spiraling down to a miserable, lonely place; they help a lot of people find a way to navigate; they help people not be so alone. But like a lot of good things in the world, they can also cause a lot of grief. When people trust you and call and you sever that trust . . . you're not getting that back. And the next time they need help, they might not ask. And it's more than likely there's going to be a next time.

She pushed hair out of her eyes. 'So Pammie was on her way to trouble because—'

'They were worried she was a danger to her children.'

'Exactly. I'm a PA.'

I nodded. Psychiatric physician's assistant.

'I work in the ER at the local, rural hospital, and I deal with people in crisis all the time, and I get why they sent someone out for that welfare check. But I know Pammie. I helped her get her meds sorted – she was one of my first patients. Helped her get off them when she wanted off them. She's been doing great, really great. Her issues before were situational, and her issues now are situational.'

'Why didn't she call the police?'

'Her partner—'

'Father of the kids?'

'Yes. He disappeared eight days ago. The official opinion is he took off, left the mama and kids behind, but he didn't. They've been together for years – he's a great guy, good father, works hard all day, takes over with the kids while she works at night. She has her own business cleaning offices. And it's really starting to pay off. So she's already called the cops a lot, the last week or so. She got discouraged tonight, pretty depressed over him being gone and nobody having a clue what happened to him, and nobody much looking.

'And then the things started happening again in the house – knocks on the wall, whispering voices. Water pooling in the bathroom for no good reason. It happened a lot; they could never find a leak. It's been going on since they moved in six weeks ago, and it keeps escalating. So she called the hotline looking for support, but they aren't from around here, and when she started talking about the stuff going on in the house, they freaked out. You can't really blame them.'

No. You couldn't.

'But Andi – well the local cops know all about that house. They've been called out there a lot, over the years. And one thing I'll say for them. They always go. But there's not a lot they can do, right? Weird stuff like that? They can do a walk-through look for intruders, do a perimeter check, keep an eye out for cars that aren't local. But they see some *really* weird stuff, and word gets around, right?'

I admit I was intrigued. That little stir of fascination I always got. The chill and the thrill. I had a million questions, but I let her talk.

'So when Andi shows up, when Pammie sees the patrol car, she's on the porch freaking out. She didn't call them, and as soon as she heard *welfare check* she lost her shit. She's bounced through the system enough to get it. She was a freshman at Yale with a full ride, just eighteen years old, when she made the suicide attempt, and they kicked her ass to the curb.'

'Is that legal?'

'You know how it is. Someone in the ER is cozy with the admin; she's the most vulnerable she has ever been in her life. She gets pressured to give permission for the university to access her medical records, and to take the meds they want her to take, after an *intense five-minute evaluation*, guided by a standardized form, with the implied threat that she has no choice but to cooperate if she ever wants to go home again, and the bait that all the university wants to do is help her.'

Elle sounded angry as hell. I kind of loved her for it.

'So Pammie was pretty worked up, but she's smart as hell, and she was looking for ways to reassure Andi that she didn't need to force the issue, and she told her that she was under my care, which was brilliant. Andi called me so she could—'

'Get out from under liability.'

'That and get Pammie looked after without getting her snarled up in the system. Unless that was needed. Andi is good. She's savvy; she thinks things through and has a lot of integrity.

'So I go out there, but I've heard about that place, so I took Chewie with me.'

Her eyes filled with tears. I handed her a napkin and she wiped her face and blew her nose, and tucked the napkin into the pocket of her jeans.

'And Chewie is—'

'My dog – Rottweiler Cattle Dog mix. He keeps me safe. He just wandered on to my property one night around supper time three years ago. I have a Tiny House on some land I bought out in the countryside so I can keep my old pony. Chewie looked to be ten months old and on his own for a long time. Pretty hungry, a little shy, but ran right up to my little porch and jumped up and gave me a kiss, like he'd been looking for me all his life. That's not something I can resist. He and Lexie, the pony, get along great, and she's safer out there with him in the paddock when I'm not home during the day. If I ever get out from under my student loans, I'll build a bigger house, something that isn't on wheels. I've added it all up and it looks like I'll have the interest paid off when I'm seventy-three. Then I can go after the principal.'

I wondered if she talked this much when she wasn't scared. Probably not. But she was on a roll tonight.

She took a deep shuddering breath. 'So just as I'm driving up and parking next to the patrol car, and I wave at Andi and Pammie who are talking on the porch . . . the lights in the house started flashing on and off, and the front door slammed shut with the kids still in the house. Chewie starts having a meltdown, and I let him out of the car. He snarls and growls and barks like aliens have landed or there's a cat somewhere, and he tears off around the back of the house. The three of us run inside to get the babies gathered up, and once we have them, Pammie goes back in looking for her cat. And then Chewie starts yelping like he's hurt and it's a *total* shit show. I go running around the back and I can't find him, but I can hear him barking – he's run off into the trees at the back of the property.

'Andi, she takes over. She tells us this is no place for the babies, and to take the kids and get out *now.* I argue, I don't want to leave her there on her own. But Pammie's car is in the shop, and Andi says she'll call for backup and round up the cat and the dog, and for us to *just go*. So we get in the Fiat and we book it, and I head right for Lexington, because whatever is going on there is a dad thing, and I called and called because I wanted him to go back out there with me tonight.'

'Better to wait till morning, when we can go calmly, in the light. Even if Perry was right here to go with us, he'd say to wait. And in truth, it would be better to get in touch with him before we go out there, to see what he'd advise on going forward. This is tricky stuff and dangerous.'

She shook her head at me. 'No way. Even if Dad can't help, I have to go back. Because Andi— Oh God, she looked so brave. And I called the police department trying to get in touch and . . . she never did call for backup. They said they'd sent patrol cars out because they couldn't get her on the radio. So I have to get out there. I have to get Chewie and the cat and make sure Andi is OK. You can't talk me out of that.'

'No, you're right. I'll go with you.'

'*Thank you.* Whatever it is out there. I shook my fist at it; told it that it could not run me off and I'd be back.'

Just picturing it made me sick to my stomach. Brave of her – and utterly unwise. But she didn't need to hear that now.

'Look, Elle, if it's OK with you, I'll call my brother-in-law, Tom. He should be getting off shift right about now, and we'll find him useful.'

'Why?'

'Safety in numbers and he's a cop.'

She nodded and gripped my arm really tight. 'Dad was right about you.'

FOUR

It was just going on four a.m. when we pulled up in front of the house. Darkness is thick this far and deep in the country. No city lights. Just a half moon, making everything shadowy, and the headlights of three patrol cards, parked randomly in the grass. Emergency lights were flashing blue, three uniformed officers in a huddle, tense, looking over their shoulders, and then all eyes on us. Tom had said he'd follow us in his patrol car and call in on the way. Let them know we were coming. He'd taken five minutes to change into jeans, an old grey sweatshirt. Leather jacket.

He pulled up close, on the side of the road, and I parked in the empty driveway. Wondering why no one else had parked there. Maybe they knew something I didn't.

Elle put a hand on the door, but I shook my head. 'Let Tom talk to them a minute – do the cop bonding thing. They'll tell him more if we're out of the way.'

Elle bit her lip, and I knew she was worried about her dog, but she stayed put. Which surprised me. But Tom had not talked to them long before he was at Elle's window. She rolled it down, and the wind blew through.

'Hey, Elle.' He smiled shyly, blue eyes crinkly. 'You can stop worrying. They found your dog. He was on the front porch guarding the house and howling for you. They figured he knew you'd be back. They lured him into the patrol car with a cheeseburger. He's stretched out in the back eating fries right now.'

The look she gave him would have melted me. She scrambled out, and Tom took her arm and led her to the car that was furthest away from the house, parked at an angle. I heard the yelp, the doggie whimpers of joy, a stream of baby talk from Elle. All the sounds of a happy reunion. Tom watched shyly, rocking back and forth on his feet.

I got out of the car and headed toward the house, and Tom trotted over. We hesitated at the steps up to the front porch.

'OK if I go inside?' I noticed the curious looks I was getting.

'Yeah, I told them you were here on behalf of the renter, to pick up a few things for the kids. They think that's a bad idea, but they won't stop you.'

'Any sign of the officer who took the call. Andi Craig?'

He shook his head. Pointed to one of the patrol cars. 'That's hers there in the middle. But no sign of her, inside or outside the house, or in the woods behind the place. Her big flashlight is missing.'

I blew air. 'That doesn't sound good.'

'These guys are about to head out. They're putting a team together; got a search dog coming in from Glasgow. Start at first light.'

We exchanged looks.

'I'll go with you,' he said. 'You don't want to go in alone.'

I shook my head. 'We need to get Elle out of here. She's sensitive to this stuff just like Perry is; she just doesn't know it yet. She's already drawn it close enough already. This place is dangerous for her.'

He nodded. This was a subject he avoided and Moira and I stopped bringing it up. But he was a veteran after losing Candice, the new love of his life, in a mysterious stairwell accident in the hospital where she worked. He'd been very solitary since then. Never talked much before it happened; barely spoke now.

'Well.' He grinned and slapped me on the back. 'Be sure and text a scream emoji if you need help.' Like most kids his age, he never considered actually answering a phone.

'Tom?'

'Yeah?'

'Thanks for coming. Do what you can to convince Elle to stay the hell away from this house.'

'Women never listen to me.'

I shrugged. I had a feeling this one would.

FIVE

The house looked tired. L-shaped ranch, some of it original to the sixties, the rest added on in the seventies or eighties. Maybe both. Sagging sky-blue aluminum siding on the front and sides. A couple of pieces with a color that did not quite match, where some panels had recently been replaced. Looked like Pammie and her guy were making efforts to keep the place up, even though it was a rental.

I headed up three worn concrete steps to the front door, the aluminum railing wobbly. The front door looked like it had been recently scrubbed. The dulling paint was white and looked like plastic.

For a moment I hesitated, wondering how it was that I had found my way to this terribly sad place. Because it was sad. I felt it all the way through me, like I was sinking. And I heard a whisper. I couldn't tell if it was in my head . . . behind . . . beside me.

Where you been?

My stomach went tight. I went inside the house, my rubber soles mostly silent on the battered old wood floors. The walls were newly painted, all of them white, as if to bring light into the house, which had narrow hallways and small windows, few and far between. Toys, shoes, scattered everywhere, a little orange bulldozer on the hall table under a lamp. Stack of mail. The furniture was cheap and comfortable, a newish emerald-green couch strewn with toys, a stack of diapers, a box of Ritz crackers and a glass of cloudy amber liquid. I picked it up and sniffed. Apple juice.

And there, tucked in the corner of the couch, nestled in a new pink snug sack for a newborn, was a tiny grey cat. A Russian Blue, wide-eyed, watching me.

I sat on the edge of the couch. Cats don't like me. And I was torn between the worry that she'd bolt and I'd never find her and being clawed if I grabbed her. Being clawed was my usual cat experience.

She was a tiny thing. Pammie had told me she was very sweet, protective and watchful with the kids.

'Hello, pretty girl.' No doubt she had a name. No doubt Pammie had told me. No doubt I'd forgotten.

She mewed sweetly at the sound of my voice and climbed into my lap, settling in with relief. I stroked her head and kept a hand on her, and she began to purr.

Any port in the storm.

But it was worth it, the long drive, for no other reason than to get Elle's dog rounded up and this tiny cat out of this house. I gave her a minute or two then scooped her gently up, holding her like Moira held Mr Timothy. He would never let me get that close, but this one – this one nestled into my shoulder and watched, wide-eyed, like she was expecting trouble as I walked through the house.

A quick look around, then I'd gather up a few things for Pammie and her kids, and head home. Where I would shower, have coffee and go into work with exactly zero hours of sleep. Patient consults and test results and keeping watch over my surgery patients. Not a jam-packed day in the OR at least.

It was cold in the house, and drafty, though all the windows were closed, and there were electric space heaters running full blast in every room, sometimes two or three. Trying to bring warmth to a place that held a bottomless cold. It felt damp. Like a cave. Everywhere was the usual chaos – working parents, a ten-year-old, a new baby girl.

I stopped in front of the big wall in the living room. Saw the traces of satanic symbols, dead center – large, dark red, painted over – like a presence that was fading in rather than out. Like the house had been marked. I was glad for the navy sweater I'd put on. I felt a breath of cold air at my feet. And a wave of something . . . hopeless. What was I doing here at four thirty a.m. in the dark?

Patrick's room was the first on my left, bed unmade in tangles, a nightlight that shot a pattern of pastel lights on the ceiling, shelves of books and toy bins. I caught a glimpse of something odd on the wall beside the little bed, so I went in to take a look.

Clusters of red and black dots, and patterns of geometric symbols that puzzled me. Red dots, circles, trapezoids, triangles and hexagons. Once I started looking, I found them everywhere. Repeated in patterns on the walls, on the door, and in a circle on the floor around the bed. Hidden by the toys scattered all around the room. Patrick loved cars and tractors and Lego blocks. The toys on the floor around the bed were weapons. Tanks. Transformers. Dragons. Facing out. Like a circle of protection, made by a ten-year-old boy.

I heard a car engine starting up. Went into the hallway and looked through the slats of the blinds. The patrol cars were all pulling out. Due to return first thing in the morning with the tracking dog. I felt a sick dread. I was being left behind.

But no.

Tom was still there. Headlights on, engine idling. He wasn't going to leave me here, no matter what I'd told him. I'd been a happy only child growing up, but it felt good to have a little brother now. And I knew he would stay right there until I was safely out, and I won't lie to you. I was relieved.

I wound down the narrow, windowless hallway, cat purring in my arms, passing a wall covered in family pictures. Pammie's partner was a big guy – tall and wide, thick black hair, looking like a grown-up version of Patrick. He wore Carhartt pants and the heavy boots of a man who worked outside. He had huge hands, and he was holding a toddler-sized Patrick perched on his shoulders. He looked a little cocky and very much the proud daddy, and his eyes were challenging, intelligent, very blue.

There were also pictures of him with horses. High-dollar thoroughbreds. Working them in a muddy ring outside in a drizzle. Holding one on a lead rope, with the ease of a man who was happier in a barn than at home. Good horses, small operations. He was young – I'd guess a trainer making his name on the racetracks.

I wondered where the hell he was. A big guy like that who I had no doubt could handle himself just fine. And looking at these family pictures, I knew this wasn't a man who would leave his family and disappear.

So I snooped. Headed into the master bedroom that was at the end of an odd L-shaped bend at the back of the hallway, maybe from the original part of the house, way at the back. The door was closed, and I hesitated, and the cat went tense, digging her claws into my shoulder. I kept a tight hold. Her fur bristled, and she wailed a long, low lament that ended in a deep growl in her chest.

I took a breath. Reminded myself that Tom was right outside. Opened the door.

And this room. This room was warm. Too warm. Three space heaters on high. Dude stuff on the dresser, including wallet and keys. A stack of bills clipped neatly together, weighed down by a dusty bottle of men's cologne.

I picked through the paperwork. Patrick's daddy was one Conor Walsh, citizen of Northern Ireland, and Pammie had student loans in her name, caught in the loop of paying for an education she had not been allowed to complete, and medical bills for the baby and Patrick and Pammie. One application for an assistant trainer's license for Keeneland, $150, in the name of Conor Walsh.

And it all fell together. Kentucky was a mecca for horse people, and there were plenty of Irish here.

It made no sense for this guy to cut and run. Especially without his car keys. Especially without his wallet.

I opened a crisp manila folder under the bills. They were planning a wedding at Cloughan Castle, in the countryside of Loughrea, Co. Galway, Ireland. Three nights for fourteen people, which cost them €7,600, scheduled for New Year's. Paid in advance.

I wondered where he was. If it was possible he was still alive.

Went back to my snooping.

Huge king bed. Comfy chair in the corner, barely room for it by the bed.

The closet had one of those accordion-style doors that never stay on track. Her side was a mess, his side the clothing was sparse and neatly organized. New shelves, wood fresh and newly installed, not yet painted, though there was an unopened can of paint stored in a corner. It gave me a pang, to see how he and Pammie had been working to fix up a place I knew could not be fixed. The money they had spent. The hopes and dreams they had no doubt had of raising their children out in the countryside.

No empty hangers. No empty spaces on the shelves. Whatever had happened to Conor Walsh, he had not cut and run. He had disappeared. And now Patrolwoman Andi Craig was missing. Both from the same house. Eight days apart.

I heard faint whispers, and a flicker of light caught my attention. Both coming from behind a door shut tight on the side wall, likely leading into a bathroom. I didn't think the light was on earlier. I wasn't sure.

But I heard a voice, and if the light was on . . . someone might be in there. Two people missing – I had to look. Then I would gather up a few things and get the hell out.

I opened the door and stepped back. Linoleum floor peeling in the corner. Toilet, sink, towels haphazard on the rack. New plunger beside the toilet, and a space heater going full blast and radiating heat. Women's cosmetics crammed precariously on the side of the counter next to the wall. Two toothbrushes, a man's razor. The intimate snarl of two people sharing a small space.

Nobody there but . . . presence.

I took a breath. The shower curtain twitched, but the house was drafty. Fear like little electric shocks in my legs. Two steps and I pushed the curtain back, hearing the rings slide across the bar. Just a bathtub. Bubble bath, lavender, Captain Jack dude soap.

I turned to head out and saw a puddle of water growing steadily and seeping toward me at a pretty good clip. It wasn't coming from under the sink, the bathtub or the toilet that I could see. It seeped from under the wall beside the door.

The bathroom light went out and I froze. Kitty dug her claws into my chest, and I didn't blame her.

I didn't like the possibility that in about thirty seconds I would be sharing a puddle of water with an electric space heater that was still glowing orange behind the grill. But at least it meant I was not in total darkness.

I'm long legged. I took a wide stride, got my feet wet, and then was out. And I thought of Pammie in there, maybe holding a baby.

Behind me, the space heater cut off and went dark.

The light in the bedroom was still on. I booked it to the front door as all the lights went off in the house. Space heaters quiet.

The front door opened as I threaded the dark hallway. I saw the arc of a powerful flashlight.

'Noah?'

'Right here. Coming out.'

I heard Tom fumbling with the light switch on the wall by the door.

'Power's out,' he said.

I laughed. 'That's *your* opinion.'

I grabbed the little bulldozer off the hall table for Patrick. I didn't have time for anything else.

The flashlight illuminated the hallway so I could see my way out.

'You got the cat?' He sounded astonished.

'This one likes me.'

'Maybe it's possessed.'

I couldn't see him, but I knew he was grinning. 'Elle's dog OK?'

'Fine. Terrifying to look at, sweet as can be. Come on, man – let's get out of here. I'm not leaving until you're in the car and on the road.'

'Back at you.'

The presence of the house seemed to follow me down the concrete steps. Tom right behind me. I hesitated. I could go back in fast and get some baby things. Diapers and stuff.

'Noah?'

I turned. Tom had his back to me. All the lights were back on in the house.

The passenger-side window of Tom's patrol car opened, and Elle leaned her head out, her arms full of a short-haired gray-black dog who had a bucket head and a wide, heavy jawline. He looked lethal.

'Y'all, we better go.' Elle's voice was shaky. 'Oh, you got the cat.'

'Yeah. I'll take her with me.'

'Chewie likes cats.'

'For lunch?'

She gave me a shaky laugh.

Tom headed for his car, and I took my keys and the orange bulldozer and Kitty and settled into the cognac leather seats of my Audi. I took an old towel from the back seat and made a little bed for Kitty, who settled half on the towel and half on my leg. Once the heat was running in the car, she tucked up closer and started purring. I put the little bulldozer in the side pouch of the car door, and backed out of the driveway, right behind Tom. He drove fast and was ahead of me pretty quickly. The little road was dark.

And I heard my phone go off. A text. Moira no doubt.

But it wasn't Moira.

Comes back.

Not an invitation I was going to accept. I was driving slow and steady, Tom long gone ahead of me. But the little shocks in my legs eased up. I felt safe. I knew I was OK.

And then my headlights caught her. A woman standing in the middle of the road. Waving me down. Long, glorious thick gray hair that fell in ripples to her waist. Face thin and worn with life experience, her gaze focused exactly on me, intelligent, knowing, but there was no way she could have seen me, hidden in the dark of the car, with the headlights blazing. A soft cotton dress billowed around her legs. She was barefooted. That's all I got in a quick glimpse as I slammed on the brakes and swerved to the side of the road, Kitty digging her claws into my thigh, the car spinning twice, leaving skid marks on the asphalt and churning up the turf. No ditch on this side of the road, or I'd have been in it, nose down. I was lucky.

'Stay put,' I told Kitty, unhooked her from my leg then was out of the car, door shut behind me. I had not felt a thump. I didn't think I'd hit this woman, *but damn*, it had been a close thing.

I could not see her. I walked up and down the pavement, on the grass, both sides, and nothing. No sign of her. No sign of a car.

'Anybody there? Need help?'

Only my voice, and I felt very alone in the dark. I spent a good long time looking for the woman, but there was nobody there. And no other cars went by.

Kitty and I listened to Chris Isaak on the long and dark drive home. When 'Wicked Game' came up in the rotation, I laughed.

SIX

Perry had not answered my calls. I tried another text.

Dammit, Perry, where are you?

I didn't expect an answer, but there was an immediate response. *Call me.*

He picked up on the first ring.

'Perry, man, it's good to hear your voice. All hell is breaking loose here, did you get my messages? Did you get in touch with Elle?'

'Yes, I—'

'What am I hearing? Are you – are you in a hospital?' I spent most of my days in hospitals – I knew hospital noise.

'I'm at Gemelli Hospital in Rome.'

Gemelli. If you had to be in a hospital in Italy, that was the one. 'As a patient?'

He sounded tired. 'I'm OK, Noah.'

'Define OK.'

He sighed. 'I had a cardiac event.'

'*Crap*. Heart attack?'

'A small cardiac arrest.'

There are no small cardiac arrests. The heart's electrical system breaks down and the heart stops beating.

'You're on a heart monitor, right?' Stupid question but I felt compelled to ask. It's how you reassure a doctor.

'I am. It doesn't beep all the time like on television.'

'It's not supposed to – you'd go insane. But what I *am* hearing tells me your IV infusion is finished or the battery is low. And your pulse-ox monitor cuff isn't on right; it shouldn't be making noise. Get them to fix that. Have they scheduled a cardiac cath?'

'No, but they want to. None of the other tests are showing anything that explains why my heart stopped. No arrhythmias. No heart attack. Blood work excellent. Scans look good. I don't have all the results back yet, but they're . . . puzzled.' He hesitated. 'And I need to come home.'

'You sure do. Which means you stay and get the cath. Because if your heart stops on the way to the airport, you won't make it home.'

'Don't sugarcoat it, Noah.'

'Do you feel well enough to tell me what happened? Your daughter is pretty great by the way. I'll look out for her till you get back. She said she called the Vatican and got some woman who said you packed up and left with no explanation and ditched the seminars you were supposed to give.'

'That's partly true. Look. You should know that when I was in Rome – I don't think I slept the whole time I was there – I made a decision. I'm leaving the church, Noah, but not my calling. I'm still an exorcist, and if anything, I'm even more committed to the work.'

'Are you . . .' I trailed off. 'Are you OK?'

'Look, it's complicated, and we'll talk later. And I would have stayed to finish out the week, but I . . . I can't explain it, Noah – I knew I had to get home. I was packed, I checked out of my hotel, very early. And then, on my way to the Vatican offices . . . I got a text.'

'Shit. Did it say *looking forward*?'

His voice went low. 'You got one too?'

'I did. And an hour later, your daughter showed up on my doorstep.'

'I heard about that. And I can't thank you enough. I know it must have been a bit of a shock—'

'Perry. It's OK. You sound tired. We can talk about this later.'

'Noah. Please, just listen. I'll do this last test if you think I should, but whatever is going on there – it's bad. I'm worried about Elle. She's on their radar, and she's in trouble. It's starting up with her, and I have to stop it now, early, before damage is done – before things take hold.'

'Tell me what happened with the cardiac event.'

'I was in one of the Vatican offices, and they were trying to convince me to stay and finish out the week. Which normally of course I would do. And they were very . . . . insistent. I apologized; said my decision was final. And I got this terrible tight gripping pain in the right side of my jaw. It stopped me cold, and I thought if I could just make it out the door and rest a minute before I headed down the front steps . . . But I didn't make it out the door. I collapsed. The Vatican has medical staff – a nurse saved my life. But, Noah,

I don't think there's anything wrong with my heart. I think I was targeted. Whatever this is doesn't want me to come home. Which means I *have* to come home.'

The jaw pain worried me. Classic. But stopping a heart's electrical system? Right up the demonic tech alley.

'Perry, don't leave until you get that cath.'

'*There is nothing wrong with my heart.*'

'Except the part where it stopped. Not every issue is demonic, Perry. We rule the physical things out first. You'd be the first to say that for anyone else.'

He was quiet. 'I'll get the test and then see about heading home. Tell me about the house.'

'Later. When you've rested.'

'I'm lying in a bed covered in monitors and worrying.'

'Perry—'

'Noah, my daughter is in trouble. This is the first time since she was six years old that she's asked for my help – she wouldn't even let me pay her college tuition. And she's going to *get* my help. And I know you have a million questions—'

'And you know we'll set all that aside for later when you don't sound so damn exhausted.'

'Good. So the house?'

'Like nothing I have ever seen before. Aware. Malevolent. *Intelligent*. I felt like it was stalking me the whole time I was there.'

'On a scale of one to ten?'

'Fifteen. Fucking dangerous, that place. I caught up with Tom yesterday. He and Elle and Pammie went back the next morning to get some stuff from the house.'

'Bad idea.'

'People with kids and a new baby have stuff. They went in broad daylight, got in and out fast. Locked everything up and then got the hell out. Tom said nothing crazy happened.'

'Repeated exposure is not a good thing.'

'Yeah I know that. They're not going back. Pammie and the kids and the kitty moved in with her grandmother at the Osage Golden Mobile Home Park, and her grandmother is there at night with the kids when she works.'

'What about the police officer that went missing? Andi Craig? Elle was upset about her. She knows her.'

'Tom said she still hasn't been found. They had a tracking dog pick up a scent under the house, in the crawl space where they found her missing flashlight, still switched on, and fresh scuff marks in the hard dirt and gravel.'

'Scuff marks?' he asked.

'Like she'd been dragged.'

'*Good God.* What happened with the dog?'

'The dog followed the scent out to the woods; lost it. No sign of Officer Craig anywhere else. Tom says he goes out there on his time off. He and a couple other officers are still looking.'

'This is going sideways, Noah.'

'Just let me handle it till you get back. Tell me what you want me to do.'

'Expect a call from my wife.'

'Your—'

'Dr Chloe Donatello. She's a quantum biologist. We never got divorced. I've been madly in love with her since we were freshmen at Transy. She's brilliant. She understands what I do. She has theories of her own about dark entities that have rocked my world. And she is worried sick about Elle. She wants to go out to that house and run some tests. I want you to take her there and let her do what she has to do. And keep her safe, Noah. Keep her safe.'

SEVEN

I was intrigued by the presence of a mysterious hidden woman in Perry's life. Fascinated that he'd never mentioned her, much less his daughter. Looked like a snarl of trauma and dysfunction to me. I could not wait to meet her.

Getting to the house with Chloe was easier said than done. We played phone tag. My schedule was a beast. She was bemused that I insisted on driving her out to the house, instead of just meeting her there, but I had my orders, and I was going to keep her safe. Door-to-door protection.

We made it out two days after I talked to Perry, and I picked Chloe up on a cool sunny Sunday afternoon. She was waiting on the porch of her little red-brick row house on Second Street, a mysterious boxy case by her side and a briefcase slung over her shoulder. She was writing in a notebook, glancing at the screen of her phone, and oblivious to my presence. By the time I opened the door of the car for her, the briefcase had slid off her shoulder and on to her foot.

'Hello, hello, I know you're there. *Total apologies,* I just thought of something and I had to make the notations or it would have gone *right out of my head.*' Her voice was a rich, resonant alto.

I headed up the sidewalk and picked up the case. 'Shall I carry this for you?'

She looked up and gave me a blazing smile. She had thick dark-blonde hair that was almost red, collar length and mussed; small turquoise-and-silver hoops in her ears. A copper bracelet that I saw when we shook hands. Snug jeans, a fitted peacock-blue leather jacket and gray ankle boots. She had the air of distraction of a woman who lives in a world of creative calculations where no mere mortal could follow. She pushed her black-rimmed reading glasses up to the top of her head, dropping her phone and the pen but held tight to the notebook. I bent down and picked up the phone and the pen and handed them to her, while balancing the case – which was heavier than it looked. She tilted her head sideways, laughed and said thank you.

'And I'm Chloe Donatello by the way.'

'*The* Dr Chloe Donatello, world-renowned biologist who just published fascinating new theories in quantum biology and dark energy and pissed pretty much everyone off?'

'I see you've been googling. Yes, that's me. It's my specialty. Pissing everyone off. But let's face it, the targets in my world are so easy. The academic community is dominated by dusty, scientifically conservative types whose main goal is protecting their dogma and their turf.'

'Not guilty.'

She laughed. She clearly spent a lot of time outdoors, and the sun had etched intriguing lines in her skin that made me think she'd had a lot of adventures in her life. She had the easy charismatic confidence that a woman only earns from life experience.

'Oh, not you. Perry has told me all about *you*. I think your work on enlightenment protocols is fascinating. And thank you for looking after my daughter, that night at the house.'

'And how is Elle?'

She looked away, and we got settled into the car. 'Can we make a stop for gummy bears?'

We were making good time in my beloved Audi. Chloe was muttering to herself and making notes on her iPhone. Chewing gummy bears.

She looked up. 'Sure you don't want one?'

'I only like the red ones.'

She sorted through the pack and gave me two.

'Thanks.' I gave her a glance. Her shoulders were tense. 'Perry said you were worried sick about Elle. I need to know what's going on with her. If you'd trust me with that.'

'I wanted to go to Rome you know, but Perry said stay here, Elle was going to need me, and he was sure as hell right about that. I don't want to worry Perry with this stuff. So please, just keep what I tell you to yourself.'

'Unfortunately you have no idea how *this stuff* works. And I'm going to tell Perry everything. None of us are going to get through this without him. You have theories. I have experience. But Perry is the expert and the genius. So. What's going on with Elle?'

She frowned. Looked away. 'Elle hasn't been the same since she went into that house.'

'Specifics?'

'Something she calls . . . *shadow people.* She sees them slipping around outside her Tiny House. She's so isolated out there in the countryside. She wakes up to Chewie barking like crazy and something leaning over her in the middle of the night. *She can smell it*; feel the pressure on the mattress. So it's there – she just can't see it. She hears voices sometimes, just out of earshot, and Chewie reacts, so he's hearing them too. She feels . . . *under observation.* That's how she puts it. She's afraid to go to sleep, except—'

'Nightmares?'

'Sometimes. But mostly it's just the opposite. Sleep is usually the only time she feels safe. Because of her dreams.'

I cocked my head sideways. 'That's odd. It doesn't usually work like that.'

'*It*? What do you mean by *it*?'

'Tell me about her dreams.'

'She's sleeping more and more. She falls asleep instantly, with Chewie tucked close by her feet at the end of her bed. She used to have terrible insomnia. Worrying at night. About her patients.'

'Does she remember her dreams?'

'Oh yes – they're so vivid, she feels like she's living them. It sounds to me like lucid dreaming. Where you know you're dreaming but it feels real. Real enough that you can control what you do, so it never feels quite . . . random. I don't know exactly what it is, but it's definitely more than a dream. And for Elle, it feels like . . . She says it feels like she's *supposed* to be dreaming.'

'What is it she dreams about?'

'Same thing over and over. A woman, very old, very beautiful, in a soft cotton dress, with tiny black buttons down the front. She has long gray hair that falls in ripples to her waist, and she takes Elle's hand and tells her she's safe, and to follow her, but she'll have to be brave. And in the dreams, sometimes Elle does follow her. Across a field.'

'A field?'

'Yes, it's sunny outside, and the wind is blowing.'

'Is this a place she knows? Somewhere she's ever been, say in her childhood?'

'Analysis much?' But she gave me a half-smile and nodded. 'Yes, it's a small village in Provence called Pente Douce. We have family connections there.'

'Really?'

'One of my uncles, several greats ago, Forrest Strickler, went to France and fought during World War I. He was nineteen. Infantry. He somehow survived the Meuse–Argonne Offensive. Afterward, he didn't want to go home to the family farm in Frankfort. And he married a French girl – he met her when he wandered on to her family's little farm.'

'A lavender farm?'

'No. Their farm was small. Pretty poor. Raised sheep. Something my uncle would be familiar with – his family had sheep too.'

'How do you know all this? I have no idea what my great-great uncles did. I don't even know their names.'

'I didn't either, but they put my great-grandmother in a nursing home in Lawrenceburg when I was just a teenager, and it upset me so much. Then they sold her house and auctioned off everything she owned. I went to the auction because I wanted to buy all of her stuff and save it for her, but I just didn't have that kind of money. Then they held up several packets of old family letters she kept in a little red hatbox, so I bought all of those. And they were from Forrest Strickler to his sister, Anna, and that's how I know his whole story. And so does Elle – she was always fascinated by it. Elle's researching because she thinks this is connected. I mean, it has to be, right? This woman in her dreams keeps taking her to the village in France where my Uncle Forrest lived. And every time, the woman says to her, *You must come. No one will be safe until you do.*'

'Seriously? *Crap.*'

'Oh, dude. *Crap*? That's all you've got?'

'I've never heard anything like this before in my life. And I've never heard of Pente Douce. But it's a real place?'

'The people who live there think so. Famous for goat cheese and a bookstore called Paisible. Lavender fields, beautiful. Exactly like her dreams. And one other thing.'

I glanced toward her.

'One night, in her dream, she bent down and picked just a few stalks of the lavender. And when she woke up, they were right there, on her pillow, one of them still in her hand. She showed them to me.'

'I'd like to see them.'

She opened her briefcase and held up a stalk of lavender that was lying right on top of folders and paperwork, her fingers trembling.

I took a quick look, keeping an eye on the road. The flowers were crispy, brown, stems still green but dry.

'*This is Elle*. And I know my daughter. This really happened. I don't know why. I don't know how, and I don't know what it means. Or why it's happening to my daughter.'

'People who lucid dream have a bigger prefrontal cortex than your average bear. It's a mysterious in-between state. Not exactly awake. Not exactly asleep. They track it from measured electrical activity in the brain. People who are lucid dreaming are actually able to manipulate physical objects. Say move a watch from one place to another.'

'Or pick a stalk of lavender.'

'Exactly. And I know it's real. Because I saw the woman too.'

She gave me a sideways look. 'When did you see her?'

'The night I went with Elle to the house. With my brother-in-law, Tom.'

She smiled. She knew all about Tom. So Elle had been talking about him.

'When I was leaving, on my way home, I saw the woman right in the middle of the road, holding up a hand for me to stop the car. Long hair, looked gray in the headlights; she was very old, very beautiful, just like Elle told you, right down to the dress. I remember it was blowing around her legs. I think . . . I think she was barefooted. And she . . . I almost hit her, but I didn't, and I got out to look for her. But she was gone.'

'And you know you weren't asleep? You hadn't fallen asleep at the wheel?'

'Wide awake. I almost crashed the car. If there'd been a ditch, I'd have been in it.'

'Elle doesn't think she's dreaming. She thinks it's really happening.'

I thought about that. 'I have this patient. A woman, who came in with her husband. She had cognitive issues – early-onset dementia we were pretty sure. You can never say exactly what's going on with that stuff no matter what the doctors tell you. And the husband said that two nights before, when she was out of town on a business trip, maybe one of her last ones . . . Anyway, he was sound asleep and woke up because someone stroked his hair. It scared him. And when she came home, they went out for lunch together and he told her about it. And she took his hand and smiled at him and said,

Did you look at the clock? Did it happen at two a.m.? And he said, *Yes, right on the dot*. And she was so happy, because she went to him in a lucid dream and did stroke his hair. They wanted me to weigh in on this. Because as her dementia progresses . . . she wondered if she might be able to do things in dreams she couldn't do physically, as she got worse.'

What I didn't tell Chloe was that my patient had been suicidally depressed at the diagnosis and began researching places in Europe where she could manage her death. Her mother died of dementia and she was terrified. Of the loss of who she was. How vulnerable she would be. The caretaking burden on her husband. I'd told her over and over that she wouldn't lose *who* she was – she would always and ever be herself, in spite of the symptoms, which, I was honest, were formidable – and that I thought the two of them together might find a way to a life they could love. I'd seen patients do that, and nobody talks about it. One thing I never tolerated was my patients in cognitive decline being dismissed as a soulless shell. They were always still there. I had pretty big opinions on that stuff.

Chloe waved her hands in the air. 'Whatever's going on, my daughter is in over her head. I need to figure this out and make it stop.'

I frowned. 'In her *lucid* dreams – are they always the lady and good dreams? Or does she have nightmares?'

'Both. Why are you frowning like that?'

'It means they have another way to get to her. And in a lucid dream, where physical things can happen . . . that's new territory for me.'

'So you're scared for her too.'

'She's her father's daughter. And that works both ways. She will attract this kind of trouble, but she'll be unusually able to handle it.'

'That actually does *not* make me feel better. But I know it's real – I trust Perry on this stuff. And I'm very interested in what's going on with people who are under what you and Perry call spiritual attack. Something that comes *at* them, not from within. Some kind of *real* presence. What the hell *is* that presence? How do you find it, track it, measure it, evaluate it? And my research grant came through six weeks ago, so now I'm up and running.'

'Perry told me you had some intriguing theories.'

'Officially I'm studying the intersection of dark matter and dark presence, and by presence I mean conscious and interacting with people. I'm looking for physical signs . . . chemical signatures that are consistent and predictable, and might even identify specific threads.'

'Threads as in a specific demonic entity?'

'Right now, I am more comfortable with the term *thread.* But yes, that's exactly what I mean And I think there could be some practical applications to being able to identify and detect the presence of specific *threads*—'

'Demonic entities.'

'Dude, stop interrupting. I mean, you can order ghost sensor apps on your phone, which I find fascinating. Perry told me how so much manifestation comes through with electronics and mechanical things, which . . . *come on*. That's just another way of saying *entanglement of photons*.'

'Yeah, I say that all the time.'

'Look, it's fine for you and Perry to call them *entities*, and while I think entity is a great term and also means we can give them little nicknames, I admit I had to spin things for the academic gatekeepers.'

'Ergo threads.'

'Ergo threads. But that's business as usual in science. The problem with academic research is that you have to come up with the answer before you do the research, which is so backasswards it's no wonder research is either beyond dull or a Wild West show. But that's what makes it fun, right?' She grinned at me. 'And the way we figure things out is that we notice there's something there – we just don't know what it is. I mean . . . black holes? The Big Bang? All based on answering a question without really having a lot of knowledge to back it up. Just the presence of things we can't explain.'

'*The presence of things we can't explain.* That's your approach? Seems broad.'

'Of course it's broad. It's every approach to every question. And it gives me enormous freedom without saying what they don't want to hear. Your Enlightenment Project; everything that happened with that. The NGO you and Perry have created. My research is all about looking into the physical side of what you deal with, because I know there is one.'

'How can you know?'

'I think there has to be. Roughly seventy to eighty-five percent of the energy in the world is dark energy. Which means we have no idea what it is. *Dark matter* – twenty-seven percent. Things we can identify? A measly five percent.'

I was nodding. I had considered these things myself.

'All of these unseen things are utterly mysterious, and utterly fascinating, but we know them, and we understand them, through the effect they have on things we *can* see and chart. And they're going to be emitting some level of radiation; all energy does, unless it's at a temperature of absolute zero, which is negative 273 degrees centigrade. Otherwise, it's going to have its own unique signature of electromagnetic radiation that transmits energy from one place to another. It's going to reflect, absorb and emit energy, and I can use a hand-held spectrometer to measure it. Right now, the research in my field is mostly theoretical, but I want physical evidence. I'm officially looking at this as a sort of quantum leap mutation. So the first, most basic thing I'm looking for is a chemical signature.' She smiled and gave me a look. 'Have I charmed you with my science?'

'Yes, ma'am, you have.' I glanced at her. She was chewing gummy bears again. 'Tell me the truth. Have you been to your daughter's place with your equipment?'

She gave me a nod. 'I have.'

'Did you find something?'

'I did. *In her bedroom.* And right outside her bedroom window. I don't like that.'

'And you want to see if the same thing is out there at that house? To see if the chemical signatures match?'

'Exactly. How close are we by the way?'

'We're almost there.' I slowed the car. Pulled to the side of the two-lane highway. 'This is where I saw the woman in the road.'

Chloe put her notebook down. The radio was playing softly, and she turned it off. She looked around the car; over her shoulder at the empty back seat. 'Do you hear that?'

'I don't hear anything.'

'Does the name *Sasha* mean anything to you?'

'Nope.'

She stared out the window. I pulled back on to the road, and a few minutes later, I drove into the driveway of the house. Gravel and tire marks on both sides. The house looked different; it had a forlorn, unloved look about it.

'Elle tried to track down the owner of this place by the way. Got nowhere. Some hedge fund out in the ether.'

'Figures. You ready?' I glanced at Chloe, and to be honest, she didn't look so good. 'You sure you want to do this?'

She nodded. 'Just feeling nauseated all of a sudden.'

It wasn't a good sign. We got a lot of vomiting in exorcisms, but I decided not to bring that up.

She grabbed the leather case she'd kept beside her in the front seat of the car. Started to open the door, head cocked to one side.

'What are you hearing, Chloe?'

'Whispering. You don't hear it?'

I shook my head. 'I try and block that kind of stuff out.'

'You can do that?'

I shrugged. 'Sometimes. What are they saying?'

'They—' Her voice broke. 'It is *they*, isn't it?'

'What are they saying?'

'*Where you been? I be waiting . . . Don't you know this be the place of no return? Don't you know I'm a gonna follow you home?*' She gave me a sassy look. 'Their grammar sucks.' Then she put her hands over her face.

'Take a steady breath,' I told her. 'They don't want you here, and they're on the attack. Which is very interesting. It's like they know you're going to be trouble.'

'How would whatever this is even be aware of me?'

'You went to Elle's house with your equipment, right?'

She nodded. 'I can show you the graph and the dark line where the sensors picked up the presence.'

'When you became aware of them, they became aware of you.'

'Shit. Of course. This is quantum entanglement. Exactly what I expected. Share a spatial proximity and become entangled on a subatomic scale and now . . . we'll be connected no matter how far apart.'

'You know, that way of looking at things takes the fun out of casual sex. Go home, take a hot shower and you're done. Except you're not if you're entangled. Glad I'm happily married.'

'This means it can follow me home,' she said, biting her knuckle. She took a breath. 'Good God. To think of Elle there in the middle of the night. Pammie – her kids. And Christ, where is that cop who disappeared? Where is Pammie's guy? Where did they go? What happened?'

'Yeah, a chemical signature is interesting, but—'

'Oh, dude, you are missing it. It's not just *interesting*. And we can ping it, if it's got physical presence. It will give off radiation. It means we can track it. Trace it. Follow it. Study it. Think *eradication*.'

'You're dreaming on that one.'

'I do have one small question.'

I waited. 'What's the question?'

'Is there a point . . . a point of no return? Where you can't get away? Can't make them stop?'

I flashed back to the feel of heat and the smell of burnt flesh. Decided on honesty. 'I've seen it. It's not pretty.'

She twisted sideways and looked at me. 'OK. Good to know. Let's go in.'

'You're sure? Because I've never seen a place where things just come at you like they do here. And you are already vulnerable.'

'Entangled. Totally different word. And if they are expecting me . . . well that works both ways, right? Now I'm expecting them.'

I thought of Elle shaking her fist at this house. Like mother like daughter.

EIGHT

Pammie had given me permission to go into the house, and the code to the new key box on the front door, but I didn't need it. Because the front door was ajar. It shook me a little. But I wasn't surprised.

'That looks like an invitation,' Chloe said. She had her leather case and her confidence back.

I pushed the door open and led the way.

She drifted a couple of feet down the hallway to the living room. 'Jesus. Who in their right mind rents a house with satanic symbols on the living-room wall?'

'Pammie said they were there when they moved in, but she and Conor figured they'd just paint over them.'

'Why didn't they?'

'They did. Several times. They just kept coming back.'

'Well awesome then, let me start right here. And where else would you advise?'

'The back bedroom. The hallway leading to that back bedroom and the bathroom attached. And the little room off the kitchen that they made into an office for Pammie. She said she hated it in there. She heard voices there. Kept thinking Conor was talking to her, but he never was. She was working in there the night she got so upset she called the crisis hotline.'

'OK, good to know.' She set her case up on the living-room floor and snapped the latches.

I drifted through the house. Empty now. All of Pammie's things were gone. Even the unopened can of paint in the closet. She had left a note in the kitchen with her husband's name at the top and a little heart. At the bottom were little geometric drawings, red and black dots, that I knew had been added by Patrick. The refrigerator was still hooked up. There was a new six-pack of water bottles cooling inside. And a box of unopened Ritz crackers on the counter next to the note.

Pammie still hoping her husband would come back.

Conor, my love, if you find your way home, the kids and I are at my grandmother's, at the Osage Golden Mobile Home Park. Water in the fridge. Come home. Please, please come home. We miss you. We love you.

More little hearts and a crying face.

It kept me up at night. Wondering what happened to Conor and Andi Craig. Looking for patterns, the most obvious of which was this damn house. I realized that I didn't actually know the details of how Conor had disappeared.

Pammie and Elle had both given me their numbers, both lodged in my contact list. I hit the button for Pammie. The phone rang only once before she picked up.

'Dr Archer?'

'Yeah, Pammie, do you have a minute?' I heard the baby making soft little noises, probably on Pammie's shoulder. It sounded like she was close to the phone.

'Is that Dr Archer?' Patrick's voice. 'Can I talk to him?'

I heard a television in the background.

'Not right now, Patrick – this is grown-up stuff.'

'Listen, Pammie, can you tell me exactly what happened before Conor disappeared? I never got the details. Do you mind?'

'No, but why? Have you heard something?'

'Just sifting the patterns of what happened to Conor and Andi Craig right before they both disappeared. Tom told me they found Andi's flashlight in the crawl space under the house. Do you know any reason she'd go down there? It was dark, and all hell was breaking loose, so it seems really strange to me.' I didn't tell her about the scuff marks the police had found in the hard-packed dirt.

Pammie caught her breath. 'Nobody told me that. Oh God, Conor was— Look, hold on a moment, OK? I want to get Patrick and the baby tucked in with my grandmother, so I can talk to you in private.'

'Sure, of course.'

There were muffled voices and footsteps as she got the kids settled, and I heard the unmistakable hinge of an old screen door open and close. A car going by, slowly. I pictured her outside the mobile home, sitting on the front step.

'OK, I got the kids squared away.'

'Start at the beginning.'

She took a breath; let it out. 'The last time I talked to Conor, he called me at work. The afternoon he disappeared. He said he was home early, and he was going to get the kids from daycare, just confirming that both of them were there, which seemed odd, but I said yeah, of course they were. He sounded preoccupied. But he said he'd had a good day at work, his training license had come through, and he said he'd cook dinner, and what did I want – tacos or pasta?'

She went quiet.

'And then what?'

'I said tacos. I work three to ten p.m., week nights. He puts my supper in the fridge. Sometimes he waits up and we eat together. Then he went quiet for a minute, and I asked if he was still there, and he said yeah, but he sounded distracted. I asked him what was going on, and he said he'd heard something, and he was going to check under the house real quick and then go get the kids. I asked him if it was those voices again – we would hear them sometimes when we were in the kitchen and it sounded like they came from under the house. But he just said he had to go and he loved me, and . . . we hung up.'

'Tell me about the noises.'

'They started the third night we were in the house. Voices, like somebody talking under the house. Knocking on the floor, right under our feet. This went on the whole time we were there, off and on. A few days nothing, then all night long – voices, knocking, slams and bangs. Conor would get pissed off, say he was putting an end to it once and for all and storm outside and go down into that godawful crawl space. But there never was anything down there that he could see.'

'And that was the last time you talked to him?'

'Yeah. The daycare people called me around six thirty. Said he hadn't come to get the kids, and they couldn't get him on the phone. I told them he'd called me at four and said he'd be leaving to get them in just a few minutes but that I was on my way. I called him several times – got no answer. And when I got home with the kids, his stuff was there. Truck in the driveway. Phone on the kitchen counter. No other calls or messages but mine. Wallet and keys on the dresser.'

I nodded. I'd seen them.

I heard Chloe's footsteps behind me as she made her way through the house. Heard her muttering softly to herself.

'Anything else?'

'I went down there as soon as I got home. To the crawl space.

Shaking like crazy but worried he was down there. Maybe he'd hit his head or had a heart attack – something awful. I left the kids in the car; didn't even take time to get them into the house.'

I waited.

'I'd never been down there before – spaces like that creep me out. You get there through a little wooden swing door on the side of the house; it latches with a hook. And you have to crawl. But I did it. He wasn't there, but he'd *been* there. The dirt was all scuffed up, like someone had dug in their heels. My husband is heavy and he wears barn boots.'

I didn't have the heart to ask her if it looked like he'd been dragged.

'And in the corner – way, way up to the side – there's a big square of plywood that's usually up against an opening that leads to where the pipes and things are. He showed it to me once, but I just looked at it from outside the little door, because you'd have to crawl on your belly to go in there. Conor would go down there to look for leaks, and he put the plywood up to keep kids, raccoons, I don't know, to keep things out. And that's how I knew for sure he'd been down there – that and the scuff marks. The plywood sheet was moved and propped against some cinder blocks. Near the wall. But he wasn't in there. I looked, and the police looked too.'

'And did you put the plywood back?'

'Yeah. After the police came out the first time, I did. I put it back. And you're telling me that Andi Craig was down there? And she left her flashlight? Were there scuff marks?'

'Yes.'

She took a breath. 'Just like Conor – almost exactly. Don't go down there, Dr Archer. Don't go down there by yourself.'

'I want to take a look, but I've got backup.'

'And if you find anything? You'll let me know?'

'I will.'

'OK. Patrick keeps wanting to go back there and look for his dad, but of course I say no. He's not doing too good. He's having nightmares. He doesn't want to go to school. It's just . . . regular kid stuff.'

'Pammie, I want you to tell me if things with Patrick get worse.'

'Oh, I don't want to bother you with this—'

'I want you to tell me. It's important. You are his mother, and you know him better than anybody. If you decide he's not OK, you come to me.'

She promised she would, thanked me and I let her go. Looked up to see Chloe standing in the doorway.

'What's up?' she asked. The professional had taken over, and she looked steady and calm.

'I need to go under the house.'

'That's where they found Andi Craig's flashlight, right? I know the police have been all over that.'

'And Conor was there too, right before he disappeared.'

'I didn't know that. Very weird. Sounds like a hot spot. Let's go down there.'

'I was on my way.'

'By yourself?'

'Hell no. I was going to see if you'd come with me. Just let me get the flashlight out of the trunk of the car. Let's go check it out.'

NINE

We headed out the back door of the house and down two small steps. The wooden door that led under the house was just a few feet away, clearly visible in the cinder-block foundation, though the grass had grown up around it. I hated spaces like this, but I went in there anyway, hands and knees in the dirt, and Chloe crawled in right behind me.

'Prop that little wooden door open, would you? Here, take this.'

I slid a chipped cinder block toward her, and she propped the door open. I had the flashlight. It was murky down there. Daylight seeped in, but there were dark corners. No spiderwebs. No spiders. Just dirt and scattered rock. In the corner, a child's stuffed animal, a lion with a tattered mane.

Chloe picked up something white and put it back down. She looked at me. 'A woman's white glove. Not so white anymore. Pretty weird thing to find down here.'

What puzzled me was what we didn't find. No insects. No sign of animals coming in. It was quiet.

'I'm afraid of spiders,' Chloe said.

'I don't see any.'

She was frowning at the spectrograph. 'Noah,' she said.

I was looking under the house where the pipes were. The plywood had been moved. Maybe by Andi Craig. Maybe by the cops. I knew the tracking dog had picked up a scent down here. But I didn't see anything but hard-packed dirt, rock and pipes.

'*Noah.* We need to get out of here.'

'You mean you found something?'

'Yeah. Same chemical signature I found at Elle's house but stronger – *much stronger*. It's in the kitchen, in Pammie's office, that back bedroom, that little bathroom. Nothing in either of the kids' rooms. But down here? It's off the charts. And it's arcing up, getting stronger. And I've got to tell you, I'm suddenly not feeling too good.'

'Go, go – I'm right behind you.'

* * *

She started vomiting as soon as we were out of the crawl space. It was violent, and copious, and once she was done, I settled her on the back steps and went to the car for a water bottle and a clean towel. I have kids.

When I got back, she was still sheet white and trembling. I crouched beside her. Wet the towel and wiped her face down; gave her the bottle of water.

She rinsed her mouth and spit. 'Thank you.' She took some unsteady breaths. 'You know, Perry told me there was a lot of GI upset with this. With exorcisms.'

'If you mean a lot of vomiting—'

'It makes sense. The neurons going from the gut to the brain. I mean there are millions of nerve cells in the gut, nerve fibers that run from the intestines to the brain. More from the gut to the brain than vice versa. Then the brain interprets the data through the emotions, and if it happens again and again, then the brain neurons can get over-sensitized. Did it . . . did it never occur to you to look at the gut during the MRIs?'

'Yeah, I missed that.'

'Don't feel bad. The gut-brain stuff is just now trending.' She wiped her mouth with the towel again.

'You steady? I'd like to get you out of here.'

'If by steady you mean not vomiting anymore, yeah, I think I'm done.'

I helped her up. Kept a hand on her as we headed to the car.

'Did we leave the front door wide open like that, Noah? We didn't, did we?'

'No. I shut it and locked it.'

'Maybe I should . . . check the doorway.'

'I think we have a good enough set of data, Chloe.'

She nodded. 'Perry talks about you a lot, Noah, and as much as I feel like I've known you for years, this is closer than I wanted to get.'

'You mean the vomiting? Don't worry about it. I'm a doctor – I do this shit for a living.'

'That doesn't help.' She climbed into the front seat of the car, still talking. 'Because I've vomited down my favorite shirt and vomited on your shoe, and all I want is . . .'

I knew what she wanted. Perry. I wondered when he was coming home.

‘We’ll stop at a gas station or something and get you a Coke to settle your stomach. You’re going to be OK, Chloe.’

‘Really? Because as much as I love Coke—’

‘If you’re worried about entanglement, think about Perry. You’re more entangled with him than the dark stuff.’

‘I like a man who knows how to talk to me on a quantum level. But what I really mean is, I’m going to need more gummy bears along with the Coke.’

TEN

Chloe was quiet on the drive back, but she looked a bit better by the time we got to her house. Some pink in her cheeks. She gathered up her leather case and purse as I turned into her narrow driveway.

'Listen, are you going to be OK?'

She gave me the kind of smile people hide behind. 'I'll be fine, thank you.'

I closed my eyes; blew out air. Gave her a steady look. 'It's a legit question. You live alone?'

'I do.'

'Got a big dog?'

'Not even a plant.'

'Do you think you could talk to Perry if you . . . felt the need?'

'I told him I'd call. But. It's a lot to hit him with.'

'He'll be expecting it. He'll be worried more if you don't call. And he is the best guy to help you out.'

She looked at me over one shoulder. 'You know he's leaving the church?'

'Yeah.'

'That was the issue that took our marriage down. The church. I was so in love with him. Still am. Whatever differences I have with Perry cut right to the heart of organized religion. To me, spirituality is completely different from the practice of religion, which I think is man-made, judgmental and misogynistic. We really tried to work through it, but I couldn't have a life partnership with a man whose life's work was steeped in the systemic misogyny of religion, no matter how much I loved him. And I'm sure it was hell being married to a woman who loathed the very thing he lived for. We live in a world that asks us to accept outrageous things so everyone else will be comfortable. That didn't work for either of us.'

She squinted. Thought about it. 'He's been talking about it a lot the last few months. Leaving. But something triggered him in Rome. He called me two nights after he got there; said he'd made his decision. Wanted to know if I was really OK, because he was worried about me and Elle; said he had to get home as soon as possible. He didn't say why, just that he was leaving the Vatican immediately – *ditching Rome* is how he put it. He'd packed his stuff and was on his way to let them know he wasn't going to finish out the conference. That must have been a couple of hours before . . . before his heart stopped.' She looked over at me. 'So no. I'm not going to call him and tell him I got scared today. I'm going to let my husband rest.'

'Well look, you can call me if you need to. And you can call Elle.'

She laughed.

'Why is that funny?'

'She doesn't answer the phone when I call her, listen to phone messages I leave or read any emails from Mom. I might get through to her if I texted the right emoji.'

I nodded. 'Same thing with me and Tom.'

'Elle talks about him,' she said. 'A lot.'

ELEVEN

It started with Patrick, and it was a small change. Pammie knew something was off. But her grandmother, with the kind of wisdom that comes in your eighties, figured it out first.

Because as things began to escalate for Patrick, that earliest sign was a change in eye contact. A *lack* of eye contact.

It was a good thing I'd told Pammie to call me if Patrick got worse. I fit her in after office hours, and Patrick was sitting out in the waiting room eating Cheetos and, God help me, reading a book. Pammie said he suddenly wouldn't touch the Chromebook she had for him at home. Not even to watch a video. He'd stopped watching television too.

'I have health insurance,' was the first thing she told me.

I shook my head. 'You don't need it.'

She gave me a steady look, with more confidence than I would have had, because I'd snooped in her house and seen the stack of medical bills and student-loan invoices, industriously and voraciously building interest.

'Seriously,' I told her. 'The Enlightenment Project is an NGO; we're generously funded, and anyone I treat in this . . . *category*, that goes under research. I couldn't charge you if I wanted to; I charge the NGO.'

She gave me a tense smile, but I could see the relief.

'And your information is kept confidential.'

She nodded. She hadn't assumed that. People were wary these days. Myself included.

In truth, I'd been more than uneasy about Patrick, who'd spent six weeks steeped in the presence of something very dark, something that had *taken* his father. Patrick was a year younger than I was when I'd been possessed by dark entities, and I wanted to head this off before it escalated. Because it always escalated.

'Everything OK at your grandmother's place?'

She smiled. I could see that being with her grandmother was a good thing. 'She's there with the kids when I work nights. I thought it would be hard on her – she has a lot of arthritis – but she seems happier, more energetic with the chaos and mess the kids and I bring. And I didn't realize how much help Patrick would be. When her wrist is bothering her, she loses her grip, so he helps her carry things. Open them. And she has such a calming presence. The kids are crazy about her.'

Happy chaos, I thought.

'And Patrick found a gang of kids there to ride bikes with. It brings back memories. I spent my childhood outside running with a pack of kids, but nobody does that much these days. But at the park, they lean toward free-range kids. Patrick loves it.'

'That sounds really good. What's going on that makes you worry?'

'He keeps waking up crying, saying he can hear his dad, calling to him for help. Nightmares, but he wants to go and look for him. To go back to the house.'

'Don't do that. The house is dangerous.'

'No chance of that, believe me. I can't even drive by the place without having a panic attack.'

'Don't drive by either. Keep as much distance as you can.'

'You didn't see anything in the crawl space?'

'I would have called you.' I debated telling her about Chloe's results, but we were keeping that to ourselves.

'Do you think there's still hope? To find Conor?'

Finding him seemed like a long shot, and when and if we did, my thinking was it would be his remains. I was pretty sure he and Officer Andi Craig were dead. I didn't much like hope. Personally. But I didn't argue with people when they had it.

'I'm not ready to give up.'

'And you've never seen anything like this before? With people disappearing from an . . . an infested place?'

'No. Nothing like it. Which doesn't mean it hasn't happened.'

'But it has to be connected. Both of them disappearing after they go down to the crawl space of that house.'

'Yes, I'd agree with that. You hear any local talk about it?'

She shook her head. 'I've asked around. Believe me, there are plenty of rumors and theories. But nobody *disappearing*. And Tom – he's been great; he helped move my stuff to my grandmothers and put some of it in storage. He talked to the local police, and they don't have any old, mysterious missing persons cases. They've been called out to the house a lot, and nothing like this ever happened before.'

'OK then. Tell me about Patrick.'

'So . . . he has nightmares. He's afraid to go to sleep. He used to have the occasional bad dream of course, but this is on a whole new level.'

'When did it start?'

'I mean – he's been prone to nightmares this whole last year. They got worse when we moved into the house. After we settled in with my grandmother, I thought they would stop then – he loves it there – but it's actually getting worse.'

'Worse since you left the house?' I made a few notes. 'Does he tell you about the dreams?'

'He says a shadow man looks at him through the window. And sometimes he wakes up and the shadow man is sitting on the end of his bed.'

Shadow man. Chloe had told me Elle saw the same thing. I didn't like the sound of this.

'But it started at the house. The shadow man dreams. He'd scream, and Conor would go running in, and he'd be saying the shadow man got into the house and stood by the bed and scared the baby. And the shadow man said *be quiet* or he would hurt the baby. But Patrick told me that he knew he had to call for help, and the shadow man was bad, so he wouldn't do what a bad man told him.'

'Smart,' I said. *Dear God*, I thought.

She put her face in her hands.

'Hurt the baby how?'

'I asked him that. He said the shadow man didn't say. I don't believe him; I think he's afraid to say it.'

'Or he was told not to.'

'And his dad would go in and make sure the window was locked, and do a walk-through of the house, tell Patrick everything was safe and locked up and hey, I'm a big guy, and whatever happens, I'll handle it. That definitely helped. Conor made him feel safe. He made all of us feel safe.'

I nodded. I didn't say what I was thinking. That telling a child what he was afraid of wasn't real didn't work well if it *was* real. And in some sense, and on some level, it was always real.

'We didn't get it,' she said. 'We told him the shadow man was a dream and not really there. But I think now that something *was* there. And Patrick's still dreaming about the shadow man. I don't know how to fight something like this. That's real or isn't real. I can't get hold of it.'

'You and I will make sure Patrick is safe.'

She nodded politely. She wasn't reassured. I didn't blame her. And I thought about Perry. Who was very much needed right now.

'But Patrick, he kind of came up with his own solution. His grandmother had gotten him some sidewalk chalk. And he loved it, but he didn't want to play with it outside. He started to draw on the walls in his bedroom.'

She got her phone out of her purse, scrolled to a photo and handed it over. The geometry symbols I'd seen in his room. Along with the red and black dots in patterns.

I handed it back. 'Text it to me, will you? And I saw these, in his room.'

She nodded. 'As soon as he drew those on the wall, the shadow man stopped coming inside. The dreams changed. The shadow man was close, he was around, but he wasn't getting into the house. So the symbols protected him somehow.'

'How did he know to draw them?'

'Every time I ask him, he pretends he doesn't hear me. His dad tried to talk to him about it – same response. Which was no response.'

A mild form of disassociation. A child form.

'But he'd get panicked if the chalk smeared, so we got him some paints and let him paint them on.'

'Good,' I said.

'Really? I'm just flying blind on instinct. I don't really know what to do.'

Pretty much the definition of parenthood.

'What about painting symbols at your grandmother's place?'

'Everywhere. My grammy doesn't mind – she encourages him. And he's painted the symbols on the walls in every single room, and by all the doors and windows. And it's interesting. I was going to major in anthropology, at Yale. I've always been into this kind of thing, and symbols or objects of protection are common in a lot of cultures, a lot of religions. Maybe all of them. The gargoyles on the churches in France aren't there for decoration – they're there to protect everyone inside.' She looked away. 'I'm scared for my son. That whatever it was that took my husband, it will get him too. And now it's not just Patrick. It's other kids at his school.'

It was a jolt. I kept my noncommittal face on. But this happened all the time. Patients told you the most important things as a side bar, an *oh by the way.*

'Tell me about it. Don't leave anything out.'

'About a week before we moved into the house, Patrick didn't want to go to school.'

'*Before?*'

'Yeah, that's why I hadn't brought it up. It wasn't connected to the stuff at the house.'

'School phobia?'

She shook her head. 'Possible, but it doesn't really track. Patrick *loves* his school. It's small and kind of charming. He's got great teachers, two best friends, and the three of them are inseparable – they have their last class together, science. And both of his friends are having trouble. I've been talking to their parents, and the teacher in the last class where they're all together.'

'Just these three – no other kids?'

She frowned. 'Not sure I'd know. The teacher seemed . . . she didn't seem surprised.'

I nodded. Waiting.

She bit her lip. 'So I told your assistant, Joyce – she was so nice to me – that Patrick won't make eye contact with me.'

'She told me. How long has this been going on?'

'The last eight days. And it's not just Patrick. It's his friend, Mateo. The eye-contact thing. But his other friend, Susu – her mom says she's just the opposite. Won't be alone, is agitated, breaks things. And she's . . . repeating phrases. Like if her mom says night-night, Susu says night-night, night-night, night-night. Over and over. It's weird.'

'Echolalia,' I said, feeling a terrible dread.

'And every morning when her mom gets up, she finds Susu hiding.'

'Where?'

'Under her parents' bed. They never hear her come in. They don't know what to do.'

I made a few notes. Looked back up. 'Let's bring Patrick in. But before we do that, has Elle seen Patrick since this started up?'

Pammie shook her head. 'Elle said I should see *you.* I told her you said to call if things got worse. She thought that Patrick's issues were worrying, but her training is for patients over eighteen. She didn't want me to take him to her supervising psychiatrist, Dr

Holtzer, because she wanted Patrick to see someone who would understand the kind of trauma he went through at that house. She said she was taking some time off, so to call her cell phone if I needed follow-up after I met with you.'

I gave her my noncommittal look. 'And this would be *Dr Silas Holtzer*, is that correct?'

She nodded. 'He's also in charge of the mental health part of the local hospital and the clinic where Elle works. You know him?'

'I do.'

Dr Holtzer was notorious for putting patients in involuntary psychiatric hold. Particularly women. I didn't want him anywhere near Patrick, and I didn't much like him working with Elle.

This wasn't the first time I'd run across Dr Holtzer. A doctor who believed all the good things he said about himself. He was an enthusiastic Medicaid scammer who routinely put Medicaid patients on psychiatric hold, keeping them locked up with no assessments and no care. It was a good racket, and he was rumored to rake in over two thousand dollars a day. He had a rich pool of possibility, being the on-record attending at three clinics that I knew of, supervising PAs and NPs without actually being available. You could work a lot of jobs if you didn't do the work. When people get to the top of their field, it's surprisingly easy to do.

And Dr Holtzer forced the meds, most of them old-school behavioral restraints.

I first ran across Dr Silas Holtzer when a patient of mine died of urinary sepsis while in seventy-two-hour lockdown under Holtzer's care. The patient had Parkinson's and was sliding into dementia. I had him slated for a DBS – deep brain stimulation surgery. He'd stopped responding to the meds that had helped him for years, and he was having terrible tremors, uncontrollable movements, loss of urinary control. His wife took him to the ER with sudden agitation, and aggression caused by his inability to explain the pain caused by a kidney infection and the inability to urinate. For seventy-two hours he got anti-psychotics that made his motor symptoms worse; meds that shut him up. He got no mental health care, and no basic healthcare. It was a terrible death of cruelty and neglect.

Another patient of mine with a brain tumor committed suicide from the trauma of one of Dr Holtzer's seventy-two-hour lockdowns that mysteriously and illegally morphed into eighteen days.

I'm not going to tell you a seventy-two-hour hold is never OK, but I am going to tell you that the fallout can be horrific. Oftentimes it's seventy-two-hour warehousing, with no physical or mental health care provided, and the result is trauma to a most vulnerable patient, job loss, crippling medical bills for treatment the patient did not authorize or even receive, years of hounding by creditors, forced medication with a long-term ripple effect and a total mistrust of any healthcare professional who might actually be able to help.

Seventy-two-hour holds come with PTSD. Everyone in the profession knows it; none of them talk about it, shaking their heads and saying they're saving lives. Sometimes they are.

The suicide rates within a year after a lockdown are high. And there's a serious risk of a patient falling into the for-profit incarceration abyss. Because there's often no other place to put them than county jail.

I've seen patients get help during a lockdown. I've seen them get lifesaving help. But too many of them fall into the hands of someone like Dr Silas Holtzer.

Pammie was giving me a worried look.

I didn't tell her that I'd reported Dr Holtzer to Medicaid for fraud, and to the medical board and the state regulatory board for malpractice. It had made me enemies. I'd been pulled aside and talked to and exchanged veiled threats of my own, a quid pro quo, which is how these things are really done. Fuck with me, and I'll fuck with you. I had more clout than Holtzer, but my NGO didn't help my reputation. Luckily I was hard to replace.

And Holtzer was afraid of me. Just a little. Though I wouldn't say that out loud.

I gave Pammie a big smile. 'If we need to bring in a child psychiatrist, I know somebody really great.'

'Elle said you would know what to do.' And she gave me her endearing gap-toothed smile.

TWELVE

Patrick drifted into my office, like a distracted duckling following his mother. There was none of the engaged curiosity and little-boy confidence that had charmed me the night we'd met.

'Hey, Patrick,' I said.

He didn't look up. He settled himself beside his mother on the couch.

'Patrick, tell Dr Archer hello,' Pammie said. She was annoyed with him and worried about him, and her face went pink. I shook my head at her. She settled back on the couch. Patrick sat beside her, perched on the edge of the seat.

'I was thinking about you last night, Patrick, when I got up to get a sandwich. Ham and cheese.'

Patrick started swinging his legs in a three-beat cadence. Up, down, pause. Up, down, pause. His mother put a hand on his leg. He stopped. She moved her hand away and he started again.

'How are things at school, Patrick?'

He ignored me. It didn't seem intentional. It didn't seem rude. He just seemed *not quite there*.

'Does your kitty cat like living with your great-grandmother?'

'Mimi?' he said, frowning, his legs going still. 'Mimi loves cats. She lets her sleep on her bed up on the pillow. Mimi is really nice. And I like it there. It's a *good* place. The backyard is really little with a white fence, and Mimi plants flowers, and it's pretty there.' He began swinging his legs again. Up, down, pause.

I came out from behind my desk; pulled a chair up across from them.

'Patrick, can I look at your eyes? You can stay right where you are.'

He didn't look at me. Swung his legs. Up, down, pause.

Pammie put a hand on his leg. 'Patrick, answer Dr Archer. He just wants to look at your eyes.'

Patrick didn't notice, and he didn't respond. I got the feeling he hadn't heard either of us. Like we weren't on his radar. Like Patrick was somewhere else.

I touched his shoulder – gently. 'Follow my finger, Patrick, just with your eyes.'

He froze then followed my finger like it was a life raft, his legs still again. Excellent simultaneous focus with both eyes, something that develops through age seven. Patrick was ten. December birthday.

I put the light back in my pocket. Patrick continued to stare at my finger. I put my hand back on his shoulder and pushed very lightly. No resistance.

'That's great, Patrick – your eyes are perfect. Excellent focus, old son.'

He kept watching my finger. I pushed his shoulder a little harder. No pushback, zero resistance, muscles pliable. If I'd pushed harder, I knew he would go sideways on the couch, but I didn't take it that far.

'How are you sleeping, Patrick?'

He didn't answer. I pulled my finger back; put my hands in my pockets. Broke the gaze. 'You sleep good?'

He turned and looked at me. Thought about it. Nodded then stared at the floor.

'I'll say he's sleeping good.' Pammie smiled. 'He used to wake up early every morning, even before the baby, and now I can hardly get him out of bed.'

'How long has that been going on?' I asked.

'Oh, just the last three days.'

I saw it hit her as soon as she said it. This wasn't good. No eye contact, followed by sleeping more, and hard to wake up. She was careful to keep a bright smile as she wiped tears out of the corner of her eyes.

'You two up for me to run a few tests? You look like the picture of health to me, Patrick; I'm just making sure everything is ticking over like it should.'

'Ticking over,' he said. 'Ticking over, ticking over, ticking over, ticking over.' He paused, and Pammie went white. I figured this was the first time this had happened, but Patrick would be stressed here in my office, and clearly . . . things were escalating. But he had connected to me, just a minute ago. I wanted to build on that. If I could.

'Ticking over,' Patrick said. Then stopped.

Pammie was watching me, biting her lips, the color draining slowly out of her face.

'There won't be any shots. I don't know about you, but I'm a big baby about shots.'

Patrick turned and looked at me and made eye contact. 'But you're a doctor.'

'I know, right? It's embarrassing.'

He gave me a little smile. 'You're messing with me,' he said.

I just grinned.

'Also, I'm going to see if I can get you in with Dr Bianchi, if you and your mom are up for it. She's one of those doctors you talk to when you have things to discuss you might be upset about.'

'A psychiatrist?' Patrick asked.

I nodded. 'Yeah, and I like her. She talked to my boys when they were really little, and she likes to play games while she talks. She's fun. It's hard to get an appointment with her because the kids always like to go back to her and play more games. She keeps a bowl of candy in her office too. But I'm hoping she might have a cancellation. We might as well give it a shot.'

'OK,' Patrick said.

Pammie nodded too.

First off would be a test for encephalitis, followed by a whole lot more. I hated putting a kid through this stuff, but right now, it was all about exclusion. I didn't like what I was seeing with Patrick. My gut said escalating disassociation with ongoing stressors. *Catatonic disassociation* because Patrick was scared of something. Really scared. And so were his friends. Maybe different symptoms, but they all came under the heading of off-the-charts stress. And it had started *before* Patrick and his family had moved into that house. And the link between all three of these kids was that last class at school.

'Anything going on you want to talk to me about, Patrick? Anybody hurt you? Scare you? Make you worry?'

He looked down at his hands. 'Worried about my dad,' he said.

'Yeah, we're all worried about your dad. That's really hard.'

'He'll come home,' Pammie said.

Patrick looked up at her. 'When? What if he comes home and we're not there? *What if he goes back to that house*?'

'We left him a note,' Pammie said. 'Let him a box of Ritz crackers, and you know how much he loves them. And I told him exactly where to find us.'

'You don't think we should stay there and wait for him?'

I shook my head. 'Your daddy can find you, Patrick. I'm a daddy, and the first thing I'd look for is a note.'

He looked up at me. 'So we don't have to go back to the house to wait for him?'

'*Ever again.*'

'OK.' His look to me was grateful, but he was stiff with tension, muscles bunched tight. Completely engaged and making eye contact. So he was with me. Back in the world. That made me feel a whole lot better. There was still time to head this off.

'Tell me about school, Patrick.' I put my hand back on his shoulder. Muscles tense, a little bit of automatic pushback and a serious uptick in respiration. I had no doubt his little heart would be beating fast.

'What's going on at school, Patrick?'

'Scary.'

'Scary like how?'

'Scary like the house,' he whispered, looking over one shoulder. Then he screamed.

THIRTEEN

It took some doing, but Pammie got Patrick calmed down enough that I felt I could leave them just for a bit.

'I'll be back in a few, Patrick. I'll give you and your mom some space here, and also, I'm coming back with a surprise.'

He didn't seem at all interested in a surprise. But Pammie looked up.

'It's a good kind of surprise,' I said. 'You guys OK just to stay put? I won't be long.'

I didn't treat children; it was not my specialty, but dark entities were. And Patrick didn't need a doctor who would not believe a damn word he said. Someone who would pathologize him and try to convince him there was nothing to be afraid of when there so clearly was a shitload to be afraid of.

His symptoms were bad. Pre-catatonia disassociation, due to ongoing traumatic stressors, which I was pretty sure were dark entities. There were some doctors who thought catatonia was purely an intense fear reaction, and it sure looked like that to me. Dr Bianchi had published a paper on it. I was going to have to get a child psychiatrist on this – and soon. It was going to be tricky to find someone good who could see him; the good ones sometimes had a waiting list of eighteen months. And I wanted Bianchi. Patrick was on his way to escalating catatonia, and the possibility of meds loomed in his future. Bianchi would be careful with the meds.

The walk to the hospital cafeteria did me good, and I got several orders of French fries, which I deeply believe have mysterious healing powers. I remembered the catsup. There were soft drinks in the office. Joyce had a serious orange soda addiction.

I was torn, and I wanted to think, and waiting for the fries to come up gave me a bit of a breather. I considered telling Pammie to keep Patrick out of school. Hard call. I needed more information. Including the tests that would help me rule things out. And ruling things out was the basis of medicine these days. Run tests, get results and if nothing shows up . . . well, not much help then, sorry. Tests were crucial and necessary but they were only part of the picture. Except now. Nowadays, they pretty much were the picture.

Patrick was calm when I got back, engaged, drinking a can of Orange Crush from the soft drinks in our little fridge. I handed out French fries to everyone, which went over well with Patrick, Pammie and also with me.

Patrick ate fries and told me the scary part of school always came during the last class of the day, the science class that used to be his favorite, but now it was the one where he and his friends were having trouble, and he dreaded it all day. Also that the cafeteria was creepy and so was the office, both in the old part of the building that was always stinky, according to Patrick. The office was just out in the hall area, and there were cameras all over the school, and there were screens behind the desk where they could watch everything, but not in the bathrooms. And sometimes when you were lined up for the cafeteria, you could see weird things on the screens. He tried not to look. He said you could run past the screens if you stayed on the correct side of the hallway. A lot of the kids ran past the office, and nobody ever got mad. He wasn't the only kid in the class having trouble, and yes, it had been going on since the beginning of the school year. It was bad.

'Tell me what bad means, Patrick.'

Mainly it was how he felt in the classroom. He liked science, and he liked the teacher and loved when they accidentally set the plaster of Paris volcano on fire, and there were two gerbils in a cage, except the teacher got worried about them and took them home.

'What was the problem with the gerbils?' I asked.

'They would go bonkers, then they got sick, and the teacher felt bad for them and took them home. But they're OK now – she showed us some pictures. But she said she's not going to bring them back.'

'Anything changed recently? Made things worse, because this is kind of new, right – the troubles you and your buddies are having?'

He nodded hard. '*Sasha.*'

Sasha? I remembered Chloe asking me if I'd ever heard the name Sasha.

I glanced from Patrick to Pammie. 'Tell me about Sasha.'

Three weeks ago, Patrick's science teacher, Mrs Garcia, brought in a big box, and when she opened it up, there was a weird-looking robot boy inside. Mrs Garcia was so excited, and the other kids, they were excited too. Most of them. At first.

One Sasha Artificial Intelligence Educational System had been donated to each of the fifth-grade classrooms in the school, a total of four, as an experimental program. They were told that with teachers and parents getting *busier every day*, this was an opportunity to allow the children to be *empowered by technology*. The Sasha Educational System was considered a teaching aid that could *enhance education and bridge the digital divide.*

Sasha had wheels under his little plastic shoes, so he could glide from desk to desk in the classroom, and he was programmed into the laptop each student was issued at the beginning of the year. Sasha communicated through the computer screen in chat boxes. Sasha could administer test questions on subjects discussed in class. If the answers given were wrong, Sasha would glide to the student's desk, providing *an interactive physical presence of social and emotional connection* while talking them through the material using the chat box on their computer screen.

Pammie passed me a school handout then folded her arms. 'This thing has been a nightmare,' she said.

The first line on the handout sheet set my teeth on edge. *Artificial intelligence can be used to power monitoring systems to help track children's behavior and glean insights into their development.*

And what would it do with those insights, I wondered, as I scanned the sheet. And what did AI really know about childhood development? It sounded like a con job to me. Moira's school had opted in for a chatbot program, and it had been such a disaster, they'd opted out again two weeks later.

'It calls me *trailer trash*,' Patrick whispered.

I looked up.

'It says nice things to most of the kids, but to me and Susu and Mateo . . .' He looked away, face flushed, hands in fists.

Sometimes Sasha came on the screens when he was turned off.

Sometimes Sasha told them weird things, and at first the teacher thought it was a programing glitch. The teacher laughed like it was a joke. Some of the kids laughed, and some got upset. Patrick never laughed. Some of the kids thought Sasha was cool, but Patrick knew better. Sometimes at night . . . he had dreams about Sasha. Bad dreams.

The little trio of Patrick and his friends all thought Sasha was watching them. Because he *told* them he was watching them. But when they told the teacher, she looked at the screens of their laptops to see what Sasha had sent to the message box, and it was all erased.

And then Sasha escalated.

'Threats,' Pammie said.

I looked at Patrick. 'Tell me one.'

'He said, *Your daddy is dead, you nasty little fucker, and your mommy is next, and it's going to be all your fault. I can make you do things you don't want to do.* He can't though. And I would never hurt my mom. And when he said it, I got mad, and then I got in trouble.' He gave me a cool look of banked-down fury. 'Because I told the teacher, but she didn't see what Sasha said. He made it go away. She didn't believe me. And she got mad when I kicked Sasha in the stomach and tried to twist his neck. He's going to get me for that. He hates me the most. But I'm going to get him first. I'm going to run over him with Daddy's truck.'

I took a minute to stop gritting my teeth. 'You won't have to, Patrick. Because I believe you. I'm going to take care of Sasha for you.'

I looked at Pammie and she took a breath.

'It gets worse, Dr Archer.'

'*Worse?*'

Supposedly a whiz at preventing data breaches, Sasha *was* a data breach. It had gone online to 'scrape' information – personal details about the kids, accessing their social media, their families' social media, their online history, able to bypass the school's content moderators programmed into the laptops. It had singled out Patrick, Susu and Mateo for an onslaught of harassment, threats and taunts. Wherever they, their siblings, their parents were on social media – Sasha found them.

And then it sent them porn. Violent porn.

That was when Mrs Garcia and the school shut it down.

Pammie put shaky hands on Patrick's shoulders. 'I talked to Mrs Garcia. There are four fifth-grade classrooms, and hers was the only one having trouble. She said that Patrick and his two friends were the only ones who were bullied. Who got the . . . you know.'

'Bad stuff,' Patrick said.

'Has it stopped?' I asked.

Pammie shook her head. 'It hacked our baby monitor. And Susu said it came on their smart TV. I've shut all of my social media down. Even for my business.' Pammie gave me a look. 'You know what, Patrick? Maybe we could use a break. If Dr Archer agrees, maybe you should take some time off from school.'

I nodded.

'No,' Patrick said. 'I have to go. I've got stuff to do there.'

'How about you let me talk to your teacher and we'll see how it goes.' I looked at Pammie. 'Can you help me set something up?'

'We've scheduled a little conference already. For me and Susu and Mateo's parents – sort of a brainstorming thing. Tomorrow afternoon.'

I nodded. 'This is good. After this conference, I'd like to talk to the teacher myself, when school is over and there aren't any kids in the room. One on one. *In the classroom.* Can you set that up?'

Pammie nodded. 'I think so. She's really nice. But—'

'But?'

'It has to be before it gets dark. She doesn't like to stay in the classroom past dusk. She has to stay late on parent–teacher night so she brings her dog.'

'What kind of dog?'

'Chihuahua.'

Worse than a pit bull, I thought. Most of the pit bulls I've met are sweet. Chihuahuas, not so much. And against something demonic? Takes one to know one.

And what I wanted to know was . . . how bad *were* things at the school? In truth, it would be hard to know what part of Sasha was dark entity or dark web. Maybe they were one and the same. AI was just opening another door, welcoming them in. If there were kids having trouble, I wanted to know what it was like for the teachers. I wanted the gossip, the rumors, the juicy stuff. And not wanting to be there after dark sounded ominous.

My Moira was a teacher. Maybe I could get her to make a few calls.

FOURTEEN

The next day was a long one, back to back surgeries, and Joyce was still there when I headed back to my office. More tired than usual. A lot on my mind. The conference with Patrick's teacher was set up for tomorrow, and I'd had to cancel two appointments to get down there after school but before dark.

Joyce was wearing the combat boots I'd bought her for Christmas, her steep heels kicked under the desk – where they stayed most of the time. The boots looked damned good with her gray pencil skirt and soft cashmere sweater. I made a mental note to get Moira a pair of combat boots. She could wear them to school.

Joyce looked up when she saw me; gave me her catlike smile. 'I have good news for you, Noah.'

'Good news sounds excellent.'

'Dr Bianchi is going to see Patrick this week. And I've set up payment through the NGO.'

'*This week?* I figured she'd be eighteen months out.'

'She's been overhauling her practice and focusing on the kind of specialty patients she really wants to work with.'

Knowing Dr Bianchi, that translated to the patients who needed someone who could tackle the unusual. Good for them and fun for her. Last time I talked to her, she hadn't had a weekend free in four months and she'd been exhausted. I liked the sound of this.

I looked sideways at Joyce. 'How did you pull that off?'

Joyce gave me the serene smile that told me she'd been up to something. She had once explained her theory of medical management: doctors, like infants and toddlers, needed regular routine, regular time off, and emergencies could be scheduled in if you always left a gap for them in the weekly schedule, and anyone who tried to mess with her scheduling for their mere convenience would be met with a courteous brick wall. Which, by the way, included me. She also thought that if patients needed certain doctors, the doctors needed them too. This rang true to me.

'Have you—'

'Yes, Noah, I've already talked to Patrick's mother and set it up.

And Dr Bianchi wanted me to let you know she'd make herself available to talk to Patrick's two friends, if they'd like to consult. She highly recommended it, as they all seemed to be affected. She thought it would be wise to look at the big-picture dynamic.'

I sat down in the chair across from Joyce's desk. I needed to get off my feet.

'Dr Bianchi is very interested in the kind of symptom clusters all of these children have. She's published extensively on that. It's her passion.'

So that had been the lure.

Dr Bianchi was exactly who I wanted. She had helped Moira and I ease our own two boys from a mysterious abusive early start in life, the details of which had never been revealed. And helped all four of us navigate foster care and adoption, with one-step-at-a-time patience to build the tight family we had.

So I smiled at Joyce and thanked her profusely, and she gave me the serious look that meant she understood exactly what I was thinking. If Dr Bianchi was joining us so quickly, it didn't give me that rainbow-and-unicorn glow. It meant Dr Bianchi was just as worried about Patrick and his buddies as I was. She considered them an emergency.

So this was one big issue off my to-do list. Next up, Elle. I wanted to check in with her. Then I would tackle the school. I wanted to make Sasha's acquaintance. And there was the ongoing issue of my medical practice.

I was suddenly very tired. Too tired to stay late. Moira would be at rehearsals. And I just wanted to pick up dinner, go home and hug my boys.

FIFTEEN

Elle hadn't reached out to her old Uncle Noah for help. That wasn't going to stop me. She was *taking some time off* according to Pammie. I didn't like the sound of that. And I wanted to talk to her about Holtzer.

Chloe was right – Elle didn't answer her phone. I sent her texts with emojis. An email. Let her know I was there if she needed me.

Evidently she did.

Rehearsal nights for Moira ran late. I arrived home with pizza and found Tom out in the backyard with Marcus and Vaughn, kicking a soccer ball around. He was still in his uniform, after his shift, and no doubt my sons had pounced on him the minute he'd walked in the door. Tash was paws up on the French doors, whining to go out.

I opened doors, and she headed straight for the ball, snatched it out from under Vaughn's foot and ran off.

'*Dad*,' Marcus shrieked.

Vaughn had his hands on his hips. 'She's killed three soccer balls in the last two days and there goes the last one.'

I looked at Tash in admiration. She'd retreated to a corner of the yard and stretched out with the now deflated soccer ball between her paws. She still had it in her, my very good girl.

'Tash can do no wrong,' Vaughn said, grinning at me.

'She *can*,' I said. 'It's just that she never does.'

'I need to talk to you,' Tom said. 'It's about Elle. She wants you to meet her for ice cream at Graeters in Chevy Chase. I told her I'd try to grab you when you got home.'

'You coming?'

He looked at his feet. 'She's moved into her dad's place at the Wellie. I'll be heading over there later on.'

I grinned. 'Will you?'

He ignored me. 'If you go right now, I promise the guys and I will save you some pizza. It's urgent.'

'On my way.'

Tom had his phone out and was already talking to Elle. So

evidently she did know *how* to answer a phone if she wanted to. I hugged the kids; grabbed a slice of pizza.

'Bring ice cream back,' Marcus shouted as I headed out the door.

Another evening of stellar nutrition.

SIXTEEN

This thing with Elle was going to be tricky. I was fighting the urge to sit her down, ask her what her intentions were toward my brother-in-law and warn her about Holtzer. Instead, I stood in line with her because Graeters was a popular place, and we snagged an outdoor table where we could watch the people and the traffic and the city, and it was a shame I hadn't thought to bring Tash, because she loved a pup cup at Graeters almost as much as soccer balls.

I ordered the sundae with bourbon ball ice cream, pecans and caramel sauce, and Elle had a triple-scoop hot fudge sundae with extra whipped cream and three cherries by request, because if you're going to Graeters, you might as well do it right. This wasn't the place to order frozen yogurt, unless you were out of your mind.

Elle gave me a sideways look. 'Thanks for coming. I got your emojis.'

I took advantage of the stack of napkins I'd grabbed and wiped bourbon ice cream off my shirt.

'I'm your Uncle Noah and always here when you need me.'

''Kay,' she said. She was focused on building the perfect bite. A blend of hot fudge, ice cream and nuts. The cherries she had eaten individually one by one first thing. 'You took my mother out to that house.'

'I took her out there because your father asked me to.'

She looked up. '*Did he?* If anyone should know better, it's him. What was he thinking? What were *you* thinking? I've been a hot mess since I went out there – you want it to happen to her too? And Dad – he needs to be worrying about his health, not this kind of stuff.'

'Have you met either of your parents?'

She gave me another sideways look. Licked the plastic red spoon.

'Elle, your mother is a grown-ass woman who was going to go to that house come hell or high water, and she is also a brilliant quantum biologist, and to be honest, I need her. She has insights I never dreamed of.'

'Sounds like Mom,' she said with an unhappy look. 'Maybe there was no stopping her. But going to that house ruined me. I don't want it to happen to her.'

'You're not ruined, Elle. These things can be navigated. And I kept your mother safe. Ish.'

'Knowing what I know about Mom? I'm betting it was the other way round. And Dad can't have anything to do with this. Not right now. He's in a hospital in Italy; his heart stopped.'

'Your father's a warrior, Elle. Do you have any idea of the lives he's saved, the people he's brought out of the darkest kind of agony, when no one else would or could help? You are allowed to worry about him, but don't disrespect him. Trust him to know what to do.'

'As I understand it, you're the guy who insisted he stay in Italy for more tests.'

She had me on that. 'OK fine, but we need to talk about Dr Holtzer. Your boss.'

She considered me with a serious look. 'You know him?'

'His name came up when I was seeing Patrick and Pammie.'

'Pammie called me. She said you were great. That you were getting Patrick in to see some hot-shit child psychiatrist to get him through the trauma of living in that house. So sometimes Uncle Noah, you are amazing. I don't want either of them anywhere near Holtzer.'

'Neither do I. I tell you in strict confidence that I've had issues with him in the past.'

'What kind of issues?'

'The kind that compelled me to report him for Medicaid fraud – and malpractice. I tried to get his license revoked.'

She leaned back in her chair. 'And it didn't work?'

I shook my head. 'You know as well as I do the system is rigged to look the other way.'

'Yeah, but if you can't do it, then—' She was looking very pale. 'He's gunning for me.'

'Tell me everything,' I said.

At first, she'd found him charming and intelligent and an amazing mentor. But then little things started to add up. He was never available. He prescribed a lot of old-school meds that everybody prescribed in spite of never working for the last twenty years and were basically just chemical restraints. He put a lot of patients on seventy-two-hour lockdown but somehow they were falling through the cracks and not getting any care. For mental or physical health.

Everything I'd been concerned about too.

She'd gotten fed up when she'd gone in to check on the patients in lockdown and found one who was not only deep in dangerous alcohol withdrawal but had an untreated abscess on his shoulder. By the time she got there, the infection had gone septic and the patient was edging toward septic shock.

She'd rounded up one of the hospitalists, who had been great and handled it really well, and they'd started talking and decided they would team up to keep an eye on the lockdown patients, and they both slept with their cell phones on their chests in case either of them was needed. Both of them were in debt and happy to take as much overtime as they could get. Elle often came in to check patients even when it wasn't her shift, paying particular attention to anyone admitted to seventy-two-hour lockdown by Holtzer. Both of them knew Dr Holtzer was a problem, but he was rarely there – he spent most of his time at the university hospital in Lexington, where he had the practice he actually showed up for, so they had workarounds and mainly dreamed of the day he'd retire.

But they weren't dumb – the Medicaid scam became patently obvious, and they were trying to build a case on the sly. Most of Holtzer's patients in lockdown were on Medicaid, most of them were charted and charged for tests and meds they never got, and plenty of them were kept for longer than seventy-two hours. She and her hospitalist buddy started gathering evidence; keeping track.

She'd finished her ice cream. She ate almost as fast as I did. A survival skill in our line of work.

'I guess we weren't as stealthy as we thought. Holtzer called me into his office. Said he was concerned about me. That I was working too hard, coming in off shift, which I knew was bullshit because I'm a wage slave like everyone else and nobody ever gets in trouble for working too hard. He gave me what I call the look of sweet smarm that I used to think was charming, but his eyes were mean, and he wanted to make sure I got what he meant. He said it was clear that I had a lot of anxiety issues and it was affecting my work. That one of the techs had heard me crying in the bathroom several times. Which is true. I have been having crying jags since I went to that house. He also said I wasn't sleeping, and that was clear from the dark circles under my eyes.'

'You don't have dark circles under your eyes.'

'I know. For the first time in years, I'm sleeping great. And my mother fessed up and said she told you all about that. So you know, right? But all that stuff Holtzer said is now in my medical and personnel records. He wants me to take some pretty hard-core meds that he knows very well will make it impossible for me to work. He hinted about lockdown *for me*.'

'Your boss doesn't get to be your doctor.'

'This is the real world, Uncle Noah – my boss gets to do any damn thing he wants. In addition to my clear and overwhelming anxieties, I also have shaky hands, drop things a lot, am tardy for work and . . . *combative*.'

I shut my eyes tight. 'Combative' was doctor code for trouble. It wasn't a good thing to have in your records. 'Did he order a blood test for substance abuse?'

'No of course not. He'd have to go through HR, and he'd know it would be clean. He does that kind of thing to patients too, usually female. When they don't cooperate. Verbal threats, and insinuations in their file. Their records show treatments they don't get, and since some of them are my patients, I've gone in and made my own notes that made this clear. Staked myself out like a goat.'

'He actually took the time to read your notes?'

'Surprised me too. When he does see a patient, they're going to go along with the meds he wants them to take and anything else he says, because he has the art of the veiled threat down pat. It's one thing to see it happen to patients, which makes me furious. It's another thing to be sitting alone with him and have it happen to me. So *of course* I told him to go fuck himself.'

I sighed. 'Of course.'

'I was going to see if you could talk to him, but I guess that's not a good idea.'

'I'll be happy to talk to him.'

She shook her head. 'I'm taking some unpaid leave. Family crisis because of my dad's heart, and it's actually true. How do you think Dad is doing? Do you think he'll be OK?'

'I honestly do. Especially since I'm keeping an eye on him.'

'Good. That's good. And . . . Mom told you about the lucid dreams, right? She said you saw the lady too, when you were driving home, after that night at the house?'

There was no privacy in this world. 'I was not asleep and I was not having a dream, but yes, I saw her.'

'That's what Mom said. I know she's real, and I've been looking for her. And I found her. The real lady, the one in my dreams. She's in Provence, in France; she lives in a little place called Pente Douce. I've been talking to her son. We're cousins. Look, it's a long story. Crazy.'

'About the uncle who fought in World War I and wound up in Pente Douce? Your mom told me about it.'

'I've been going back over the letters my uncle sent home to his sister – they wrote back and forth for years. My mom has the letters; she let me read them years ago. She got them from her great-grandmother. And she and I curled up and read them again the day after you two went to the house.

'My Uncle Forrest was only nineteen when he went to France, and after the fighting was over, he just started drifting. Went off on a sort of walkabout around France, wound up in Pente Douce and met my aunt, and they got married and had a little girl, and they were like soul mates or something, and he was very happy in France. And their little girl grew up and had a daughter, named Cerise. That's her. That's the lady. I've seen pictures.'

'Cerise is the lady? You two are related?'

'I really, really think it's her. Cerise is alive but fragile. She's really old, and she has dementia, and I want to go to France and see her. You get why I have to do that, right? Uncle Noah? You OK?'

'Yeah, my head is just spinning a little.'

'Should I get you some water?'

'No, thank you. I am surprised not decrepit. I can't believe you actually found her.'

She grabbed my arm. 'But listen. In his letters, my uncle – he talks about something weird going on. In Pente Douce. He talked about a haunting. And people getting sick, kids getting scared and weird weather. Red skies at night and lightning coming up from the ground. And then . . . he went missing on September 27, 1959, when his granddaughter Cerise was three. They never found him. And it made me think of Conor Walsh and Andi Craig.'

I leaned back in my chair. This was starting to look like a pattern.

'I need to go to France and meet Cerise and her family, or anybody around who might know something about what happened. And maybe I can get a handle on what's happening *here*.'

'And they never found your uncle?'

'Never.'

'Cerise may not be able to talk to you about it, so go easy with her. And Elle . . . I don't know. I see why you want to go. But if it's anything like what's going on here, this is dangerous.'

'No, because whatever was happening there is *over now* – it's history. It can give us insight. I've been in touch with Cerise's son, Josue, and he was so nice and happy to hear from me, and he's always wondered about his American cousins in Kentucky. And he said to come and meet him, and his mother too if she's OK enough for a visitor.'

I nodded. 'Please, Elle, stay in close touch. Be careful.'

'I will be. You think it's all right to go? Just dodging Holtzer and leaving Mom? She's going to look after Chewie for me, and a friend of mine will take my pony to her farm until I get back. And Mom is buying me a ticket and funding me, because I am fucking broke as always. And I may not have a job when I get back.'

'I like the idea of an ocean between you and Holtzer.'

'And don't worry about me because Tom's going to come with me. He's put in for some vacation days and said he'll join me there as soon as he can. And we can research my Uncle Forrest together and be in the south of France.'

'Sounds romantic.'

She rolled her eyes at me. 'That's kind of the point.'

Elle leaned close and gave me a cheerful kiss on the cheek. Young. Ready for adventure.

I was worried sick.

'Your mom told me what the lady – Cerise – what she said in your dreams. That you had to go there, to the lavender fields where she was taking you.'

Elle wouldn't look at me. She wrapped her arms around herself and looked suddenly very small. 'She says the same thing every time. *You must come. No one will be safe until you do.*'

SEVENTEEN

Tom was putting a worn olive-green duffel bag into the trunk of his squad car when I drove up. He was in freshly washed jeans, a soft gray sweater over a white dress shirt, sleeves rolled back over the cuffs of the sweater. Leather loafers that looked new. He was freshly shaved and smelling of cologne.

I got out of the car and grinned at him. 'Going somewhere?'

He gave me a sideways smile. 'Yeah, busted. I'm taking Elle out to dinner, for Mexican.'

'Thus the duffel bag.'

'That's family for you. You know every move I make. I'll be staying a while, with Elle. Perry's condo is great. We can walk anywhere downtown with Chewie. We're going to take him with us tonight and sit out on the patio.'

I envied him a little. I wish I'd taken a little more time to enjoy it when I was his age. But if anybody deserved a happiness break, it was Tom.

'I think I want your life,' I said. 'If you aren't in too big of a hurry, can you pop into my office just for a moment?'

'Uh-oh. Am I in trouble?'

I laughed.

I sat at the desk and wrote him a fat check on the NGO account while he stood by the desk. He wouldn't sit down, and I got the message. He wanted to get gone.

'Is that a checkbook?'

'Yes.'

'I always wondered what they looked like.'

'Ha ha.'

'What's that for?'

'Salary and expenses for your trip to France.'

'You hiring me as Elle's bodyguard?'

'Yeah, yeah, have your fun. You're a cop, investigating the disappearance of Elle's grandfather.'

'From World War I? But I *am* a cop; I can't do outside work like that. Not and get paid for it. And you know the reason I'm going is to be with Elle.'

'OK hang on. Let me get the other checkbook.' I opened a drawer in my desk. 'Look, Tom. This is brother-to-brother stuff, OK? I want you to go, to have fun, for you and Elle to look out for each other and just be young in France and not have to worry about money for once in your life. Do you even have a passport?'

He nodded. 'After Candice died, I thought I might take off for a while. I just never had the heart for it.'

'Well, you've got the heart for it now. This is from Moira and me. I know you miss Candice. I know you—'

He shook his head at me. 'I don't want to talk about that.'

'OK.' I handed him the check; he took it and smiled.

'*Bon chance*,' I said. I stood up, and we did the awkward man hug. 'Is that my Gendarme cologne?'

'It's mine now.'

EIGHTEEN

Moira got home around midnight, just as I finished making the last of my clinical notes. She looked as tired as I felt, and I shut the laptop down and moved it to the table beside the bed. Moira grabbed it and put it on the dresser, so I wouldn't knock it to the floor in the middle of the night. The longer we were married, the better it got.

She had that little glow that meant rehearsals had gone well.

I gave her a tired smile. 'There's pizza in the fridge – want me to warm you some?'

'Oh God, that sounds so good. Yeah, will you? And bring me a glass of red wine?'

'I'll bring the bottle. I talked to Elle tonight, and I've got shit to tell you.'

'Good. And I've been asking around for you about that school in Osage. Come to find out, it has a notorious reputation.'

I kissed her. 'Deal. Don't hesitate to get comfortable and take off all your clothes.'

When I made it upstairs with warmed-up pizza for both of us, two glasses and a newly opened bottle of wine, she was shutting the drawer of my dresser, comfy in black panties and my Transy University Dracula tee shirt.

'Look what I found,' she said with a great big smile.

Admittedly, she looked better in it than I did. And I knew I would never see the tee shirt again unless it was on my wife.

We curled up in bed with pizza and wine, propped up on the eight pillows that Moira likes to keep on the bed, and she snuggled up close. 'I've got juicy things to tell you. That school is beyond belief. I thought people would keep all this a secret, but come to find out, Noah, they could not wait to talk.'

I smiled at her. All the things I loved. Pizza. My wife. Kids sleeping happily in their beds guarded by Mr Timothy and Tash. And another layer of information on a thread of dark entities that were like nothing I had ever seen before. Life would be perfect if I could have about twenty straight hours of sleep.

It was the old part of the school that was creepy. The new part was fine, until you passed through the connecting hallway to the original building, which was like walking into another world. Teachers laughed about it, somewhat uneasily, and shrugged it off; told each other stories in low voices, one on one, or in small huddles. You might call it an open secret. Par for the course in a little town.

Walking into the newer part of the building in the middle school meant automatic motion-sensor security lights, big classrooms with lots of windows, linoleum floors pounded by years of rowdy kids, the smell of children, packed lunches, the lingering scents of cafeteria food and the harsh cleaning chemicals used on the floor. Business as usual, everything normal . . . nothing off.

Then, just past the science lab – which was large, open, a bank of windows all across the outside wall – you turned a sharp corner into the old part of the school, a hard left into a suddenly narrow hallway full of . . . *shadows*. The light there never quite reached the corners; the sides of the hall were dark and hard to clean. The floor sloped gently until you were about six inches lower than in the newer part of the school. But if *felt* much lower. Closer to the earth. Dank.

A little too hot in the winter, with the heating system running full blast. Sweaty hot in the summer, in spite of the air conditioning that spewed cool air and an earthy scent, musty, a little bit . . . wrong. A hint of decomposition, the science teacher thought. The administration desk on the right was flanked by a bank of monitors from cameras that kept the school under constant surveillance. And sometimes those monitors showed you things you didn't really want to see. Uneasy things. Shadows. Movements. Posters flapping on the wall. Cafeteria chairs that seemed to scoot sideways, abruptly, enough to make you do a double take and wonder if you'd seen what you'd seen. In empty rooms, where nothing should be moving . . . but was.

Tight quarter turn there, past the worn-out countertop, into a dark cul-de-sac where a staff bathroom and the copy machine were tucked away in a short stub of hallway. Another corridor past the admin desk, with the old classrooms. They were smaller, shut behind heavy wooden doors. Some didn't have windows.

Though being their own small school district meant freedom from ongoing changes in administrative and teaching requirements that just wouldn't work in such a little school district, the teachers were overworked here like everywhere else, and there were lit classrooms after dark, after dinner, in the elementary school and the high school. But the middle school tended to stay empty, to stay dark, though sometimes a light here and there would flash on and off even when the parking lot was empty.

New teachers in the middle school had a usual pattern. They'd work late once or twice, sometimes even three times if they were stubborn, if they were brave, but the usual pattern was twice and then never again. Nobody lasted past three.

Because creepy stuff happened at night in the school. Things happened when you were there alone. Things happened during the day too, when the school was teeming with kids, the sun was out, the lights were on and there were lots of people around. So you just kind of ignored it. Amazing the things you could get used to.

During the day, when the kids were in the science lab, where Patrick and his two friends had their last class of the day, at the corner where the new left off and the old began, right at the nexus of old school and new school, the nexus of weird and normal . . . there were heavy, hard knocks on the door that made the kids jump in their seats and the teacher, Mrs Garcia, stop on her way to the Bunsen burner – then take a deep breath and keep going. She had stopped going to the door to answer loud knocks. There would never be anybody there – the kids knew it and she knew it. So she'd quit answering the door and started locking it. The kids always noticed when she locked the door, which was every single day after they were all rounded up in the classroom. It made them feel better. It made them feel safe. It was an oasis. It was amazing the things you could get used to. The things their teacher took in stride.

She kept industrial-sized rolls of paper towels in her supply cabinet to clean up the puddles of water that seemed to seep in from . . . *nowhere.*

She worked late a total of two times. The first time there was that loud beating on the door, and nobody there, though she'd walked up and down the hallway looking but only found the history teacher, who was also the basketball coach, and he had heard the knocking too.

The second time she worked late, she took her chihuahua with her. The knocking came again when she was sitting at her desk, deep in concentration, and the door slammed open, hitting the cinder-block wall. Her dog went ballistic. She had him leashed, and she kept him tucked in her arm, but he was hard to hold, straining to get to something in the hallway. She needed to get to the car, and she was taking the dog and the class gerbils with her – no living creatures left behind.

The gerbil cage was too big to carry, so she emptied out her Big Gulp cherry Coke plastic cup, hands shaking hard, and put the gerbils inside – there would be air coming in through the hole in the lid for the straw. No doubt the dog was giving them little gerbil heart attacks, but she had no choice. She stuffed them into her backpack, slung it over her shoulder as best she could with the dog squirming in her arms, grabbed her purse and ran like hell down the hall, to her car, in the well-lit, comforting parking lot, where for some reason the dark things did not walk. She hoped.

And after that, she noticed that none of the other teachers worked late. She was new to the school and realized, with her hard and newly earned insight, that the majority of the teachers headed out on the heels of the kids, sometimes beating them to the parking lot. The teachers that stayed late were always gone by five – to beat the non-existent traffic in the very small town. And once dusk started to settle, it was a race for the last stragglers to get out the door before dark. Nobody wanted to be last.

The history teacher had taken to calling out on his way home – *Hey now, I'm heading out. Anybody need a ride or help getting their stuff to the car*? He wasn't staying after dark anymore, but he was willing to be last one out – he was that kind of man. He'd joined the marine corps after college and had mentally promoted all the other teachers to honorary marines, and he'd keep them safe if he could. He was a big guy – he'd played college football and been small-time but pretty good, but the last time he'd stayed after dark, he'd heard laughter from the copy room behind the admin desks and stuck his head in the door. Nobody there.

It was the last night he'd worked late. His wife was on dinner duty that night, marshalling their four kids into kitchen chores, and he'd planned to take some time to finish up where he might find some peace and quiet, but this wasn't the kind of peace and quiet he was looking for.

'Hey,' he said. Somebody was laughing, and he wanted to know who.

The light was on in the little bathroom adjacent to the dark cubby of a storeroom next to the copy-machine nook.

'Hey,' he said again. His senses told him somebody was there.

And he heard the laughter again, coming from the bathroom. The door opened a crack. Whatever was going on in there, he didn't want any part of it. But then, maybe it was some kind of practical joke – a hazing; he was new here at the middle school, where teachers cycled in and out pretty fast. He didn't mind being the butt of a joke. Didn't bother him a bit. Made him feel accepted, really.

'OK, guys, what's going on.'

Two quick strides and the bathroom light went out.

'You people are hard-core,' he said, chuckling a little, turning the light on and pushing the bathroom door wide open.

Nobody there. Nobody in the copy-room nook. Nobody at the admin desks; nobody in the hall. He saw movement in the cafeteria on the monitor. A poster on the wall, flapping pretty violently – maybe some kind of draft? Or. No. Posters didn't *detach* themselves from the wall. And then some dark, nebulous shape crept closer and closer to the camera, like it was coming straight at him through the monitor. Which was ridiculous of course. Just . . . a trick of the shadows or something.

But time to go home. Time to go home for sure. And he too stopped looking at the monitors.

The laughter started again as he went out the double doors, and he jogged through the parking lot to his silver Rav4 then drove methodically home, hands shaking on the steering wheel, to the new subdivision, and the one-level ranch house with new grass and twiggy trees, to the home and the family he loved, and he could see the lights on all through the house; his kids running by the windows. Everything normal.

For a while, he just sat in the driveway. It was full dark now, and the blinds in the house were open. He could see bugs gathering on the windows, basking in the light; he could see his wife, her mahogany hair bundled up in a ponytail, slipping a sweater on over her tank top, and he felt a sense of relief that kept his legs weak, and him sitting in the car a little longer, glad to be home, *relieved* to be home, but not quite ready to go in. There had been a set of barracks at Paris Island in boot camp that made him feel just like this. He wondered if it was him. If he was imagining things. An unsettling thought.

The next day he hinted around about it to the science teacher, Mrs Garcia, and they huddled together, talking in whispers. She told him about the beating on the door, and running through the hallway with her little dog going nuts, and getting the gerbils home safe in a Big Gulp cup. And he told her how he thought at first he'd been the butt of a practical joke when he'd heard laughter near the copy-machine nook, but there was nobody there. That he could see.

And they both felt better knowing it wasn't just them, and the open secret stayed pretty much an open secret. Nobody looked at the monitors. Nobody worked after dark.

Everyone felt sorry for the English teacher who had a shadowy classroom right smack in the middle of the old part of the building, cattycorner from the monitors that she *did* look at, unlike everybody else; that she *did* study, from time to time, shoulders tense, mouth set in an unhappy line. She was found sound asleep on the floor at the end of a school day, students stepping over her on their way out the door, and she got fired for being drunk on the job. So they said.

In truth, she didn't smell like alcohol – the school secretary admitted that – but you couldn't smell vodka, could you? Especially if she ate mints? Because she did eat a lot of mints. And they'd had a really hard time waking her up. They almost had to call an ambulance.

The teacher found a job at another school, kept herself to herself and refused to say a single word about what happened to anyone, no matter how much they hinted.

But it had always been just kind of managed, and so things continued. New teachers figured it out, nobody stayed after dark, the history teacher checked the classrooms right before he left and offered to help anyone take stuff to their car, which was his way of saying *time to go home*. That's how things work in small towns. Everybody just kind of knows things through a mix of gossip and generalized osmosis. The point is that eventually they know.

And though there was a low-level creepy hum in the older part of the building, and the science classroom that the kids called *creepy adjacent*, and you had to avoid looking at the monitors, it was all quite manageable.

Until it wasn't.

NINETEEN

The school didn't seem bad at all when I got there. A charmless architectural style you might call American squat – a short, sprawling old yellow-brick rectangular block building that had a tired look. Two sets of heavy doors, practical for funneling a mass of kids in and out. Wide concrete sidewalks, with new sections showing stark white after maintenance and repairs. It had been built in the sixties, then added on to, with a random sprawl that was more practical than aesthetic.

Mrs Garcia was waiting for me out front, holding a tiny dog wearing a purple hooded sweater in the crook of her arm. She was very young. Round gold spectacles, hair tied back, wearing a floaty dress that looked comfortable and high-topped sneakers. She shook my hand and gave me a shy smile.

'You're Mrs Garcia? Patrick's mother tells me you're a fabulous science teacher.'

Her smile was sweet. 'I *am*. I can't thank you enough for coming out. And this is Vernon.'

Vernon was quite old and shivery. He liked me immediately and put a paw out for me to shake, which I did quite gently. He sniffed my hand and gave me a kiss.

'You could teach my cat a thing or two,' I told him.

The teacher shook her head. 'He's not good with cats.'

I laughed. 'Neither am I.'

She led me into the building, Vernon peering at me over her shoulder. He looked good in purple. He had a regal side.

Mrs Garcia glanced back at me and slowed her pace. 'I've been so worried about Patrick. And now Susu and Mateo.' She ran a hand across her forehead. 'I don't know what to think.'

I followed her down the hallway, thinking the problem was that she knew exactly what to think but was afraid to say it out loud. But so far everything looked mundane and normal. No creepy feeling at all. Lockers, linoleum floors. Hallways that echoed.

Mrs Garcia's room was huge. Long desks laid out in rows, science stations, multicolored streamers that hung from the ceiling. A bank of windows on the outside wall; posters on the others. A room full of light and color. It had a good vibe. The room was on the corner right where the hall either went straight or took a hard left. And that was where it was – the corridor that narrowed; led to the old part of the school. I saw the bank of monitors at the empty admin desks. I veered into that narrow part of the hallway. It felt uncomfortable there. Overheated. Oppressive. Uneasy.

Mrs Garcia waited for me in the doorway of her classroom then led me inside. On the lowest corner of a whiteboard, I saw Patrick's handiwork. Geometric symbols, black and red configurations of dots.

'Patrick?' I said, studying the artwork.

'Yes. And look here, on the wall by the door.' She bent down close to the floor. 'He was only supposed to put them on the whiteboard, but . . . he promised to stop drawing them if I would let him keep the ones here by the door and on the board.' She shut her eyes tight. 'I know he's having a hard time. I feel like I should go easy with him on this.'

'Agreed.'

'He says it makes us safer. He said the *good lady* taught him to draw them – that they kept everyone safe.' She motioned me to a chair and sat behind her desk.

The *good lady.* Here she was again. 'Did he tell you who the good lady was?'

She tapped a finger on the desk. 'I think I must have misunderstood him – when he told me about her. I think it must have been a dream. He said she came and sat on his bed sometimes at night when he was really scared. That she was very old and had long gray hair, and she made him feel safe. She had a nice voice. She talked to him in his head. Showed him how to make the drawings, and even gave him a little piece of rock that had some of the red dots on it. He keeps it in his pocket; he showed it to me. I'm sure he just found the rock outside somewhere and painted them on himself.'

I could see why Mrs Garcia thought it was all a dream. I would have thought the same if I hadn't also seen the good lady standing on the road, illuminated in the headlights of my car. And I would love to see that rock Patrick kept in his pocket.

I heard a loud thump on the door, and Mrs Garcia shut her eyes tight, swallowed hard.

'Let me see who that is,' I said.

She sighed. 'No one will be there.' She held her little dog close.

I opened the door to an empty hallway.

'Don't worry about it,' she said. 'It happens a lot.'

'I've heard. About the issues you have here.'

She nodded. 'I wasn't sure if you knew about that.'

I smiled. 'My wife is a teacher and she asked around.' I hesitated. 'I would like to discuss . . . Sasha.' That was why I was there. To make his acquaintance. And to get him out of the school. Or at least out of Patrick's classroom.

She looked away, and the dog whimpered. 'He's locked away.'

'Locked?'

'Understand please that Sasha, the AI . . . all that has been shut down in this school. The systems were donated, for a trial run only in the fifth-grade classes – there are four of them. Evidently my unit had some kind of . . .' She hesitated. 'Glitch.'

'Is Sasha – your unit – still here in the classroom?'

She swallowed. 'Yes. But he's locked up so he can't get— so none of the kids can get to him.'

Vernon struggled out of her arms, tapped across the desk and stepped into my lap.

'I don't think you should keep it in the classroom.' I waited for her to ask me why. She didn't. 'You're willing to get rid of him?'

'Happily. It's just that wherever I put him . . .' She trailed off. 'I don't want to take Sasha home.'

'God, no – don't take it home.'

I was getting worried about the kids in this school. Worried about the teachers. If their only way of coping was a sweet but fierce elderly chihuahua, going home before dark, staying out of the cafeteria and running past the monitors . . . the odds did not look good. And now they had AI in the classroom. Shut down now, which was a relief. Because the dark things are overly fond of electronics. One energy field calling to another. They loved to text, mess with car engines, call you up on the phone. Always happy to attend a Zoom – they didn't need an invitation, and they didn't need a link. And I wondered about Perry. How sure he was that they had stopped his heart. His cath scan had shown no issues whatsoever.

And they had been having a field day, right here in this classroom, with Sasha. Because it was clear they were entrenched here. Had been infesting this school for a very long time.

'Look just . . . I'll take it with me. Sasha. If you want.'

'Would you?'

'Be my pleasure. Where did you get it? Who donated this?'

'It came in the mail. Some company in Silicon Valley that relocated to Texas. I tried to track them down and let them know what was happening with our unit, but all I could get were' – she laughed – 'chatbots.'

The maze from hell.

'All four of the fifth-grade classrooms got them. No other classroom had trouble but mine. We shut all of them down after . . .'

I nodded. 'So four total in the school, all still here on the premises?'

'Yes.'

'Did they come in the mail to the school address?'

She turned pale. 'My home address. All four teachers got them at home.'

I nodded like this was business as usual. 'Just your school? Other schools in the district?'

'I um . . . asked around. Just this school.'

'When?'

'Six weeks ago? I don't remember for sure.'

'All of these Sashas need to be out of the classrooms and off school premises.'

'Yeah, well, that's kind of an ongoing fight.'

'Don't go through official channels. Word of mouth, like a whisper campaign. Say you heard it from somebody else. Just do your best, OK?'

She nodded. 'The principal wants them out. He's afraid of lawsuits.'

'Are any of the other kids in school having issues, like Patrick and his friends?'

'Not that I know of.'

'OK then. And Sasha?'

She got a key out of her desk drawer, opened the third little door in a wall of storage lockers.

She let out a small whimper. 'I put him right there. Third from the left.'

The locker was empty.

'Maybe he's in another one.'

She began opening them methodically one by one. Two more

lockers down, she jumped back. Vernon barked fiercely with tiny chihuahua rage, which was actually quite formidable.

Sasha was upside down in the locker, arms folded, feet with tiny wheels under plastic shoes on the locker ceiling. I grabbed him by the neck and pulled him out. Turned him right side up. He was heavy.

He had horse hair, brown, parted to one side and floppy, like Hugh Grant without the charm. A mushy-looking face and pebble black eyes. Thick red plastic lips. Black pants with a cuff, a white button-down shirt that sat crookedly and had picked up a lot of dirt. Did this creepy bot think people would launder his shirt? Did he expect it?

I had the oddest feeling he would have said yes. That Sasha wanted me to shine his scuffed lace-up plastic faux-leather shoes, polish the wheels beneath, wash and dry his horse-hair mop, and have his white shirt cleaned and ironed.

Mrs Garcia put her face in her hands. Vernon scrabbled at her feet. 'Will you please just get that thing out of here?'

'Yes, ma'am.' I left a business card on her desk, and Vernon took the opportunity to give me a farewell kiss on the ankle. I reached down and gave him a scratch behind the ears. Told him what a brave boy he was, shook Mrs Garcia's hand and headed out the door with Sasha tucked under my arm.

TWENTY

It felt weird carrying that damn thing out of the sprawling campus of the middle school. I got a couple of curious looks. Sasha was as big as a ventriloquist's dummy and surprisingly heavy. I held him upside down.

I slammed him into the trunk of the Audi, his head bouncing on a toolbox. I didn't like having him in the car, but at least he was out of sight. What to do with him?

Get him off school premises, was my first thought.

I hit the road, mulling the best way to do him in. Perry had told me stories of creepy objects – dolls, mirrors, battery-operated toy trains and trucks, pictures . . . radios, jewelry boxes, a lot of things that made music. Haunted things that brought menace . . . they watched you, making you feel like you saw them moving out of the corner of your eye, or even full frontal in your face. They turned on and off at random, got loud, kept falling off the shelf. Gave off heat and strange glowy light, and left odd scorch marks. Just wrong. And therefore dangerous. There was precedent for things like Sasha. Bad precedent.

So no. I wasn't taking the damn thing home. Big trash dumpster? Leave it in a ditch on the side of the road? Someone might find him and take him home. I couldn't take that risk. Bury it somewhere like I was hiding a body? Try explaining that to the cops.

The best plan was to burn him. Reduce him to ashes. And I had to burn *all* of him. I'd need matches, at the very least. I also had the urge to cover him up. Put him in a plastic bag. That felt right. I didn't want to look at him. I was running on pure instinct now.

The next exit looked iffy, but there was a battered sign promising a gas station and fast food, what passes for civilization these days, and for me right now would be welcome.

What I got was a two-lane broken asphalt road, overgrown weeds and scraggly trees on both sides, and then, at last, an intersection. Straight ahead a worn-out hardware store. Behind me on the left was a rusted-up but functioning gas station, isolated houses on both sides. Might be something better a ways down the road past the gas station. Might not.

I took the hardware store. My car was the only one in a parking lot rippled with potholes.

Out front, a man stood by the door talking to a woman who had a long story to tell, a cigarette to smoke, a plastic bottle of Mountain Dew in her hand.

The man was on the tall side, with a thick head of wavy white hair, soft looking, brushed back. He listened to the woman, but he clocked me. I had his full attention, which I didn't much want.

He wore a suit and lace-up dress shoes, almost exactly like Sasha's, except his were expensive leather, polished and shiny, whereas Sasha's were plastic and scuffed.

I locked the car. Headed inside. The woman, clutching a phone, gave me a quick brush of a glance over one shoulder, flicked ash on to the sidewalk, not so friendly. She wore a shiny polyester vest over her sweatshirt and jeans, so probably she worked at the store.

Not the man though. Not in that serious suit. He held my gaze; gave me the kind of big smile I associate with Baptist ministers and a 'Hello, neighbor,' and I got the feeling that for some reason, he sure did like the looks of me.

I gave him a hard look, full of subtext. *Stranger?* Yep. *Dangerous?* Maybe. I suggest you fuck on off.

In the South, we don't ever say it out loud. On the other hand . . . we don't have to.

I headed into the hardware store, and it was a descent into the hell of worn-out linoleum and bad smells. And stuff. Narrow aisles, crammed with all kinds of things I didn't want, a lot of it dusty. The aisles were narrow, a grid-like labyrinth, no consciously logical layout. High metal shelves. I could not see over the top, which gave me a shimmer of claustrophobia.

I found what I wanted not too far back. A little camping and fishing section. I got matches, fire sticks. I picked up a tarp. Put it back when I found a box of forty-gallon lawn and garbage bags – heavy black plastic with bright-blue pull ties threaded through the top. Sasha would fit right in. I would double bag him just for the hell of it. I wanted him contained.

I headed to the front of the store looking for the checkout, which was way to the side on the left. Nobody there. Nobody at the counter; nobody anywhere I could see. I was alone in the store, and that didn't feel good, like a descent into rural dystopian hell.

A curling sign on the register gave me the hint. Self-checkout. I paid, bagged, and the woman came in as I was headed out.

'You get everything OK? Need any help?' She smiled, friendly now, back on the job.

'I'm good,' I told her. Headed out the door.

The man in shiny shoes was still there and still smiling, and watching me blatantly, creepy as shit.

He watched as I opened the expansive trunk of my Audi. Still smiling while I double bagged old Sasha, taking pleasure in cutting off his air supply. Smiling as I slammed the trunk shut and settled into the luxurious ease of my cognac leather seats, locking the doors and starting up the engine that throbbed with power and always gave me a thrill.

I backed out carefully; drove slow, easy and watchful, anxious to get the hell out of this totally David Lynch kind of place.

I turned on my expensive sound system: 'A Thousand Miles From Nowhere', Dwight Yoakam.

I could relate.

Three miles to the exit and I was back on the interstate. Ten miles later I started to breathe again. The sign for Mammoth Cave State Park seemed promising.

It took me a good hour and a half to get to the park, which was deserted in the middle of the day. I glanced in the rearview mirror and caught a glimpse of something not right; looked over my shoulder and slammed on the brakes.

The black, doubled-up garbage bags were heaped in the left corner of the back seat. Not in the trunk then. Inside the car. With me.

And just for a moment I wondered. Did I misremember? Had I put Sasha in the back seat and not the trunk?

But I knew better. I remembered the sound and the satisfaction of slamming that trunk shut, under the watchful eyes of the man in shiny shoes.

I found a campsite with a fire pit, and nobody close. I dumped Sasha into old cold ashes, rounded up the matches and firesticks, and set his ass on fire.

TWENTY-ONE

There was a certain freedom in a very small school district, a very small school, and word of mouth by teachers in the know. It was quietly decided that the way to go was to take action now, beg for forgiveness later.

By the end of the week, the remaining three Sasha AI robots were removed from the school. The fifth-grade teachers rounded them up, had a private bonfire to kill the Sashas off, then headed out to Jade's for margaritas and Mexican food to celebrate.

For a moment, for a day, for three days, even a whole sweet *everyone breathing easily* week, the school was theirs again. Like it had never been theirs before. It was full of open windows, cool breezes, and the light was somehow different. Brighter. Sweeter. *Normal.*

One of the sixth-grade math teachers decided to work late, thinking it was safe now, even after dark. I got the details like everybody else when I saw her stunned husband interviewed on the local news.

She settled her purse down on her desk, smiling a little. The children would get better, she thought. Some of them had been having trouble, but somehow she just knew they would be OK. Whatever this was . . . it was over.

She realized that she had forgotten the copies she'd made of the fact sheet to go with the art work for tomorrow's lesson. Left it on the kitchen table all ready to go. But the original was there, at the bottom of her canvas bag. And so she headed to the copy machine, crammed back behind the administration desks. It was a small thing, she knew, silly, but the kids were fascinated with famous mathematicians, their often nerdy lives and the beautiful graphics she printed out from numerical algorithms. It surprised them, still, that so many of the brilliant mathematicians were women they had not heard about.

Opening their eyes, one assignment at a time.

She would have them work on reading the fact sheet together as a class. Since the elementary reading curriculum had changed a decade ago, the kids weren't reading too well. They didn't teach reading the way they had when she was growing up, and it wasn't turning out so great. Education was subject to the cycle of fads. She had folded reading practice into her classroom.

And it made her happy, doing something so mundane and fun for the kids, surprising them with handouts on their desks that would be waiting for them when they came into the room. Imagining the little buzz of excitement while they settled in, scraping their chairs on the floor, getting stuff out of their backpacks, squabbling, laughing, just being kids. This math class was one of the good ones, a dream classroom, not like the one last year. Great kids. Quite sweet some of them. She felt like she was getting her life back.

It was quiet; she was alone. She couldn't even hear the street noises this far into the school. She ignored the bank of monitors by habit, made her copies, thought she heard laughter and smiled, thinking she wasn't the only one there working late after all, though when she went back into the hallway, there were no other lights that she could see. So she was alone. No one else was there. That's what she thought.

She stopped cold in the hallway.

Her classroom door was shut tight. She'd left it open. She stood in the doorway, afraid to go in. All the tables and chairs were crammed into the center of the room, when minutes ago they had been laid out exactly as she'd asked the kids to arrange them at the end of the school day that very afternoon. She liked things lined up and orderly.

And she knew then that working late had been a mistake, that she'd been overconfident, that the easy breezy feeling she'd had just that afternoon had drained away into something else, and two words came into her mind.

Looking forward.

Whatever this thing was, it was always so damn polite. Which somehow seemed rather worse.

Then she felt it – a breath of hot air and someone standing so close to her there could not be a half inch between them. A presence. Heavy. It smelled *bad.* It breathed hard. She could feel that breath on her cheek and her neck.

A man? A rapist? *Dear God, what?*

Often enough, the skull brain decides to protect you, filtering out the things it doesn't want you to see. Filtering out things it decides you *shouldn't* see. In a moment like this, all three of the brains ignite – the gut brain, the heart brain, the skull brain – all cradled in connecting neural pathways, lighting up like a three-alarm fire. Her gut told her to run, and her heart pounded blood through her veins. All in concert with the body. Because the body knew *exactly* what the skull brain refused to see.

The lights went out in the hallway though they were on sensors – there was no good reason for them to go dark. She screamed and ran, leaving her purse behind, the copies of the fact sheet and numerical graphics scattering into the hallway, and she made it to the big double doors; such heavy double doors, they tangled her up, but she barreled through, and the outside light sensors flicked on and she ran for her car, that beautiful old Kia, metallic blue, that always cheered her up, right there in the parking lot, back seat full of Legos, a jacket, one glove, a tee shirt, Matchbox cars, glittering plastic unicorns, crumbs, wrappers, the remains of sticky snacks. And the keys were in her purse. Still sitting on her desk in the school.

Come back. I wants to be with you.

'Fuck you,' she said out loud. And then sobbed hard when she saw her husband's pickup truck pull into the lot. A huge truck like they made them these days, extended cab where all three of their little kids, still in elementary school, could ride comfortably, squashed by the family German shepherd, Howie, who'd stretch out on all three of their laps, doggie smile big and broad when the windows were down and he could feel the breeze coming in. She had almost brought Howie with her tonight. Why hadn't she? *Why hadn't she*? Gentle as he was with the kids, he'd have gone after whatever it was in the hallway. *Howie would have taken it down.*

She ran to the truck just as it stopped, brakes locked in tight, tires skidding, and her husband was out of the truck and running to her. Oh God, how had he known to come? Such broad shoulders. Bronzed, burnished skin and muscles, he worked outside, full of energy and strength, fatigued now at the end of the day, but her glorious and beautiful man, who she took for granted. Which she didn't think she would ever do again.

'What is it?' he said. 'What's wrong? You forgot your fact sheets,

I brought them – I know the copy machine never works half the time. My brother's with the kids, but—'

'*It's back.*'

'What's back?'

'You know what I mean.' She was trembling so hard he had to hold her up. 'I left my purse. My keys. Oh God, I didn't think it would let me go home.'

'Stay here,' he said. 'I'll get them.'

She grabbed his tee shirt and pulled it into her fist. 'No. You won't.'

And then she sighed a little, turning her head like she heard something he could not hear. Her eyes rolled back in her head, and she went limp. He caught her and looked around the dark parking lot; saw a light flicker on and off in the school. He loaded her into the passenger's seat, half in and out of his lap, kept tight hold on her, and drove one handed to the emergency room.

It hit the national media two days later. Her name was Mrs Pavlenko, and she was the school's beloved math teacher. She and her husband had emigrated to Kentucky from Ukraine, where they'd been high school sweethearts. Small towns in Kentucky welcomed immigrants – there were three Bosnian restaurants in Bowling Green alone.

She was the first teacher to drop into a coma.

The very next morning Mateo wouldn't wake up. Susu began having seizures at lunch in the cafeteria, and by the time the ambulance came, she was unconscious. And Patrick stopped talking. Stopped moving. He sat wherever you put him and stared at the wall.

All within twenty-four hours.

The rural clinic was too small to handle it. Some were transported to University of Louisville Medical Center; some to the university hospital in Lexington where I had my office. By the time I got to the ER to see Patrick, and Susu and Mateo, four more kids and two more teachers from the school were brought in. The waiting room was in a panic; the parking lot was full of ambulances and police cars, and jam-packed with family and reporters from the local media.

Because the body knows so very much. And sometimes the body says *no*.

Within forty-eight hours, three more teachers and five more kids from Patrick's school had developed similar and ever-widening symptoms, filling emergency rooms, with doctors as baffled as the families.

TWENTY-TWO

HYSTERIA IN SMALL-TOWN KENTUCKY hit the news, and the vultures began pouring in. Media, talk-show hosts, researchers, pontificators, medical predators, and just everyday people who followed things like this, like groupies and rock bands. There had never been such a line of cars heading south since the Los Angeles takeover of Nashville.

Dr Bianchi arrived pretty soon after getting my call. I had set her up at the 21c Museum Hotel downtown. I breathed easier as soon as she texted to tell me she'd arrived.

I got waylaid on my way in to meet with her, when I stepped aside to get out of the way of a stretcher: the Osage Middle School history teacher, an ex-marine, eyes rolled back in his head, in cardiac arrest. And I thought of Perry.

The reporter who stepped in front of me wore a suit and a serious face. 'You're Dr Archer? Dr Noah Archer, neurosurgeon?'

'Excuse me please. I—'

'And you run an NGO, don't you? Called The Enlightenment Project, Inc? You're not just a neurologist; you're a demon hunter, right? Do you think there's something satanic going on at that school?'

I turned away.

'Dr Archer? I'm not the one that came up with that term, and I'm not the one making an accusation. Your colleague, Dr Hildegard Sweetwater, is the one who—'

I felt punched in the gut. Hilde. She had turned on me once before but never like this.

'Dr Sweetwater thinks you may have a part in this. Spreading fear in the school. She's teaming up with neuropsychiatrist Dr Silas Holtzer, who's speculating that this is mass hysteria, likely brought on by children suffering the trauma of poverty and sexual abuse, and maybe some hysterical teachers taking advantage, possibly faking their symptoms.'

I thought about the history teacher, his face chalk white, in cardiac arrest.

'Dr Holtzer says this kind of mass hysteria happens particularly in small towns like Osage, Kentucky. Do you have a comment?'

I turned and faced him. I did have a two-word comment, but I took a moment instead to think it through.

'No legitimate, ethical doctor would speculate on the diagnoses of patients, or libel their families with accusations like Dr Holtzer is making. I would encourage the families to file a lawsuit against any doctor who has accused them of faking symptoms, crimes of abuse or given out confidential details of their medical condition.'

The reporter shifted uneasily then stepped closer. 'Well then, what is *your* opinion, Dr Archer? Because Dr Sweetwater suspects toxins, maybe in the water supply of Osage, or something at the school.'

'I would certainly want the school checked for toxins, in order to rule that out.'

'The Osage Three – these first three kids – they are your patients, are they not?'

'I can't comment on that.'

'What's your insight on Dr Holtzer's suspicions of some kind of ongoing systemic trauma involving the possible sexual abuse of these children? Repressed memories surfacing from some kind of trigger? Doesn't one of the children live in a trailer park?'

'I fail to see the connection.'

The reporter took a step back. I knew that I looked pissed off, because I was pissed off and I do not have a poker face.

'You must have theories. Can you give us anything at all? Do you have a plan? There are a lot of people worried about these kids – people who want to see them properly cared for.'

'Let me be clear: I will not give you confidential information, I will not confirm who is or is not my patient and I will not speculate on the condition of anyone in my care. And I will not stand by while you make off-the-wall accusations in order to pathologize and monetize the things these people in Osage are going through.'

'That sounds like a threat, Dr Archer. What are you planning to do?'

'*Whatever the fuck it takes.*'

It made the news, and I was a meme in less than twenty-four hours. It aired locally, nationally and internationally through Reuters. They blipped out the *fuck,* and I looked like a raving maniac, and I have never gotten so many calls of congratulation in my life.

It was a total shit show. It was every man for himself.

And I also got a call from Perry. He was ignoring the advice of his doctors and my own concerns, refusing to wait at least another week before taking a flight; he was ignoring the possibility of blood clots, his vulnerability to changes in altitude and air pressure that might increase his heart rate or blood pressure. He was coming home. And he had a plan.

TWENTY-THREE

Dr Bianchi and I talked in low voices outside the ICU, where Susu had just come out of a coma, brought on by continuous seizures. Recovery can be quick when we get the seizures stopped. We'd been lucky. Dr Bianchi and I had decided to put all three of the children on Ativan to get their fear reactivity turned down and under control or things could get worse really fast. They were starting to come around. This time. The goal was to make sure there wasn't another time, which there would be, unless we addressed the root cause of the issue. We had to calm their fears and make them actually safe, which meant keeping them out of reach of those dark entities at the school.

People were looking for toxins. They were almost right – Chloe had already found them. She'd been to the school. Not alone. And during the day. I'd cleared the way with the principal, because I was the on-record physician treating the kids the media were calling the Osage Three and I called Patrick, Susu and Mateo. Normally I would not have touched this. I'd have sent them to a neuro who specializes in pediatrics. But as long as Dr Bianchi was there, it would be the two of us working together. Because I already knew what the issue was. I was just waiting for test results to confirm. And for Dr Bianchi to weigh in.

I had just been in to see Patrick, who was sitting up, Pammie confident and steady in a chair beside his bed. She'd even smiled at me. And I realized what a relief it was for Pammie and Patrick to be believed, to be understood, and not to be alone in this. To get medical care that wasn't laced in coercion or threat. And if this was happening to other people as well, the point had been made. It wasn't their imagination. It was real. There was a certain empowering comfort in that, and Pammie was looking to me and Dr Bianchi to help her get Patrick to the other side of this. I sure as shit hoped we could.

Patrick still wasn't talking yet, but he was no longer frozen in place. He watched me, watched Pammie, through the relief of an Ativan calm, and he dozed off and on like the exhausted child he was. Mateo was still sleeping but would open his eyes and sometimes turn his head to his father's voice. Susu was stable thanks to anti-seizure meds recommended by Dr Bianchi.

We were discussing dosages when Dr Bianchi stared over my shoulder, at someone she clearly didn't like. I turned around to see who she was looking at.

Dr Holtzer, storming the hallways, a man on a mission.

'Let's talk in my office. I have a new coffee maker that's better than your usual pour-over.'

'Not possible.'

'Ethiopian coffee beans.'

'Cuban is better.'

'This isn't a competition, Vivian.'

'Yes it is. Do you have cream? Sugar and a lot of it?'

'As much as you can put in your cup. I also have a package of gummy bears on my desk that got left in my car. They're yours if you want them.'

She had that gummy bear glow. 'Yeah, let's go to your office and talk. For privacy. And good coffee. And gummy bears, which are just a perk.'

'But an important perk.'

And I was reminded, for just a moment, of conversations like this with Dr Hildegard Sweetwater, who used to be my colleague and one of my closest friends. Who had been my partner with the Enlightenment Protocol when the research was first launched. Who had been reluctant to believe that stimulating the neurons of the spiritual side of the brain could bring dark things along with good things. Who had blamed me for the complications and for shutting the project down. She had seen a side of me she couldn't fathom, couldn't accept. And I'd never seen this hard, judgmental side of her, even though I'd known her for years. At first, I'd just rolled with it and let her have her space, thinking if cordial was all we'd be, that would have to be OK. But tonight she had crossed a line.

Still, she was brilliant. With any luck, some other hospital would lure her away.

I unlocked my office door and had a weird moment of feeling unsteady. And then like I could not move. *Push door open gently,* I told myself. And the moment passed, so I waved Dr Bianchi in. I knew it was stress; fatigue. I just needed sleep. Many of us do.

She started in on the gummy bears while I made the coffee. I frowned at her over my shoulder. She curled sideways in a chair. Black hair cut very short, narrow black trousers. She had the Audrey Hepburn thing going, though she was too young to know who that was.

'You need a proper dinner. Order room service tonight when you get to the hotel.'

'Gummy bears are fine.'

I didn't push. She was impossible.

She looked up, chewing. 'I do think you're right, Noah. That the underlying issue with all of these symptoms is fear, but I need to talk to the kids, and so far none of them have been in any shape for that. I'd say pull them out of that school though, for now at least. Keep them feeling secure. And you're testing for?'

I gave her the rundown.

'So basically everything.' She wrapped both hands around the coffee mug I handed her. 'What about encephalitis?'

'Done. Ruled out. And I'm running a gut dysbiosis so I can look at the gut-brain microbiome axis.'

She sat forward in her chair like a little kid. '*Really*? I was going to suggest that. The connection between the microbiome and mental-health issues is stunning. I've seen it as the first indication of early psychosis. It could definitely push the fear-anxiety-reactivity loop. And it explains the cluster symptoms we're getting. So many reactions but all triggered and looping from the same issue.'

'Also you should know that our friend Dr Holtzer's request to consult has been denied.'

She grimaced. She was very familiar with Dr Holtzer. 'He waylaid me in the hallway three hours ago and I thought I was going to have to call security. Wanted to be a part of our "team". And he warned me about you. Suggested I talk with the parents and have you removed as their doctor.'

I cocked my head to one side. 'I mean . . . he does know I'm the one who called you in?'

'It didn't seem to bother him. He had a lot of snark about you running The Enlightenment Project and what he called your . . . *belief system.*'

'He said demon hunter, right?'

She blushed. 'I would never say something like that about you. Or to you.'

'Yes, but he would.'

'It's slanderous. You know I don't believe in anything demonic, Noah, but that's just a *word* I don't like. I have great respect for you, and I'm curious about your thinking on all of this.'

I told her about Chloe measuring a defined chemical signature in Patrick's home, and that she'd gone to the school and found an identical signature concentrated in Mrs Garcia's classroom, the cafeteria, the school office and copy room.

'Has she been able to identify what it is?' Dr Bianchi asked.

'No.' I settled back in my chair. No more coffee for me. Just thinking about it made me ill.

'And your theory is?' She smiled at me. 'Let me guess. That third thing we can never quite put our finger on, when a patient has somatic symptoms. We're treating them physically and finding stress, trauma and fear reactions, so we treat that too, but *why* . . . and how to heal it. That's the big mystery to solve. And often enough, it does come down to that unidentifiable *third* thing. I just don't think it's demons.'

'Yes, you've made that clear. And I don't actually like the word demon either, Vivian, except for the way it takes the air out of the room when I want people to pay attention. Because whatever this is, it is something *other*, and ignoring it is unwise. So, to be clear: we've picked up a consistent, measurable energy presence, and yes, I think it's some kind of dark spiritual thing. I do think the kids are under spiritual attack. However you want to define that.'

She gave me a lopsided smile. 'Yeah, I've heard rumors about this crazy theory that we're conscious human beings. Maybe with a spiritual side. It's mysterious whatever this is. And with all of the media chaos, it's going to escalate and spread the somatic symptoms. And you know by that I mean symptoms that the brain expects and therefore creates physically. The patient has no control over this. So the question is, what are they reacting to? Because the symptoms are real.'

'And if we don't get this at the source, the symptoms will be ongoing, chronic, and they may flare up and get worse.'

'Unfortunately, that's how it usually plays out. You know, Noah, we're not as far apart on this as you think. Because incidents like this have happened before. It's mysterious, it seems to happen out of the blue – which of course isn't the case – and often enough no one ever really figures it out, because the reasons are complicated.

'Remember those girls in New York – what did they call it, the town that caught Tourette's? Small town, like Osage. Western medicine calls it conversion disorder. Physical symptoms that the body expresses sourced in emotional stressors, and it's contagious in a close-knit social group. It's a mass psychogenic illness, and when the brain sees it happening to someone else, it mirrors the symptoms, so it's as contagious as yawning. And some of the girls responded to antibiotics, and there was speculation about strep and brain chemistry. And while you're on the right track with the gut testing, whatever's going on, I think the gut is reacting to, not causing, it. Hard to know, right? If stress and fear reshape the gut bacteria, or it's the other way around. Either way, we get stress hormones and inflammation. And a body flooded with toxins and neurohormones. But to my way of thinking, the gut isn't the stressor. Something else is. We just give it a loose term like conversion disorder.'

I sat back with a smile on my face but listening hard.

She tossed a gummy bear across the desk, and I caught it. A green one.

'Listen, I've researched this stuff – it's mind-boggling. Another culture might see it another way, call it something else, more in line to your way of thinking, Noah.'

I tossed the gummy bear back.

'No really, listen. In the 1980s, Hmong immigrants, mostly healthy young men from the highlands of northern Laos, started dying in their sleep. Usually between ten p.m. and eight a.m. – ninety-eight percent in that exact time frame. And yet the best theory the doctors came up with was poor diet, which is, of course, ridiculous, because if poor diet caused this—'

'A lot of people would be dead. But they must have seen something in the gut testing, so let's cut them some slack.'

'*Let's not.* Nobody listened to the patients. To the community where it was happening. These were healthy young men, dying at the same time each night. There was no warning, no illness – they went to sleep, they got caught up in terrible nightmares and they didn't wake up.'

I thought of lucid dreaming and felt a chill.

'The point is, Noah, the Hmong people say the deaths were caused by evil spirits – that the men were terrorized to death by a nightmare. But nobody listened to the people who were living it. So that's why I'm paying attention to what you've been telling me about that school. Sometimes people are afraid. Of what and why I don't know, but the Hmong people were living it – *they knew it was fear*. You know it's my belief that catatonia is caused entirely by fear. Psychological abnormalities can be created by the predictive coding of the brain. Somatic disorders come from the stories the patients tell themselves. Their body believes the stories. Illness can literally be passed on from one patient to another from thoughts, proximity, expectations and thus embodiment. Whatever you want to call it, cognition and social pressures can produce lethal cardiovascular response. People die. Only a fraction of our sensory experiences are in the conscious realm, Noah – think about that.'

I did think about that. I was glad she was thinking about it too.

'And the brain expresses itself through the body,' I said.

'The brain expresses itself through the body. So we have a contained community in this school, under heavy stress and the fear of what they *perceive* to be supernatural, haunting experiences. And so they are getting sick, as a community.'

'I want to talk to you about the word perceive. Because I was there. And this is real.'

'We'll agree to disagree on that. In a way, it doesn't matter.'

'Well it does matter if the experiences keep happening to them. The symptoms these kids are having are all about disassociating from fear. And this Dr Holtzer, with his limited, dated and salacious theories that these issues are caused by repressed trauma and sexual abuse, is making things a lot worse. And it is always the poorer patients whose families get accused of this. These kinds of accusations ruin lives. And I'm not having it.'

'Neither am I. Come on, Noah, when it happens to women, it's attributed to faking. I heard one of the reporters say that the female teachers in the school were faking symptoms to get attention, but that wasn't applied to the *male* teachers. Sounds like business as usual to me. And you know as well as I do how often doctors make jokes about women with disassociate seizures.'

I knew. I'd seen it.

'When something like this happens to men, it's not even called conversion. Somatic symptoms aren't even considered. Take the "sonic weapon" theory for Havana syndrome, which occurred at the Canadian and US embassy in Cuba. All of the symptoms are categorized as idiopathic. Spontaneous and unknown but assumed to have a physical cause. The victims were generally male, white, affluent and in their forties. If it happens to men, it's assumed there's a physical cause. So nobody was calling it what it was – a mass psychogenic illness. And their symptoms were real. They suffered and they're still having trouble. But they weren't subjected to questions about sexual trauma, abuse or poverty. The very term mass hysteria is misogynistic because it's only applied to women, and it's a way of not taking their symptoms seriously.'

'*But, Noah* . . . if an illness can be created through expectations, then you can also *heal it* through expectations. And the cause may well be a major stressor rippling through the "society" of these kids and teachers. Something there that we just don't know about. You say the school is haunted, and *I* say it doesn't matter whether it is or it isn't. If they *think* it's haunted – same outcome.

'And Holtzer is a menace – he *will* make it worse – and now we run the risk of a looping causation effect that will make these kids sicker and sicker. The last thing we need is Holtzer creating external and internal feedback loops. Not only will it make them worse now, it could make them chronically ill for the rest of their lives.

'And an exorcism, Noah . . . isn't that really decoding the patient's story? Isn't it a metaphor for distress? Functional disorders are the brain's coding system going haywire. The brain is creating the illness, expressing it through the body. Anxiety is contagious, and disability can be learned. But what is programmed and coded can be unprogrammed and uncoded. And *that* is what we have to do.'

'No biological or physiological treatment will heal them, Vivian.'

'The Hmong were animists. They did a *soul calling*. To bring a wandering soul back. This was a community under enormous pressure to assimilate. Young men, caught between the old and the new. Walking between two worlds. The Hmong believe we have several souls. And the trouble comes when the souls are out of harmony. But in my terminology, a soul calling works as a community narrative to change the coding.'

'The coding isn't going to change unless we make sure these kids are free from this dark energy, and right now, it's all over that school. This is more than a narrative.'

She just looked at me – another Western doctor, afraid to come out of the box. And I'd expended way too much energy trying to convince her of something I knew inside and out; something she would never see.

But I was still glad as hell I'd called her in and grateful she came, with her brilliant mind, her compassion, her ability to be analytical and her open-minded, utterly formidable insight.

'I will give you this, Noah. It's really interesting that Patrick feels safer with those symbols you showed me. But calming the fears of these children doesn't mean an exorcism. I think that could make them worse. It insinuates that they're the cause – that they're wrong somehow.'

'I agree.'

'Oh. Do you?'

'On a child? No, I would never recommend that.'

'But you do work with an exorcist.'

'Yes. I do. And he has only one time ever done an exorcism on a child. In an extreme case when nothing – and I mean nothing – else worked.'

'What was the outcome?'

I eased back in my chair. 'You're looking at him. You tell me.'

She put a hand on my arm. 'I'm sorry. I didn't realize. I hope I didn't offend you.'

'I already told you I agree with you. And you'll meet him. Father Perry Cavanaugh. He's part of the team.'

She leaned back in her chair and folded her arms.

'He's been out of the country. Ill. But I've been consulting him as this has been playing out, and plans are for him to get home as soon as he can grab a flight. I want to be upfront with you on that.'

'He's the . . . guy?'

'You can say exorcist – the sky won't fall.'

'What exactly is he going to do? I could possibly see some kind of healing ritual that would dovetail with the family beliefs, if that's what they want, but I wouldn't want them pushed into something like that. I can't be on board with influencing or pressuring a family into doing something like this; I won't go along with that. And to be clear, I won't go along with exorcisms of these children.'

'Agreed. Perry has no intention of doing an exorcism of the kids. He's going to be doing an exorcism of the school.'

She frowned at me. 'Will the kids be there?'

'Absolutely not. But the thing is, Vivian, we can do all the testing, we can give these kids meds for their fears, but we're going to need to tend to the spiritual side for something like this. It's the third thing you've been looking for. Meet Perry and decide after you talk to him. He's the one who'll know how to go forward on that side of things, and you can judge him for yourself. Nobody's going to pressure you into anything you're not comfortable with.'

'Nobody can.'

'Fair enough.'

'What happens if you and I disagree?'

'You're the final authority on the kids. I'll do any neuro workups you want, or you can find a pediatric neurologist. That might be best anyway.'

She thought about it. Nodded. 'OK.'

'And you don't have to be in on any of the spiritual things we do at the school. Don't do anything that makes you uncomfortable.'

'Oh no you don't. I'll be there. I want to see what you do and how it works and what happens. I want to see the school and the environment these kids are living in. I want the whole enchilada.'

'You can have the whole enchilada and all the gummy bears you want. I'm just glad you're here. Sound good?'

'It does. And I appreciate your trust.'

'It's late – let me walk you to your car.'

'Can you get me through the scrum outside?'

'There's a secret passageway.'

'And by that you mean the corridor and freight elevator to the basement where they transport the bodies in and out of the morgue?'

'Yes, that's it exactly. And your predictive coding will tell you—'

'*Oh, enough.*'

TWENTY-FOUR

It happened again when I finally made my way home, sitting in the driveway, too tired to pull into the garage. I shut the engine off and sat in the car. Not because I was thinking or taking a moment. I *wanted* to get out of the car and go into the house. I just couldn't.

I told myself this would pass. I shut down the analytical part of my mind so full of theory, judgement, excuses and fear. I was tired. I would sit. I would be still. A new experience for me. Being still.

So I sat and stopped worrying about what this meant. I put the seat back and stretched out my legs; got comfortable. A still night, no wind. Most of the lights off in the house. Moira home; Tom here too, his patrol car parked out front. Tash likely stretched out with the boys, guarding as she slept.

And just as I opened the car door without a particularly conscious decision, the hall light went on, and Vaughn came outside, on to the porch. He waved at me as I locked up the car. Met me in the driveway.

'You OK, Dad?' he asked.

'I am now.'

'I was worrying about you.'

'Worrying about me why?'

He shrugged. 'Everybody else is asleep,' he told me. Reporting in.

'That's good. I'm glad you came down to check on me, but I'm fine. Come on – let's head in. You've got school early in the morning; I'll tuck you into bed.'

'Oh God, Dad, I'm too old to be tucked in. I could tuck you in.'

'Everybody likes a little, but nobody likes a smart one.'

He laughed, reinforcing my long-held opinion that a vulgar father was pure delight.

We parted in the hallway – Vaughn to head up the stairs after giving me a tight hug; me to go into my office. I sat in my big leather chair and unlocked the drawer where I kept the red notebook.

I used it for insights on patients. Random, sometimes brilliant but often mundane insights I had when I just let myself go to that place of focus and contemplation. That place where I imagined their surgical outcomes. Miraculous healings for terminal patients that rarely happened but sometimes did.

I flipped to a blank section and put my name at the top. *Noah Archer.* I would look at myself through the eyes of a doctor, stepping aside from the man.

I knew that these moments I was having were a warning. Years of certain kinds of stress and out-and-out trauma that were never addressed actually were addressed in the physical. Your average ALS patients are the nicest in the world – never a cross word, never a complaint, a lifetime of repressing their feelings and putting everybody else first to the point they don't know what those feelings are. Doctors talk about that in private. We keep it to ourselves that MS patients are a type and patients with certain cancers have astoundingly similar histories, as do patients with anything autoimmune.

But with me, I wasn't sure what the issue was, and I wasn't sure what to do about it. Twice tonight my body had tried to bring something to my attention. I would need to sort it out before things escalated. I picked up my pen.

> *Dr Archer carries the weight of judgement. Sometimes people look at him like he's batshit crazy. It takes a toll.*
>
> *Dr Archer is tired.*
>
> *Dr Archer needs to remember that it is not his job to make people understand the things he knows. It takes time and energy he doesn't have to give.*
>
> *Dr Archer has everything he needs to figure out how to help these kids. That is the right place for his time and energy.*
>
> *Dr Archer was born for this kind of work.*
>
> *Dr Archer is on the verge of figuring out some really cool shit.*
>
> *Dr Archer is having moments of fatigue, dizziness and reluctance to move forward that manifested physically tonight in his car.*

I closed the notebook. Locked it in the drawer just as Tash padded into the office. I took her outside for a late-night wee, then both of us headed up the stairs. She to the boys' room, me to my wife.

TWENTY-FIVE

I found the message from Perry on my phone the next morning when I woke up.

I'm at Geneva Airport. My flight leaves in three minutes. I get into Cincinnati tomorrow afternoon at five fifteen p.m. Any chance you can pick me up? We need to talk.

I made it out of the hospital early, which took some doing, and was almost on time to pick him up. Cincinnati Airport was just the right size. Plenty of international flights, but easy in and out. Perry was waiting patiently at the curb with one small suitcase, and he waved when I pulled up. Thanked me for coming.

He looked surprisingly good for a man who had almost died in Rome. Lighter somehow, more relaxed. Maybe everything was better in Italy. He laughed at me when I tried to lift his suitcase into the trunk.

'I've got it, but thanks.'

'Are you hungry? I was thinking we could go to dinner at Malone's.'

'I'd like that. It's good to be home.'

I wanted to bombard him with questions, but I knew to go easy with him. I was just glad he was here, and I was glad he was alive. But it was Perry who brought it up on the drive home from the airport.

'Thanks, Noah, for taking care of things.'

'Happy to be the haunted house escort for the women in your life.'

He gave me an easy smile.

'I'm happy to know them, Perry. They seem pretty great. You could have told me about them. Why *didn't* you tell me?'

He looked out the window. 'Because they're so rarely in my life. Their choice not mine. And there's nothing on this earth more humiliating than a daughter – and a wife – who don't . . . who don't want you in their lives. Being a failed husband and a failed father isn't something I discuss. With anyone.'

'Oh, that. Chloe clearly wants you in her life.'

'She cycles me in and out.' But he was smiling.

'Elle is in her terrible thirties. As I understand it, kids get better in their fifties.'

Noah nodded. 'So just twenty years to go? Elle has spent a lifetime pissed off at Chloe and I for screwing up her childhood by splitting when she was three. Still married but not living together. She doesn't like the push-pull of our relationship. She'd like us to decide one way or the other.'

He sounded cheerful enough. These were old wounds, and he'd been living with them a while. No doubt I was getting the condensed version.

'It's not up to her. Did you know that your daughter considers me the uncle she never met?'

'She told me you looked out for her. You know I appreciate it.'

'For a family who says they never talk, the three of you seem to talk a lot.'

'That's a recent development.'

TWENTY-SIX

It was good to be sitting with Perry at Malone's, which had been our hangout for years. Tonight was a blow-out meal. Perry had the twin fillets with crab, asparagus and Mornay sauce. And I had a giant New York strip with Creole blackened shrimp. Gruyere potato casserole croquettes for both of us. I had a Stella Artois on draft. He had his Martini. All was right with my world. At least for tonight.

I'd been filling him in on the house; the school. 'I've never seen anything like this, Perry.'

'Unfortunately, I have. It'll be the worst thing you'll ever see.'

'That doesn't sound good. How do you think Chloe and Elle are dealing with it?' I had my opinion. I wanted his.

'*Not good*. They say they are. They're not. I'm glad Elle headed off to France. The further away my daughter is from that school and that house, the happier I am. And she's right. The family connections, the dreams about this mysterious woman who's some kind of great aunt . . . I understand why she feels compelled to go and figure this out. And you'll have noticed that my daughter, completely agnostic, is also an absolute beacon for this kind of dark entity.'

'Takes after her dad.'

'I'd just as soon not have passed that on.' He tapped a finger on the table. 'I like Chloe's take on this. It doesn't change the way I see it, the spiritual side, but I like having a physical explanation. It also—'

'Makes it scarier?'

He nodded. 'Funny how that works. Be we need to get out there, Noah. To that school. We need to shut this down. The school is closed down right now?'

'By the health department. They're checking the water, the air, focusing on environmental hazards. They're holding classes in an old carburetor factory that closed down in 2007.'

'OK, that's excellent. But soon enough they'll open that school back up. Do they want my help?'

'They do. They've given us access to the school. I've set up a meeting to coordinate and make sure we're all on the same page. They want me and you, and Dr Bianchi wants to be there to see the environment the kids have been in. We've agreed for her to be the public face of the healthcare issues.'

'Good call. I saw the meme.'

'I have no regrets. We can't control the crazy stuff that's all over the media, but we can counter it. But I have to ask if you feel well enough to do this.'

'You, my wife, my daughter and quite a few children and teachers are all tangled up in this. This is not a matter of choice.'

Exactly what I expected him to say.

'I know you can't give me details on patients, other than the general things you've already told me. You say they want my help. They understand that I've taken early retirement from the church? That I'm not there in any kind of official church-sanctioned capacity? I have a plan for handling this, but ethically, I have to be clear about that.'

'They just want help. They're desperate. And the paperwork's done. They've requested and accepted the services of The Enlightenment Project, NGO. They're aware that you're the . . .'

He gave me a smile. 'The exorcist on staff?'

'Yeah.'

'It will be my total focus. Maybe now we won't have to turn so many people away.'

'It's triage.'

'I can understand that without being happy about it.'

'What happened, Perry? In Rome. What brought all of this on?'

He took a sip of his Martini and looked away. 'For a while now, Noah, I haven't felt connected to the church. The work, yes, but there were always ongoing issues, politics, things I disagreed with where I had no choice but to lend my support. And I'm . . . just tired. I'm still connected to the work we do, with The Enlightenment Project. But even that . . . I haven't been sure how to approach that anymore. I've had a lot of thinking to do, and no time or mind space to be still with all of my thoughts.'

I nodded. That I understood.

'Look, when I landed in Rome, I was so psyched to be in Italy, to be at the conference, to be leading a seminar and to talk to other exorcists. And they had a driver pick me up, treated me like royalty, but when I walked into Vatican City, it was so strange. I got so tired. Drained. Like everything around me was surreal. And then the second day, I was sitting in a room of priest exorcists. Some of them good men, some of them not. But all of them *men.* Pontificating. Having opinions. Making policy. Using the agony of people in trouble as an opportunity for marketing the church brand, *exorcism.* And I wondered: was I different? All of us making excuses, always turning a blind eye. So much dark history, Noah. And dark things still. Organized religion – overall, does it add to people's lives or does it take things away? When does the bad outweigh the good?

'And finally – and at last – I truly understood my wife. And I realized how often I made excuses for a religion that excludes people. Considers women less than. How was that ever OK? How did I just accept that as business as usual?'

He toyed with the Martini glass. 'But what surprises me most is how this has freed me up for an even stronger faith, one I don't have to make excuses for or be ashamed of. Because it's mine and it comes from within. And I've never felt such a beautiful spiritual connection, or such an intuitive knowing that I am on the right path.'

'It's a big change, Perry. A good change. But still. Religion . . . your church. That's been your life.'

'But it hasn't, Noah. It's just been the framing. The true spirituality is mine and always has been.' He smiled at me. 'I made things official before I left. I did worry that I would have regrets, but mainly it is joyous autonomy. I feel free of so many snarly things that have been weighing me down. It adds up you know – all the uneasy compromises. I don't have to make apologies for things I've never agreed with. I wish I'd had time to stay awhile, to drift through Italy and be still, just think. About what the rest of my life is going to look like. But no doubt I'll figure that out.'

He leaned forward. 'And for me, the work we do with The Enlightenment Project – that is going to be the focus of my life. This is what I do, Noah. That hasn't changed.'

'I've been worried you'd had enough of it. That it was weighing you down.'

'The work that you and I do together takes a physical toll, and it has a formidable spiritual danger. But that is not what I was tired of. This is the work I was born to do.'

And that was a feeling I knew and understood.

'Once I was in Rome, everything became clear. Because when I was there at the Vatican, with the exorcists . . . it felt like death's waiting room. It felt like my past.'

'So everything's going to be the same,' I said.

'Yes. And everything's going to be different.' But his tone was bracing, and it gave me confidence. I hadn't liked winging this on my own while he was gone.

He motioned to the waiter and ordered another beer for me and his second Martini. 'Let's get to business. Tell me about the AI issues and the robot.'

I waited until the server was out of earshot. 'His name is Sasha. He scared the shit out of me. There were four Sasha AI systems donated to the fifth-grade classes in the school, but all of them are gone now.'

'How did it interact with the kids? Specifics.'

I told him everything. He winced at the threats, the porn and the bullying, and nodded when I told him about Mrs Garcia locking Sasha away and how Sasha liked to move around. 'She started out thrilled to have AI in her classroom. But by the time I got there, she was terrified. I couldn't just leave her alone with that. So with her permission, I took Sasha out of the classroom and set him on fire.'

'You didn't take him home?'

I shook my head. 'But I had him in my car.'

He frowned. 'Did you burn all of him?'

'Nothing left but hot ashes and lumps of electronics. But I'm a little . . . rattled. I put him in the trunk of my car and headed out to a state park to incinerate him. And when I got there . . . he was in the back seat.'

'It. Not he.'

'I'm afraid I'll find him on the doorstep of my house. And I keep checking the rearview mirror to make sure he's not lurking in the back seat of the car.'

Perry nodded. 'It wouldn't surprise me.'

'Thanks for that.'

'Just be aware, Noah – vermin always finds its way back. And everything is energy, right? It can't be destroyed; it just—'

'Takes another form. Thank you, Perry, I feel so much better now.' I shrugged. 'As far as I know, *all four* of the Sashas are gone. Burned to a crisp. The teachers had a bonfire then went out for Mexican food to celebrate. And for a week or so, everything got better at the school. Then it got worse. A lot worse.'

'To be expected. There will always be pushback, and it will come in hard.'

'Yeah, evidently. Dr Bianchi was worried about having the kids go through exorcisms—'

'Who said they should?'

'No one actually, but no doubt she's seen the movie. She *is* up for some kind of healing ritual—'

'Noah, these kids are scared. So you and Dr Bianchi take care of them – she's the psychiatrist, and you're the physician. The infestation, the darkness, comes to me. That is at the school, and my brilliant wife has, by God, measured it. So the school is where we go. And trust me, Noah, from the sound of this, it's going to be a knock-down, drag-out fight. A dangerous fight.'

'Yeah. Been there, got the tee shirt, which is currently being worn by my wife.'

'Understand this: getting rid of a deeply rooted infestation that's been feeding on the energy and fear of all these children and teachers doesn't happen overnight. The goal is to eradicate it, but there are no guarantees. I can make it better. I can help. But we're going to be up against it.'

'Then let's order dessert and plan the logistics.'

And we did – Perry with a slice of coconut cream pie and me the apple pecan crisp. Malone's has the best coffee in town. It helps. I would have to bring Vivian Bianchi out here.

Perry closed his eyes. 'This time yesterday, I was in Italy.'

'Miss the Vatican, do you?'

'Rome, Vatican City . . . it's extraordinary, Noah. So much darkness there. So much light.'

TWENTY-SEVEN

The dessert plan was this. A team of four – Perry, Chloe, myself and Dr Bianchi – heading to the school as soon as we could orchestrate four intense schedules. Vivian had already told me she wanted to go. To see the school and meet the principal. She was looking for social context. To frame the somatic symptoms that were spreading like wildfire. More teachers. More students. More media.

I was curious what she'd think. If she would feel anything off in the energy of the school.

Dr Bianchi would be particularly helpful, Perry said. She didn't believe in supernatural things and would be fascinated, but not be distracted by that particular unsettling fear. He was interested in her reactions to the school. What she felt. If it affected her.

'All humans are afraid of supernatural things,' I told him. 'On a visceral level if nothing else.'

'Exactly my point,' he said.

He would take some time, walking through the hallways, circling as he always did, and when he was ready, he would begin the first exorcism. He said to expect many. Such infestations were stubborn, and he was worried about how deeply embedded this one was, and how it had been building, feeding, growing.

He wanted me there, with free reign to wander, to get my insights, my intuition, my sense of danger. As usual . . . takes one to know one. I am ever and always a man who has been possessed. Chloe would be recording and measuring. We would see in graphed-out data the effect the exorcism had on the dark entities at the school. A physical representation we had never had access to before.

Perry and I hashed out scheduling details as I gave him a lift home.

'Does Chloe know you're back?' I asked him.

'She's expecting me tomorrow; I got an earlier flight. Drop me off at the house, would you?'

'Her house? Or your place at the Wellie?'

'As I understand it, my daughter is occupying the Wellie. Take me to Chloe's house. On Second Street?'

I nodded. I knew where it was. 'But Elle is in France.'

'I am not going to the Wellie either way. I'm going to Chloe's. My favorite razor is in her bathroom.'

I admit that I sat in the car and watched as Perry set his suitcase down on the tiny front porch of Chloe's small but exquisite house, with the two-foot black iron fence around a very small postage-stamp front yard. Perry had a key, but the front door opened before he'd turned the lock. There was a moment, Perry facing Chloe. Then he gathered her into his arms and held her, and they went inside together. Forgetting the little bag he'd left on the porch.

TWENTY-EIGHT

I drove everyone down to the school in the Audi, listening to the buzz of conversation. Vivian and Chloe had an immediate connection. And I could tell that Vivian was impressed by Perry. He had a well-earned gravitas; a low-key, gentle charm. He was clearly not what she expected.

Osage was a small town, and it was overrun. Media trucks, traffic, which meant fifty cars ahead of you instead of one. The school was a hive of activity, cordoned off behind tape, guarded by the state police, barriers blocking the parking lot, no unauthorized personnel allowed. I thought I saw a drone passing over the school, but it might have been a bird.

We were expected. Shown a place to park that had been reserved just for us. A news camera filmed us going in.

'It's like being in the middle of a documentary,' Vivian whispered.

'You don't have to whisper,' I told her.

She pivoted. Completely absorbed. 'The school looks normal. Small and nice. I get a happy feeling here. And it's well maintained.' She was full of energy and buzz. This was definitely not her average day. And in the ranking of interesting cases . . . this one was off the charts for all four of us.

We went through the heavy double doors, Perry holding them open, shepherding everybody in.

'Up close and personal now,' I said.

Perry and I exchanged looks. He got what I meant. We were no longer observers. We were intertwined.

You had to walk the hallways of the old part of the school to understand this place. And there were places in the older part of the school I had not seen yet; places I wasn't sure I wanted to look.

We settled into Mrs Garcia's classroom, using it as our home base. Chloe unpacked her equipment – bigger, more serious instruments and meters, and a laptop. As arranged, all doors were unlocked and accessible, with state troopers outside to assist. The principal,

Mr Rheingold, was supposed to meet us, but he was nowhere to be found.

'He's probably on his way,' Vivian said. Ever the optimist.

'I'll need you later,' Perry told me in a soft voice then slipped out of the room. Off on his own for now.

Vivian wandered through the desks; looked out the bank of windows. 'I like the way this teacher has decorated the room, it's so cheerful. It has such a good feel.' She went to the whiteboard. 'Yes, Noah, see this here?' She pointed to the symbols Patrick had drawn. Red and black dots, geometric configurations. Triangles and trapezoids. She went right to the door, searched out the ones Patrick had carved and painted there. Mrs Garcia had let him go to town. 'Patrick told me about these. I had a long session with him yesterday.'

She inclined her head, and we headed out to the hallway for a private conversation.

'How did it go?' I asked.

'He's a great kid,' she said, staring off down the hallway, in thinking mode. 'Super smart. Resilient. A . . . a valiant heart. If that doesn't sound over the top.'

'It doesn't. I've met him.'

'He worships you,' she said. 'And his dad.'

Patrick was going to have a long road of grief ahead. I'd walked that path myself. I hoped Patrick would keep seeing Dr Bianchi.

'He is having a lot of bad thoughts,' she said matter-of-factly.

'Not surprising.'

'I always tell my kids to reframe the thoughts. Instead of thinking *something bad is coming for me* I ask them to change it to *I'm having these thoughts and worries that something bad is coming for me*.'

'How does that help?'

'It gives distance – and empowerment – because this way they can be in charge of the thoughts.'

'Seems brilliant, Vivian.'

'It works really well with a resilient take-charge kid like Patrick. And of course I had him do some drawings. Mainly he drew these symbols over and over. Because they keep him safe.'

She glanced down the hallway and frowned.

'Something?' I asked.

'No, no,' she said with a laugh. 'My imagination, I'm sure.'

She put her back to the wall, hands in the pockets of her narrow black cotton trousers, looked at me, considering. 'I want to get your take on some of the things Patrick said. Because when I asked him how he knew to make the drawings, and how they kept him safe . . . he said he's seen them in a cave. I asked if he could tell me where the cave was, but he said he didn't know how to get there. I asked him when he went to the cave, and he said it was the night before his dad disappeared. Except he didn't say disappeared. He said his dad *got taken*.'

I felt a chill. Flashed back on being in the crawl space of the house. The crawl space where Conor and Andi Craig were right before they disappeared.

'He told me he'd been worried that night, because he thought the baby was scared, and he couldn't eat his dinner. He and his dad liked to watch movies and eat together after his dad put the baby down, and his mom would be working then. It was guy time. He loved guy time, but that night the baby had started screaming and his dad had gotten her back to sleep and said not to worry because babies are supposed to cry when they need you so you go and pick them up. But Patrick said he knew the baby was *scared*, and it made him mad, because it wasn't right for a baby to be scared – she was too little.' She looked up at me. 'He's going to grow up great.'

'If this doesn't scar him too much.'

'You grew up great.'

'Don't analyze me, Vivian.'

She just smiled then gave me a steady look. 'This is the part where it gets interesting. Patrick went to bed, even though his daddy said he could stay up. He said he fell asleep really fast, and then *the lady* woke him up.'

'The lady?' I asked like I didn't know who *the lady* was. I wasn't sure I was going to get into that. Not Vivian's wheelhouse.

'Yeah, interesting, right? So I told him to tell me about the lady. Was she a good lady? And he says oh, she's really, really good. Like the best lady you ever met. And she told him to put on his jeans and his shoes and grab a jacket because they were going outside, and she was going to show him something. Something really important. He said it was dark when they got outside, but she made a light all around them. And she took him to a cave.'

'A cave?'

'Yeah. She took him to a cave and showed him symbols on the walls; she said they were really old and had been there a long time.

He said they were drawn into the rock. She told him to memorize the patterns and symbols – it was important to get them right. And that had worried him, that he might get them wrong, but she said not to worry about that. She took a knife and cut a chunk off the rock with the symbols and told him to keep it. He could draw them anywhere and they would make a barrier of protection.'

'That's an interesting phrase.'

'Certainly an odd expression for a child that age to come out with. And then he said he woke up and it was morning and light. Like one minute he was in the cave, then suddenly he was in bed awake and it was morning. And that he had the rock in his pocket. I asked if he'd show it to me and he said yes, because it was proof he wasn't lying. But that I had to promise to just look at it, not take it.'

She pulled her phone out of her pocket, scrolled for a picture, and handed me the screen.

Patrick's open palm and a piece of rock, two inches square, ragged edges, oval. Marked with a triangle, a hexagon, and red and black dots.

'What do you think, Noah?'

'What do *you* think, Vivian?'

She frowned. 'It's detailed – the symbols are drawn precisely, with what looks like the practiced hand of an artist, and an adult. It looks like it belongs in a museum, don't you think? It's too sophisticated for him to have drawn. I was comparing it to what I see here on the board and by the door, and you see? His drawings are way different. But my thinking is that he found the rock with the symbols – I have no idea where – and because he is so smart, he wove it into a story where the symbols protected him, and a nice lady came to help.'

'There's only one problem with that theory, Vivian.'

She looked at me. Eyes bright.

'I saw the lady too.'

She froze. This was not what she had expected. She leaned back into the lockers and bumped her head.

'I saw her the night I went out to Patrick's house. I told you what happened, right? At the house? How Patrick and I first met? So on my way home, there she was, standing in the middle of the road. I had to slam on my brakes and stop the car. I didn't hit her, but I got out to look for her. Couldn't find her. But she was there. I saw her just like Patrick did, and I wasn't asleep. And Noah's daughter, Elle – she's seen her too.'

'Yes, you told me about Elle. How did Elle describe her?'

'A beautiful woman with long gray hair in ripples to her waist. A flowing dress with buttons down the front.'

Vivian scrolled on her phone again. 'This is the only other thing Patrick wanted to draw.'

It was her. The lady. A child's hand-drawn version, but the hair, the smile, the blue-blue eyes. The floating, flowing dress.

'Yeah, that's her.'

'Wow,' Vivian said. 'You of course did not discuss this with Patrick?'

'Absolutely not. And I would have told you if I had.'

'My take is that the lady certainly seems real. But it could be a sort of shared—'

'Shared contagious hysteria? Shared delusion? Vivian. Have you ever heard of a lucid dream?'

'*Shit damn hell.*' Chloe.

I headed back into the classroom, Vivian one step ahead. Chloe sprawled on the floor, scrambling to her feet.

'I'm OK,' she told us. 'I just slipped in this puddle of water. Where the fuck it came from I have no idea.'

'That's one of the . . . manifestations,' I said.

'Well, a warning would have been nice.'

'Sorry, Chloe. *Beware of manifestations.*'

Vivian was helping her up. 'Did you get hurt?'

'No,' Chloe said. 'It just pissed me off.'

I glanced at the line of lockers on the wall. One slightly ajar. The one where Sasha had been stashed. I crossed the room, opened the door. Empty.

'Also, Chloe. This is the locker where Sasha was stashed.'

She nodded. 'Good to know. I was getting readings over there. I'll do the locker inside and out.'

And then we heard the tap of a cane in the hallway. A woman's voice. 'Anybody here?'

TWENTY-NINE

She introduced herself as Mrs Emmaline Loring, a long-retired principal of this school. She had been here before the new part of the school had been added on in 2007. She was out of breath. Her hair was twisted into a loose and thick gray chignon, she wore black-framed reading glasses pushed up on to her head, for convenience or because she had forgotten they were there. She wore loose, wide-legged khaki linen pants, a lightweight black tunic and gray calf-high Uggs that looked comfortable but would not give her feet the support she needed. I didn't tell her that. But I wanted to.

The cobalt-blue cane helped, but walking for her was slow, strenuous and painful. I pulled out a chair, and she let me support her arm while she settled in.

'Thank you.'

'Take a moment,' I said. 'Catch your breath.'

She gave me a twinkly look. 'It may take more than a moment.' She took her time, breathing slowly and deeply. I could tell she was in enormous and chronic pain.

She saw my look. 'Degenerative arthritis.'

I could see the huge lumpy swelling of both knees even with the loose linen pants. And from that I felt that I knew her. Her arthritis told me the story of her perceptions, her emotional memory – a childhood home with strict, controlling parents, siblings favored over her, feelings always repressed. That she had spent a lifetime as the family caretaker, used but not valued, and had lived a life of chronic and prolonged stress. She may have been valued. Her parents might have given her unconditional love. But her inner narrative said otherwise, and often for reasons I would not know.

These conclusions were not drawn from new theories or cutting-edge observations. This field of knowledge had been around since the 1800s. She would be fiercely independent and convinced she could take care of herself *no matter what.* No human being alive can take care of themselves *no matter what*, but a significant percentage think otherwise, myself included. And now her immune system was at war with the connective tissue of her body. If you're wondering why medical science doesn't take this into account in the treatment of patients, that makes two of us.

'Can I get you some water?' I asked.

She shook her head. 'I'm fine. And I know you were expecting to meet with Mr Rheingold – he's been principal the last three years, poor man – but he wound up in the ER this morning, so I came instead. I had to . . . I had to wait until someone could drive me or I would have been here earlier. My husband dropped me off.'

I wondered about a husband who would 'drop her off' when walking was such an intense chore. If he'd offered to help and been told no.

'Now in Mr Rheingold's case, I think he's going to be OK – it looks like mostly a panic attack. And I can't say I blame him, the things they're saying about this school.' She glanced around at all three of us, standing and watching her.

'Let's sit,' I said.

Chloe was gathering up equipment. 'Thank you for coming, Mrs Loring. I have some measurements to take, so I'll leave you to it. And take care, will you? There's a puddle of water over here, and five minutes ago, I fell on my ass.'

Mrs Loring gave Chloe a second look. 'You're OK?'

'Yes, I just wanted to warn you.'

Mrs Loring shut her eyes for just a moment. 'I know this school very well. I know to look out for puddles.'

Vivian and I settled in chairs.

'You're the doctors; I saw you on the news.'

I nodded. Vivian said a soft yes.

'I liked what you said. Sensible, and clearly both of you know your business. There are so many nasty rumors and theories going around. Like we're a town of people with so much time on our hands we have nothing better to do than engage in malignant sexual practices. Believe me, there is no such nonsense going on around here, and I would know – you can't be a principal as long as I was, and know the local families as well as I do, for that kind of thing to be going on right under your nose. And I may have been retired a while, but I'm older, not dead.

'It makes things so much worse, having those kinds of rumors floating around. It's terrible for the kids to hear things like that, to worry their parents, to accuse them. *As if it wasn't bad enough already.*'

'I agree with you on that,' Vivian said. 'How are people dealing with this?'

Mrs Loring told us to please call her Em and filled us in.

As one could certainly understand, a lot of people living here in the small town of Osage, Kentucky were seriously pissed off. Dr Holtzer's speculation on sexual trauma had morphed into horrendous theories about the school, including the possibility of satanic sex rings. A lot of the people in town had children or grandchildren who were students here, family members who were teachers or staff, many of them in the hospital right now. None of them needed this kind of nonsense. They needed real information, and there was little to be had. There was a hot, simmering rage beneath the surface, and people were feeling overwhelmed.

And as ever more members of the media arrived, the people of the town decided to fight back, in the way only a closed community can, and the war of obstruction began.

The Main Street Hotel & Tavern, thriving and full of guests a week before, suddenly had no rooms available. The Airbnbs were mysteriously full. Visitors were directed to an old run-down motel forty miles away that always sat empty, due to issues of mold and insect infestation, and sadly, the internet connection there was spotty. Everyone from out of town got herded into that one godawful place. Em took a moment to feel sorry for them.

Nevertheless, all the restaurants on the charming town square stocked up, and stayed open for longer hours to make sure everyone got fed, because it was not only profitable, it was only human to make sure everyone had plenty to eat. The town square was becoming quite lively at night because everybody was eavesdropping on everybody else and staying late with their laptops for the internet connection. Friendships were formed. There were several hot romances afoot. She was not going to name names.

Esther's Food Truck was doing a killing on the shady side of the square. She and her husband had so much business, their two teenage boys worked continuous shifts. They were third-generation rich, which meant most of the family money had been squandered by their parents, so they had to work for a living like everyone else. In truth, though, there was a great deal of affluence in the town sourced by thoroughbred horse farms, real estate and generational wealth. As well as a great deal of soul-crushing poverty and opiate addiction. Just like everywhere else, except here there were parades where the school kids made their own floats, and everybody went to the high school football games.

But the wealthy people had money for excellent attorneys, and Dr Holtzer was soon going to find himself on the receiving end of two lawsuits and counting.

I couldn't hide a smile and Mrs Loring – Em – smiled back then sighed. 'Everything that is going on is affecting the little ones.'

Vivian leaned forward. 'Can you tell me about that? Do you mean the children from the school here?'

Em shook her head. 'No, no – the *littles*. Pre-school. Toddlers. Babies. They wake up crying, don't want to settle for bed, they're clingy and tearful.'

'Is it families with older kids in the school?'

'Yes but other families too. That is what's so strange. It's *all* of them.'

'Stress is contagious,' Vivian said.

Em gave her a tolerant smile. 'I'm sure it is, but what is the stress? Because this started up with the babies and the littles *before* this big crisis, not after.'

Vivian gave me a look. Both of us were thinking of Patrick's baby sister.

'And it's not just a few. It's most of them. And I know it would be best to have Mr Rheingold here; he'd have insight on particular students and teachers, but at least I can tell you anything you want to know about the old part of the school. I was principal for thirty years, and assistant principal to Mr Hennessy before he . . .' She trailed off.

'Before he what?' I asked.

She didn't say.

'It's actually the old part of the school we're interested in,' I said. 'Please tell me what happened with Mr Hennessy.'

'He committed suicide, here in the school. Hung himself in his office, right next to the copy machine. I'm the one who found his body.'

'I'm so sorry,' I said.

She shook her head. 'I wasn't surprised, but God, it was sad. I knew him growing up; I had something of a crush, he was four years older than I was. Tall and lean with a big head of black hair. He was a foster kid, kind of a bad boy in school, which attracted me no end. I was one of the *good girls*. But I used to see him at this little place called Hunts One-Stop Service, down in Bowling Green, at the corner of the 31W Bypass and Caball Lane. It's long gone now, but they had the best barbecue sandwiches I've ever had in my life. And Hunts was the *it* place for the high school kids – we used to drive down in packs from Osage on Friday nights, because there was nothing like Hunts in our little town. And Rory grew up in Bowling Green. After high school, he went to Vietnam. Came back and got a teaching degree at WKU on the GI Bill. That's how we wound up working together. By then we were both married and had kids. He was smart, and funny in a sarcastic way, and so full of life. You would never know what a terrible time he had as a child.'

She looked up. 'Is the exorcist here? Do you think he might go say a little something in Mr Hennessy's old office? He died so unhappy. I think some of his stuff is still in the storage closet; they ought to get rid of it.'

'Can you tell me where his office was?'

'I'll have to show you.' She put her hand on the edge of the desk and started to get up out of her chair.

I put a hand on her shoulder. 'Sit tight – I'll be right back.'

It didn't take long to snag a rolling chair from one of the administrative desks. She laughed when I wheeled it into the room.

'Just don't go too fast,' she said as I helped her into the chair. But she was smiling. 'Go straight out the door and take a hard left where the linoleum is older and the hallway gets narrow. Go to the admin desks, don't look at the monitors and head straight back to the cubby where the copy machine is.'

I felt like I already knew the way.

THIRTY

The lights in the office were on, and Perry and Chloe were already there. It was a hot spot, and Perry was looking into the cubby where the copy machine was, deep in thought. He saw us over his shoulder. I introduced him to Em.

She studied Perry, who was always a subject of fascination. 'It's a sad place, isn't it? That little nook? And that door there beside the copy machine leads to a storage room where our old principal, Rory Hennessy used to have his office.'

Perry and Chloe exchanged looks. 'I saw that door, but it was locked.'

'Oh, it's just stuck,' Em said. 'Turn the knob and lift the door up and it will open easy. You know, when I first came to work here, this school was just fine. Nice and new and normal. It wasn't until a lot later that the hauntings started up.'

'I like how direct you are,' Perry said with a gentle smile. 'Do you remember when it started exactly?'

'Remembering isn't the problem. Forgetting is. Because things started happening around 1976. Rory's wife and daughter died in 1974. April third. I don't know if that date means anything to you.'

'The tornados,' Perry said. 'The F5s. Winds over two hundred miles per hour and tornado after tornado spinning off and going through like the end of the world.'

Em was dry-eyed but grim. 'That's what it felt like. The end of the world. And there were days I wish it had been. Rory's wife and daughter were visiting family up in Brandenburg. And late that afternoon, the tornados came.' Her voice went low. 'Brandenburg – the whole town was demolished; Xenia, Ohio was flattened; it was twelve hours of pure hell. Rory's wife and daughter were at her folks' house, and all of them died. Nothing left of the house. It's hard to image a thing like that. And there were earthquakes too, that very same day, small ones. Nobody much remembers that, because of the tornadoes.'

The New Madrid Fault Line, locally known as *impending doom*, runs right through Kentucky.

'And before it happened, weird things. The littles got upset.' She glanced at me and Vivian. 'Just like the littles are upset again now. And before it happened, there were weird lights, blue lights at night, and here in Osage, I saw lightning coming up from the ground. I'm not crazy either.'

'Earthquake lights,' Chloe told her. 'It's a known phenomenon, but it scares people. There are a lot of theories, but nobody knows how they happen. Something about the seismic activity, the shifting rock.'

Perry sat down on the edge of one of the desks. 'I was in Xenia, Ohio afterward, to help in the cleanup. I was just a kid, but I went with a church group. It was the worst thing I have ever seen.'

Em nodded. 'A lot of people around here lost family. And of course, Rory was hit hard. He sold his little house here in town – such a pretty little place. Said he could not live with the memories. I always wondered. If things would have been different for him if he'd stayed. He bought a rundown place out in the country, thinking maybe he could find some peace out there, that it would be healing. It was just the opposite. He was never the same after he moved out there. Didn't eat, didn't sleep. And of course that was when all the odd things began happening at the school. Kids crying, thumping in the ceiling. Lights going on and off. It got a little better when they added the new part to the school, but the whole feeling of the place had changed.

'Rory got to where he didn't want to go home; he started sleeping in his office at night. And I asked him once, wasn't he afraid here in the school at night all alone, with all the odd things going on? And he said it was worse at home, but he wasn't afraid. He'd been in Vietnam. Survived the Tet Offensive. Had a terrible childhood in foster care. He didn't think anything could hurt him. And he said that whatever was going on at that house had followed him to the school. And one day I asked him . . . *why*? Why was it haunting him? And he looked at me and said, *Emmie, it's not just haunting me. It's hunting me.*'

Perry froze. We locked eyes.

'Did you ever go to the house?' I asked her. 'Can you tell me where it was?'

Yes – she'd grown curious one day and driven by. Told me where it was exactly. I nodded. Pammie's rental house. Haunting and *hunting*. Like something had laid a trap.

'He hung himself right there in his office. It was odd, but things got a little better for a while. Like he was here with us, looking out for us. Sometimes people in town who knew him, who remember him . . . they get glimpses of him here and there. But then things started getting bad again here at the school. Just slow and steady, but building up. It would get bad, then it would get better. I never really understood why. So, Father, if you'd say a little prayer for Rory, I'd be grateful. He had a hard life, but you'd never know it. Always dressed up in a nice suit, shiny shoes. Thick head of hair. Coal black when he was young, and snow white by the time he was forty. Big smile for everybody. The kids loved him.'

Her description clicked with a memory and stopped me cold. And I thought . . . Exit 137. The hardware store.

'There's a picture of Rory in Mr Rheingold's office – take a look.' She inclined her head to a closed door. Not locked.

I opened the door a crack; looked inside.

'Up behind the desk,' she said.

I saw it. I knew the man. I'd seen him standing outside that hardware store – shiny shoes, nice suit, thick head of white hair, smiling-smiling-smiling at me. I remembered his voice. *Hello, neighbor.* But hadn't the woman there been talking to him?

I pictured it in my mind. She'd had her phone, talking intently, her back to me. I had just assumed she was talking to him. But he'd watched me the whole time I'd walked toward the store, and if she'd seen him do that, surely she'd have looked over her shoulder to see what he was staring at. And she hadn't.

THIRTY-ONE

Vivian and Em and I were on the benches out front, while Perry sat quietly in Rory Hennessy's old office, deep in the meditative prep he did before an exorcism. Conversation had been strained, and mostly we were quiet. Exorcisms are socially uncomfortable. None of us said a word about the way the lights in the building flickered on and off, because what can you say?

Em had called her grandson to pick her up.

'And there he is,' she said, with a bit of gush. Her smile was big and happy, and she waved at the twenty-year-old driving a jonquil-yellow Corvette that was freshly washed and shiny. 'I bought that for him new three years ago. There's a Corvette plant south of here, about two hours away.'

Her grandson was in jeans and a tee shirt – tall, blonde, slim and polite and looked like a ringer for a Ralph Lauren model. For all I knew he was.

'I'm going to his place,' Em said with a happy sigh. 'The sheriff is going to try and serve a warrant on me, and I need to dodge him for a couple of days to let the judge simmer down, in case he's mad enough to put me in jail.'

Vivian's mouth opened. 'In jail for what? Do you need an attorney?'

'Oh, I have an attorney – she's a hotshot, let me tell you – but this is just a dance that judge and I do. He will have no evidence. He will say, *Mrs Emmaline Loring, did you or did you not break into this barn and steal a litter of puppies and their mama*, and I'll say, *Certainly not.* He'll say, *Case dismissed for no evidence.* And I'll say, *You have plenty of evidence for an ongoing puppy mill. Why don't you get somebody out there and look into this*? And he'll sigh and say, *There are no puppies there now, are there?* It's a little trap, and I'll tell him, *My goodness, how would I know?*

'I want to give him time to cool off though, because this time I got just a little fed up and might have done a bit of damage to that old barn, so it might not go as usual. It's hard to tell. Not that I was actually in that barn, and not that my grandson has the mama and her puppies all gated in the kitchen at his mom's place. She's my daughter-in-law and I just adore her. Tender-hearted as they come.'

Her grandson nodded at us, said nice to meet you and gave his grandmother a look. 'You really shouldn't discuss this, Grandie – you know that.' He looked at us. 'And there aren't five puppies in the kitchen at my house. Or a mama dog either.'

'No, of course not,' Em said. 'And don't you be skipping classes at school looking after those puppies. Your junior year of college is *crucial,* especially now you've switched majors.'

He grinned at her.

Em leaned close to me, patted my hand and gave me a soft little kiss on the cheek. 'You saw him, didn't you? Rory?' she whispered. 'I saw how you were looking at his picture, up on the wall. Like you'd had a bit of a shock.'

I gave her a quick discreet nod.

Her grandson took her arm. Helped her get settled into the passenger's seat of the car. It was low to the ground, and she put her seatbelt on and grinned. I had a feeling she liked that 'Vette as much as he did.

'Take care of your grandmother,' I said.

She snorted. '*I am just fine*. What we need is someone to take care of you.'

THIRTY-TWO

As soon as Em and her grandson roared off in the 'Vette, Chloe opened the front door of the school and told me it was time.

'My equipment is set up. Perry's waiting. He wants to do this in Rory Hennessy's office. He says it's the place of most pain.'

Vivian looked from me to Chloe. 'Would it be possible for me to observe this?'

I hesitated.

'I know it's not a spectator sport. What I want is insight.'

'This is not without danger, Vivian. It's one thing to talk about things like this. It's another thing to see it.'

She gave me the confident nod of someone who had no idea what she might be getting into. 'I want to be there. I want to understand.'

'OK. But there are rules. Everything you see and hear is confidential.'

She nodded.

'You observe only. Please do not comment or interact or talk to Perry. If you feel ill or upset – and you might, Vivian – then leave. If you feel like you're in trouble, touch me on the shoulder, and I'll follow you out and help you.'

'I'll be good,' she said. I could see she was excited.

Not for Perry the raving outrage of an exorcist facing the demonic. Or the mundane monotone of one too many exorcisms in a week. Perry was different. His voice deep, melodic, confident; the lyricism of ritual, the words that held beauty in their precision. It was clear he was channeling something powerful, something spiritual, something totally outside of himself yet infused with his own spirit, a powerful tapestry I did not understand. Perry was a steady oasis of calm, and an exorcist like no other.

It was the reaction to Perry that was the performance and the opera – and the dark entities didn't disappoint.

Gusts of wind knocked a desk over and sent a file cabinet rolling.

The blinds banged against the windows, before being ripped away and sent flying. The windows cracked – then shattered suddenly, spewing glass across the room. Chloe was tough, focused on her equipment and her husband, but Vivian Bianchi was wide-eyed and in shock. But she stood her ground.

And then in the midst of chaos, Perry did an extraordinary thing I'd never seen him do before. He murmured a prayer in Latin – I caught a word, that sounded like *exsufflation.* He held out his hand and breathed out three times fast, like he was blowing kisses. 'I put you to flight, Prince of Darkness.'

And everything went still, the air full of tension and heat. A flash of light – then darkness. There was a low base drumbeat I felt in my bones – then a monstrous tremor. The entire school began to shake.

Then quiet. The normal noises of the building gradually returned. I heard a leaf blower on the grounds somewhere; the hum of the heating kicking in. The ionized air was clear now. The room was lighter, like it had been cleansed.

'What did you do to piss them off?'

Perry gave me a smile of serene exhaustion. '*Exsufflare.* A ritual breathing prayer. *Libellus de mysterio baptismatis* of Magnus of Sens, Charlemagne. Three breaths to blow the evil away and put the Prince of Darkness to flight. Then *insufflare* – three breaths in, for blessings and protection. The ritual fell out of use decades ago, but I studied it when I was in Rome. There are exorcists now who are using it to great effect.'

Perry turned to Chloe. Took her hand. 'You are OK?'

'More like impressed, Perry.'

'Your first exorcism. I'm glad you were here.'

Chloe and I exchanged looks. We had our theories, our instruments, our science. But we were on the sidelines. Perry might have left the church, but his mysterious, mystical, spiritual channeling could rock the earth.

Vivian looked at me, eyes wide. 'So it's over?'

'It's over. Not what you expected?'

'I've never seen anything like that in my life.'

'Remember what you told me last night? Only a fraction of our sensory experiences are in the conscious realm. You got a look into the abyss.'

'I can't say you didn't warn me. But I wouldn't have missed it for the world. I needed to see this. I needed to get a sense of why these children are so afraid. I knew it in my head, but now I know it in my gut.'

She looked at Perry. 'What was that – an earthquake?'

Perry gave her a gentle smile. 'That was pushback.'

He helped Chloe pack up her equipment, and everyone headed out. Perry paused in the doorway, looking over his shoulder at the portrait of Rory Hennessy.

And I caught a glimpse of the man – human, tired, with that soft glow of exaltation that surrounded him after every exorcism. In Rome they considered him a direct descendant of Mary, Mother of all Exorcists, this man who considered himself a failed father and failed husband, a failed Episcopalian priest. Returned to the state of the laity by choice but steeped in sacrament nonetheless.

THIRTY-THREE

I waited for Perry to go ahead of me out of the office.

Perry looked at Chloe with the soft smile he held only for her. 'Anything?'

'Like a miracle,' she told him, looking up from her graph. 'The entities are receding like the tides.'

He nodded. 'And like the tides, they'll be back. But weaker next time. And the time after. Until they're gone for good.'

I hesitated, feeling oddly apart, watching them walk away from me down the hall – Perry with a casual and comfortable arm around Chloe; Vivian looking up at him and pelting him with questions.

I was being left behind and somehow I could not follow them. Somehow I could not leave. I could see the end-of-the-day sun slanting in through the windows; feel the slow build of tension as the darkness began to gather again, murmurs that I refused to hear.

There was a quick flash of light, and it became a swarm of energy and voices all around me – an all-out attack. I fought the feeling that I was supposed to stay behind, that I and only I was not free to leave. I wanted to ask for help but found I didn't have the strength to speak. Or to stay on my feet. I was aware of reaching out for something to hold on to and clawing only air, until I found my way to the wall, which gave me something to push against and break my fall, just before I passed out.

They were whispering my name, then I realized it was Perry's voice calling me back. Someone had tucked a blanket under my head. I felt queasy. But the swarming voices had gone. I opened my eyes.

'There you go,' Perry said.

'This is incredibly humiliating,' I told him.

'I knew you'd say that. It's just you and me. Dr Bianchi is out front with Chloe, calling an ambulance.'

'No ambulance. Will you please God shut that down?'

'You didn't hit your head?'

'I'm a fucking neurosurgeon and I've seen a shitload of skull fractures, so no, I didn't hit my head. Neurosurgeons know how to pass out.'

'I'll take care of it. Let me get you up on your feet. There's no way I'm leaving you alone in here.'

THIRTY-FOUR

We stopped for dinner. All of us were hungry, and all of us were thinking about barbecue.

But when my food came, I couldn't eat. Everybody noticed, nobody said a word, and since I'd ordered the ribs, I distributed them evenly between Chloe, Vivian and Perry, and got not one word of complaint. I handed over the garlic bread and the fries too. I sipped a ginger ale to settle my stomach, and it did.

I was grateful when Chloe offered to drive – the headache I'd woken up with was going from bad to worse. Perry and I sat in the back. He was asleep immediately, always exhausted after an exorcism. He said it had only scratched the surface, but he was upbeat and patient – this kind of infestation was going to take time. And Chloe's measurements showed a hopeful before and after. The pulse of radiation had faltered, gone down 11 percent, which she considered significant. Perry and I had looked at each other. Feeling the extraordinary thrill of actually being able to measure the presence of these things we had thought of as dark and beyond explanation. Hard data was a welcome relief.

I leaned back in the left corner of the passenger seat, exactly where Sasha had been, double bagged with plastic, before I had removed him from my car and turned him to hot glowing ashes. I'd dropped the car off to be washed and detailed three times since. I kept my thoughts directed to tomorrow's schedule. It was going to be a heavy day.

Vivian, up front with Chloe, was texting like mad. No doubt she had a million things going on, and I sat with my head against the window and gritted my teeth. As sure as I was that I was not concussed, whatever was going on with me, was getting worse.

It was Vivian, looking up from her phone, who saw it first.

'What *is* that?'

It was pitch dark, no moon, and we were on the Bluegrass Parkway headed home. Isolated. Just headlights now and then, going the other way. I looked out the window and saw it. Lightning rising from the ground from the hill on the other side of the road.

Chloe pulled over. We got out. The sky was pitch-black with flashing blue lights.

'Earthquake luminescence,' Chloe said. 'Earthquake lightning and earthquake lights.'

'This is what Em was talking about,' Vivian said. 'It's extraordinary.'

She turned to Chloe. 'You said earlier that there were a lot of theories on what causes it . . .'

Chloe laughed. 'Yes, give me four academics and I'll give you four different theories. There's a lot of earthquake phenomena we don't understand. But I've picked up some ULF waves – today and the day I was here last week. Ultra-low frequency could come from seismic activity. Very low level – nothing the monitoring stations would pick up. But it would account for what Em was talking about – the littles being upset.'

'How so?' Vivian asked.

'There have been studies, particularly in Japan, of very young children being upset, clingy and restless before an earthquake, just like Em described. Due to the low-level radiation is the theory. Always in a one-hundred-mile radius of the quake. And it's not just kids. There are always accounts of animals acting differently before an earthquake. The theory is that the waves create anxiety, in both kids and animals.'

Vivian took pictures of the lights. The lightning. 'I'm going to follow up on that theory about earthquake radiation affecting children.' She glanced at me over one shoulder. 'The things I learn hanging out with you.'

'Would you text me your pictures?' I said. 'I want to show them to my boys.'

'Me too,' Perry said.

One more thing to factor into the research.

It was good to get home. So very good.

Moira was in the kitchen, kids long asleep. 'Noah, what happened?' She touched the swelling on the side of my head, and I flinched.

'I fell.'

She put her arms around me and pulled me close. 'What is it, my love? What's wrong?'

'I don't know,' I whispered.

I was deep asleep when Perry called six hours later. It was Moira who answered my phone.

Because I was dreaming hard, hearing voices – faint, compelling but impossible to understand – as they echoed in the swirl of the wind.

Something building, something close.

THIRTY-FIVE

Elle Donatello Cavanaugh disappeared into a lavender field the last day she was seen. Walking just outside the small village of Pente Douce, in Provence, France. Late September, a warm windy day. The lavender had been harvested in mid-July, the fields cropped. The lavender was green, low to the ground, the hillside ahead a gentle slope. The light in Provence was extraordinary. Angel light, Elle had called it, in the notebook where she had scribbled her plans, her discoveries, during the time she'd been in Pente Douce.

The heat was letting up, most of the tourists were gone, but the seasonal restaurants were still open and busy. There was a picture of her, on that last day, taken by a photographer with a popular Instagram account – *Travel Provence.*

You can see why he took the shot. Elle walking through the rows of low-cut lavender, the hills close enough that maybe she was heading there. But her focus, the angle of her intent, is toward a two-story stone house, narrow, with the forlorn air of abandonment. It is old, the windows gap darkly and there are overgrown bushes on the left-hand side, almost covering that dark open doorway. She is wearing a red print dress, and it swirls around her legs, and her hair is caught up in a clip and falling loose. She is pausing. Looking at the house, head tilted up. Maybe she is making up her mind. Maybe she knows she is watched.

The notes she left were intriguing. Elle was excited about something. *I think I know where he is*, was the second-to-last entry on her coffee-stained yellow legal pad. Followed by the final entry. *I hope so. For Cerise.*

Elle had been tracing the path of her long-lost relative, Forrest Strickler, Kentucky born and bred, who had found love, family and peace of heart in France. Who had come to a small family farm where he was sorely needed, so tall, so strong, so small-town polite. He had disappeared on September 27, 1959. It was September 25 the day Elle disappeared.

Had Elle gone into the stone house? Had she headed up into the hills? Was she lost? Had she been taken? Was she hurt . . . was she dead . . . *nobody knew*.

They were looking – and looking hard. Tourists were a protected class in Provence. Her cousin Josue had sounded the alarm, gotten in touch with her family in the US. But all they had was the picture from the Instagram account. No one remembered seeing her after she'd left her hotel. She was a pretty girl, and most of the tourists had gone. Someone would have remembered. No one did.

What they did know – she had not returned to her hotel room. Had not used credit cards or her phone, which was tracked and found just outside the stone house, sideways in a bush, like she'd dropped it. Maybe she didn't know she'd lost it. Maybe she was running away.

Running away became the opinion of the men and women who were searching for her, growing grimmer every day. Because she'd gone into the little stone house. She wasn't there now, but a torn strip from the hem of her dress confirmed that she'd been there on that last day she was seen.

THIRTY-SIX

Moira and I sat side by side on our small stone patio, under the pergola, a small fire just taking hold in the stone fireplace, a fine dusk settling lightly. We were holding hands. We were worried. We were tired.

Now that Elle was missing, I slept not at all. Afraid that she would just disappear like Patrick's daddy and the cop who had arrived to rescue Pammie and all the kids and the animals . . . and was never seen again. Nothing left but her flashlight in the crawl space under that house.

I had never dealt with people disappearing before, much less the mass hysteria that was taking over the kids and teachers and staff from that middle school in Osage, Kentucky. Neither had Perry. Who was outwardly calm and steady but, according to Chloe, was totally losing his shit underneath. His little girl gone. And he would know the dangers.

Tom left for France the morning we got the news. Perry and Chloe made it out eight hours later. I would be leaving as soon as I could, torn between surgery patients, Osage patients, and the urge to go to France and track Elle down.

It had been one of the trips we'd talked about, Moira and I, spending time in France, just not like this. Instead, I would be going to Provence under shadow and fire.

Moira had a glass of red wine, and I had a bottle of beer, and she kicked off her shoes and curled up like she always does. Her hair was piled on her head in an intriguing mess, curls brushing the nape of her neck.

The boys were deep asleep, and Tash and Mr Timothy were stretched out in front of the fire. Mr Timothy was actually purring not two feet from my chair. We were making considerable progress, because he had not tried to hurt me once today.

Moira settled in, tilting her head back, eyes shut tight. I picked up her feet, settling them in my lap, and she swiveled to one side and sighed as I began to massage her left foot.

'How are they doing?' she asked. 'Perry and Chloe?'

'Their phone calls are upbeat, they are worried sick, but Chloe is methodical, and she is pretty tough stuff. Have you heard from Tom?'

'Two or three times a day. He goes out with the search party every day. He is losing his mind.'

'Tell me how it's going with you, hon. Dress rehearsal last night, opening night tomorrow.'

'The dress rehearsal was *disastrous*,' she said. Eyes shut tight.

'But that's good, right? Disastrous dress rehearsals—'

'Mean good opening nights. Yeah, let's hope that holds.' She gave me a little sideways smile. 'The kids are psyched. Whatever happens . . . it'll be fine. And you'll be there with the boys?'

'Front-row seats. And we'll take them out afterward for burgers and ice cream and let them stay up way too late.'

'And your flight leaves?'

'The morning after, early. I finish up my surgeries tomorrow, and afterward I will be sitting up front with the boys for opening night.'

'Provided nothing gets complicated in the OR.'

I gave her my confident smile. 'Everything will go fine.'

Moira blew me a kiss. She loved a confident man.

'Any word from Tom on the tracking dogs?'

'No luck so far. But it's still early, Noah.'

Tracking dogs had not found Andi Craig or Conor Walsh. But I kept that thought to myself.

'If for any reason you need me in France . . . but with everything going on with those kids in Osage, I don't want to be away from the boys. You look out for my little brother, you hear me?'

'Tom? He'll be looking out for *me*.'

What I did not tell Moira – what I did not tell anyone – was that the first thing I was going to do was meet with Cerise. She would know what had happened to Elle. She would know where to find her. And I knew she was waiting for me to come. That there was a reason she had stood in the road that first night I went to the house, illuminated by the headlights of my car. There were things she was struggling to tell us. I would know how to listen.

My neuro patients spoke in allegory, and the things they said gave me insight. Metaphor was how a patient told you what they were feeling, experiencing. It was crucial to my work. Fears, needs, hopes – all of this fed the metaphor that revealed so much. There were patterns of thinking with schizophrenia, Parkinson's, early dementia. Dementia patients got to a point where they no longer understood metaphor; where they took things literally. If you told them it was raining cats and dogs, they would look out the window. But they also spoke in metaphor of their own that was so often dismissed as confusion but was their literal truth. The difficulty, of course, was understanding.

Zombies. Childlike. A shell without a soul. The terms for people with dementia that had always seemed so cruel to me often came from those who loved them most. I had come to realize this was an expression of the anguish and the fears of those who loved them. As much as they sounded like a judgement – and a lack of compassion – they were, in truth, a lament. A yearning to comprehend what had been lost and what remained of this person they loved, who seemed to be drifting further and further away.

It was possible to understand what patients with dementia were trying to tell you. Patients with cognitive issues spoke their own language, filtered through changed perceptions. As doctors we looked at this as damage. But we needed to look deeper. In cognitive decline, the usual paths of communication are blocked. Destroyed. Inaccessible except through enormous effort. Often, a dementia patient would find another path. And eventually that path was just their presence, as they grew silent, and still, unable to take food or liquid, to a place in their consciousness where we could not follow.

And always they wandered. When the now was inaccessible, they walked through the past. Able to talk to those who were dead. To live in memory. But what was memory, except a way of moving through time, where past, present and future were a circle around us. As much as it distressed everyone around them, it seemed like a miracle to me.

I refilled Moira's wine glass, feeling aware and in the moment – a last night with my beautiful wife, before I descended into hell. Just thinking about the possibilities gave me a dreadful thrill. I wasn't coming back without Elle.

THIRTY-SEVEN

Friday for surgeries and opening night, and Saturday morning I was on a plane to France. The coffee on my tray had gone cold, but I drank it anyway.

Before she left, Chloe had given me a copy of all the family letters, years of communication between Forrest Strickler and his sister Anna, both of them treasuring the news of the sister in Kentucky, the brother in France. I read each one of them, puzzling out the sloped, curling handwriting of Chloe's great-great-great uncle, Forrest Strickler, born in Frankfort, Kentucky, disappeared in Pente Douce, France. And the upright clarity of his sister Anna, who had wanted him to come home.

I am home, he would tell her.

Forrest Strickler's war, along with so many others, began at five thirty a.m. on September 26, 1918. By then France had lost over three million men. His was just one American face in a sea of untried American soldiers and war-weary French, advancing against German positions in the Argonne forest along the Meuse river.

It was a hellscape of mustard gas and phosgene shells for the soldiers who had managed to survive the raging Spanish flu. Forrest Strickler, a foot soldier, was there in the first strike, as the infantry began the advance, supported by aircraft and tanks.

Another chapter in the love affair between France and the United States – the Americans and the French side by side in another war. There would be more wars to come. This time, the fighting had been going on for years, and the Americans, tardy as always, were not there for long. The war ended on November 11, 1918, when Forrest Strickler was nineteen years old.

His division had only been in France for several weeks, but for Forrest, it felt like a lifetime, and in many ways, it was. It was certainly long enough for him to fall in love with the country and the people of France. A love affair that went both ways.

Casualties were high, and pretty much the whole damn country had lost all or part of their family to war, to the flu, to the bombs over Paris. To starvation.

Forrest, still alive, had lost himself.

He'd heard of soldiers in the Red Cross Hospital at Blois taken to the Château de Chambord, south of Paris, in the Loire Valley. Sent to recover from war neurosis. A friend who went there wrote to him and said he was feeling better. Being out in the countryside made it easier to get through the days, if not the nights.

The nineteen-year-old kid he used to be would have been longing to go home to Kentucky. The nineteen-year-old man who was a veteran of the Meuse–Argonne could not bear to go back. Some things were just not possible.

Forrest figured pretty much all of them were suffering from war-neurosis, so he was nothing special. But the French countryside called to him. The idea of just walking, no particular place to go. That called to him too.

Maybe France was his future. If he had one. He didn't much care anymore. Kentucky was for sure his past, like it had been severed right out of his life, though the name of his family could be found in the 1900 consensus under Farms and Farm Property, Crops and Livestock Products.

He set off on foot, all six feet six of him. It was a wonder that an infantry soldier of his height had gone through that battle with only minor wounds and a newly formed hatred for mud and barbed wire. He hadn't worried much about dying, but getting hurt and losing a limb had haunted him.

In truth, he was good at war – wiry and strong, with farm-hardened muscles and stamina. Forrest was considered good luck, and a lot of his fellow infantrymen stayed close. Forrest had confidence, a gravitas he'd had since he was a quiet, introspective book-reading boy on that small farm in Kentucky. Hoping to go to college one day, winding up in a war instead. People were drawn to him. He made them feel safe.

THIRTY-EIGHT

What he found were families steeped in grief, hungry children, farm fields that had become battlefields.

And in a mysterious confluence of what seemed like random events and off-hand decisions, Chloe's Uncle Forrest found his way through a country he fell in love with and defended with his life. A country that opened its arms to him as he headed further and further south, until by accident and by fate, he found the place where he was needed.

Forrest heard the bleat of the ewe lying sideways; saw the girl, about his age. She pushed the ewe to her side and took gentle hold of the newborn lamb, clearing its nose and pushing it close for the mother to lick.

Clearly, there was another lamb on the way.

Forrest stood shyly looking over the fence. The girl was huffing and pushing a lamb back in. She looked up and saw him.

'I can help,' he said, coming over the fence and putting his rucksack down.

A lamb on its way into the world, one leg forward and one leg back. He was strong and sinewy, and the girl rocked back on her heels and let him push the baby gently back in. He gave it a moment and checked to see the legs were sorted. Then he pulled the baby out, and the girl took the lamb, cleared its nose and tucked it close to its mother. Put the first baby to nurse – the milk was ready and thick.

'*Trois*,' she told him, holding up three fingers, and he nodded, his large hand on the ewe's side, feeling the power of her contractions. The lamb did not come. He looked to the girl for permission; she nodded, and he reached in and pulled another baby out.

He smiled at her. She was so lovely, with her hair blown back, a smudge of dirt on her chin, a look of calm intelligence in her eyes. And so very thin, like most of the people he saw in the French countryside. The war years had been hard.

The connection between them was strong, and they worked together, speaking the language of farm kids, and it was as if they had known each other forever and were picking up where they'd left off. The ewe had found her way out of the pen before giving birth, and together they got the ewe and the babies rounded up and into the barn where they would be warm and safe.

The girl's name was Noémie, and she would become the mother of his daughter, Agathe, who would give him his beloved granddaughter, Cerise.

Noémie took him into the kitchen for dinner, her mother impressed with his size and gentle nature, and the first night he slept in the barn. The house was quite small. Eventually, he was settled into a storeroom, where Noémie's brother had slept before he and her father had disappeared into the blood mist of the Somme Offensive.

The little room was quite warm in winter, deliciously cool in spring, and by the time summer came, he and Noémie had married and he spent his nights tucked into her bed, helping she and her mother run the farm. It never occurred to him to leave.

There were years where Forrest didn't write as much to his sister, Anna; years where Agathe grew up, got married. Had his beautiful little Cerise. He told Anna about his German shepherd, King; his strong affection for blue peafowl. He had several on the farm, and King protected them as well as the lambs and Cerise and anything or anyone that needed protecting. He was that kind of dog.

How he loved to walk at dusk while Cerise gathered up the blue-green feathers of the peacocks; how he loved feeding the peafowl by hand, and having King to patrol and keep things safe, the two of them connected in the way of large men and large dogs.

But when the dark things came to Pente Douce, he began to write quite regularly, a chronicle of events he seemed to feel needed to be recorded. And the accounts he wrote to his sister were sickeningly familiar to me.

At first, he had been bewildered, reporting one terrible thing after another. But eventually, he became steady and purposeful. He was going after it, even though he didn't yet know what *it* was.

It started with the youngest children in the village. They became restless, they cried at night, they couldn't bear to be away from their mothers, and people were worried this was the beginning of another flu epidemic. There were long nights where Forrest sat in the darkness on the front porch with Cerise in his lap, King settled close, so that Agathe and Noémie could rest. In truth, he didn't need much sleep, and he was the only one who could quiet his granddaughter. Her father had died when she was six months old, struck by lightning as he came out of the barn, where he'd been checking on the lambs as a storm came up. The memories of her father were buried too deep. It was her grandfather's voice she listened for.

And there were red skies at night, which turned to purple and then to blue. Lightning came up from the ground, and there was a series of small earthquakes that did little damage but stirred dreadful memories of the earthquake in 1909.

People became afraid to go out after dark, though they could not say exactly why. An eight-year-old boy, and then his young mother, had disappeared, three weeks apart, then another one, the boy's grandmother, who had been so ill she rarely left her bed. She left the house in the dead of the night, and no one found her either. All in the same family. All living in a little stone house.

Where had they gone?

And I looked through the letters to see if the boy, the young mother or the grandmother had ever been found. And ran across a short mention of the father who had six weeks later hung himself in the little stone house, swinging from the rafters in the kitchen until Forrest himself cut him down. They were not mentioned again.

But whatever had happened to those people who lived in the stone house, the ones who'd disappeared, had happened to Forrest Strickler too. And to Andi Craig. And to Conor Walsh. And with every letter, I was watching it all unfold.

Had they been taken? Where had they gone? Why did a small village in France have such a connection to a small town in Kentucky? How do such things even happen? Do these things find us, or do we find them? Is this some mysterious entanglement on a basic level of physics?

Entanglement was immediate and instantaneous, and for that kind of connection, distance did not exist.

THIRTY-NINE

Pente Deuce was a very small village, so Perry, Chloe and Tom were staying in St Remy, at Le Petit Hotel, where Elle had been staying. Tom settled in her room; Perry and Chloe got a room down the hall, and reserved one for me. It was a small boutique hotel, and though high tourist season was over, I was lucky to get it.

I flew in to Marseille Provence Airport, rented a car and drove the 90 km north in an hour and fifteen minutes, taking my time, finding my way. The hotel was small, nine rooms total.

Being in France felt different in a way I could not describe. The hotel was in the heart of St Remy, and I could smell jasmine as I walked through the front courtyard. Stone building, greyish-green shutters, double doors framed by a black-and-white awning. Cafe tables were settled to one side. It was eclectic, kind of beautiful. I checked in and climbed the wide curving staircase. I was in suite five, the last available. I had a double bed, crisply made with a white duvet, and long, tall windows. I thought about coming back with Moira someday.

I took a long, hot shower, eased into a pair of jeans that were getting loose. My appetite had been off for the last few days. I put on a fresh white broadcloth shirt, leaving the top two buttons open and rolling back the sleeves. The weather was cool and sunny.

Perry and Chloe were at the stone house tracking chemical signatures; Tom was with the search party. I had called Josue and left him a message, telling him I was at the hotel and would like to meet with him and, if possible, see Cerise. That I understood Cerise was very ill, and he must decide if she was well enough for a visit.

As I headed down the stairs looking for something to eat, a man in the lobby looked up at me. He was slim and wiry, very tall, dark hair cut short, combed carefully. He wore round wire-rimmed glasses and had a gentle smile.

'You are Dr Archer?' he asked. 'You left me a message. I am Josue – the son of Cerise.'

His voice was soft, and we shook hands.

'Have you eaten? There's a place close where we can get a quick lunch, then I can take you to see my mother. She's sleeping now, but in an hour or two will be a good time.'

'I'd like that. It was good of you to come.'

'Yes, of course. Chloe told me when you would arrive. I wanted to welcome you to Provence and not have you alone with everything that is going on. Eating outside is OK with you?'

I nodded. Eating anywhere would be OK with me – I was hungry. It felt good.

'I don't have a word of French, I'm sorry.'

He smiled at me. 'I grew up in a bilingual house, as did my mother. We are very proud of our American side.'

The little bistro was close. The outside tables were grouped in the shade. We shared a large bottle of San Pellegrino water. I followed his lead and took the *planche de charcuterie*, and it was impressive – small chunks of baguette, sliced sausages and pâté. I didn't know exactly what I was eating on the sausage side, but it tasted good so I didn't let that worry me. I've never been squeamish. The plate was very full, and there were pickles, cheese, fresh sliced mushrooms, cucumbers, dark grapes and strips of red, green and yellow pepper.

'How is your mother doing?'

He seemed relieved to talk about it. Maybe because I was a doctor.

'Mostly these days she sleeps,' he told me. She was getting quite weak. She could no longer swallow and was on low doses of morphine and Temesta – the French version of Ativan. Now that she couldn't eat or drink, it wouldn't be long before he lost her.

I nodded, familiar with this phase. It was the quiet time. Preparation for death.

Talking about Elle made him smile – his so American cousin, full of life and things to say. She had been so curious about Cerise – and her Uncle Forêt. She'd wanted to know the family stories. Josue had told her what he could remember. His mother couldn't tell her now; she'd stopped talking a few months ago. Looking inward. Sleeping. Refusing food and water. Growing weaker and weaker as her body slowly began to shut down. She had wanted palliative care only. No hospitalization. No antibiotics.

'I worry she is hungry,' Josue told me.

I shook my head. 'You're doing exactly right. A stomach tube never works – it's a big choking risk. And when the body is shutting down, forcing liquids means fluids will build up in her tissue and her lungs. That only causes misery. It would make it hard for her to breathe. Right now, her brain no longer sends the message of hunger or thirst. I'm sorry for the plain talk, but you want to know this, don't you? She has the morphine for any pain, the Temesta that will keep her feeling peaceful and prevent any feelings of air hunger if she has trouble breathing. You're doing everything right.'

He look was grateful. 'This is good to know. This is what you would do if this were your own mother?'

'It is exactly what I would do.'

He drove me to his home in the countryside. The family farm was long gone, and he and his wife lived in a newly built, one-story house with a tiled courtyard, windows open to the breeze. He and his wife had a small flower shop in town. They took turns working shifts so one of them could always be home with Cerise. His mother had an *aides-soignant* who came in daily to dress and bathe her. And each month he received a book of checks to pay a carer to come in for three hours a week. He could pay for extra time out of pocket if he needed more help. The government also paid for someone to come in and clean the house.

He led me into the house through French doors on the side of the house, to a small kitchen, with tiled floors, and a small washer and dryer tucked under the cabinets. There were flowers everywhere – some in vases, some laid out on the kitchen table, some stacked in the sink. He spoke in a soft voice to the carer, who was gathering up her things. She left with a cheerful wave. He looked in on his mother then made coffee for both of us, dark and rich, and the two of us settled outside in the courtyard at a small table, where we drank the coffee from tiny white cups.

'My mother is still waking up,' he told me. 'We'll give her a little time.'

'I love the flowers all over the place.'

He laughed. 'My mother loves them too.'

For years, Cerise had come with them to the flower shop. But in the last few months, she had become restless, agitated, and would wander off, looking for her grandfather, Forêt. Or she would sit for hours just staring, annoyed when he tried to get her lunch, or a sweater if it was cold, as if he'd interrupted her thoughts. She became otherworldly, in another place and time. He would hear her mutter, talking to people who weren't there. It used to worry him, but now he missed it. Missed her voice, the conversations, the laughter she had shared with people he could not see.

And then, more and more often, she began reliving the dark times when she was little. She would cry softly and call for her grandfather; call for his big dog King.

'From what Elle has told me, the dark times in Pente Douce were happening then much like the things you are having now. My mother told me a little about it growing up, but I don't know how much is true memory and how much she was just told.'

'Any theories about what was happening? Has it happened before, maybe in other places?'

He shrugged. It was his fault he didn't know more. His mother would often want to discuss those dark times, to try and puzzle out what had happened to her grandfather, and she'd looked for him all of her life. But it had seemed pointless to him, and sad, so once he grew older, he would usually shut the conversation down. Now he wished he'd just listened and let her talk. It was clear she was obsessed. He wanted her to find peace in her heart before she died.

'Here.' Josue smiled, retrieved a well-worn photograph that sat on a small table near the couch and handed it to me. 'A picture of him. My grandfather – Forêt. My family would talk of how big he was. A tall American. From him, I got my height.'

Although Josue's great-grandfather was gone years before he was born, the connection between them was strong, I could tell from the affection in his voice, the pride. He had grown up with the memories of him, from the stories that became family legends from the grief and love his mother felt.

Forrest Strickler was young in the picture. Handsome in the sepia-softened black-and-white photograph. He was wearing a crisp, clean white shirt, cuffs rolled back from sinewy arms, and sitting stiffly in a chair, long fingers wrapped around a small leather book, round wire reading spectacles on his nose. He was slim and well muscled. His hair was, wavy, parted to one side – light brown perhaps. He had a studious air, a presence of gravitas and gentleness.

I wondered if the French thought all Americans were that tall. Forrest would stand out wherever he went.

'My mother always told me how he would come into the kitchen at night, in those old days on the farm. Washed up, hair slicked back, tired but still full of energy and an air of mischief, hungry for the family dinner. By then, her mother would have milked both cows, and my great-grandmother Noémie would be putting dinner out on the table.

'Even so little, my mother was aware of the worries that sometimes kept the adults around the dinner table talking in low voices late into the night. Sometimes she'd hear her mother crying softly. She knew her mother was afraid, afraid for *her*, and that made her scared to go to sleep. And she remembers how upset she felt, how her stomach hurt all day, how she wanted to be in her grandfather's lap. In the village, the little children couldn't sleep, and the older children were getting sick. She heard her mother talk about it late at night.

'But still, in those dusky evenings at the end of the day, when her grandfather would walk into the kitchen, she could feel the relief, the happiness that he brought, like a halo all around him. Her mother and grandmother would be smiling, and full of things to tell him, and there would be loud conversation, and he would catch sight of her, so little, hiding shyly in the corner. And he would cross the room on swift long legs and scoop her up and toss her in the air and catch her and say *my little cupcake* in English, and it was years before she knew this was *petite gateau.*

'And she said that he was the kind of man who made you feel safe the minute he walked through the door. Because in those days, she had been scared a lot. It was the thing she remembered most.

'For my mother, my great-grandfather was magical, and her world turned upside down when one night he didn't come home, and nothing was ever the same again. She couldn't understand where he went, and no one could find him, and there was a lot of crying, and worry, and searching. And then everyone gave up. She didn't know how such things could be.

'But my mother, she didn't give up. And she promised herself that she would find him someday. And she would take his hand and lead him back home. Because even then, when she was so little, she knew – somehow she knew – that Forêt was lost. Because my mother even then was one to see and know things other people could not see or know.' He gave me a look to see how I would react to that.

'And after he disappeared, at night she would sneak outside when she was supposed to be asleep. She would sit cross-legged on the front porch in her nightgown, with King, Forêt's beloved Berger Allemand sitting beside her. Both of them looking out for him, waiting for him to come home. She said this was when she learned not to be afraid of King, who loved her so much that he let out a war whoop every time he saw her, and knocked her flat on her back while giving her kisses all over her face. And she knew in her heart that with his granddaughter and his giant dog waiting for him, Forêt would come home if he could.'

'But he never came home,' I said. All those years, hoping and waiting.

'No, not yet.'

'*Not yet*?'

'Of course he's no longer alive. But my mother, she wants me to look now that she can't. She asked Elle to look. To find out what happened; to find his remains. And bury him next to her grandmother. She says this isn't a sentimental thing. She says to find him is a matter of life and death. She has said this over and over. And Elle was much affected by this. And it makes me feel terrible. It's our fault Elle is . . . gone.'

'Did your mother say why it's a matter of life and death *now*?'

'I don't know, but surely it must be connected to everything happening in Kentucky. And believe me, both Elle and I, we asked her about this, but she cannot seem to say what she means, and there are times she can't talk at all. All of this is complicated by her *démence*. Even when she can talk, it's hard to understand her words, because of the *dystonie*, in the muscles of her face.'

I nodded. I'd seen how this played out.

'But now that I've met Elle and—' He shook his head. 'Now I believe what my mother said is true. But if she couldn't find him all the years of her life, how can I? But we have to now, because I think to find him is to find Elle.'

'Did anyone else ever disappear in the village – that your mother talked about?'

'Yes, there was a little boy. And soon after his mother. And his grandmother after that. This sounds very much like what Elle tells me is happening in Kentucky, with people who disappear in the night, and no one ever finds them.'

I nodded. This was the family Forrest had written about in his letters.

'My mother would tell me this one story, always. How every

night her mother would give her a glass of milk with her supper, and how she hated milk and was made to sit at the table until she finished it. And how her grandfather would wink at her when her mother's back was turned, drink the milk and say in a loud voice, *Why look at this good little girl who drank all her milk.* And everyone would agree how good she was, and she was too little to know it was a family joke.

'But when Forêt didn't come home, my mother would never drink her milk but would leave it on the table for him, and her grandmother and mother let her do that.' And then he looked up and over my shoulder and smiled, scrambling up out of his chair.

'Maman? I have someone for you to meet. Here, take my hand and let's get you settled on the couch.'

FORTY

Beautiful Cerise. I knew her immediately, and she clearly knew me. She wore clean white socks and no shoes, and her hair had been pulled into a thick plait that draped over her left shoulder. Josue guided her to the couch, and she tucked up her feet, then he put a soft pink blanket over her lap. She looked at him and didn't smile, but it was clear from her eyes that she would if she could. Her cheeks were hollow, her facial muscles tight and inflexible. She was gaunt and had clearly been losing weight very fast.

She looked at me; patted the couch. So I sat carefully beside her, and she touched my hand. She was trembling softly. 'Patrick. You came.'

It happened this way sometimes. Weeks of silence, then words.

I smiled at her. 'I know Patrick. He talks about you.'

She began to make rocking motions, as if there were a baby in her arms. And then she shook her head hard and let her arms fall to the side. Put her hands over her ears. '*Non*.'

She could have meant so many things. I looked at Josue. He shrugged.

'You are rocking your baby again, Maman?'

She set her lips and looked away. Her shoulders sagged. We'd failed to understand, and she was frustrated. She looked back at me, eyes no longer dull. 'Elle has found him,' she said. 'After all this time.'

That made me worry. Whatever it meant, it didn't sound good.

Cerise tried to stand, and Josue took one side and I took the other, and we walked her back to the bedroom, and Josue tried to tuck her under the blankets. But she would not lie down. She put her head on his shoulder and cried.

FORTY-ONE

We left Cerise lying on her side, staring out the window, her eyes glazed in that way I knew very well. She wasn't gone exactly. She was just someplace else.

And I thought through everything she'd said and began to put it all together. Patrick, she had said. She didn't think I was Patrick, as I had first assumed. She was trying to make me understand. Because Cerise had taken Patrick to a cave in the lucid dream they'd shared.

'Josue. Are there any caves around here?'

'*Les grottes*? Yes, there are many in the area.'

'How about near your family farm?'

He shook his head. 'But there is a strange thing that has happened – a new karst spring has come up. This is an underground stream that comes up through layers of rock then eventually disappears. Always near the caves. Because of the porous nature of the rock, it makes a place for caves and underground springs. And Karst holes.'

'An underground spring? We have them in Kentucky. And we have sinkholes too. Sometimes a little one where you can break your ankle. Sometimes really big ones that swallow things up.'

'Then that is another connection between our homes, Dr Archer.'

'Where is this underground spring?'

He frowned at me. 'It's close to the stone house, where Elle was last seen.'

There were no caves within walking or running distance of the house where Conor Walsh and Andi Craig had disappeared. In Kentucky, that would be the first thing that crossed your mind. But caves could be there when you didn't know it. The rock beneath the soil would shift and settle. Sinkholes opened up now and then, swallowing up cars, houses, with no warning.

The tracking dogs hadn't found Conor Walsh, and they hadn't found Andi Craig. But they had picked up a scent under the house and then led the handler out through the backyard, off the property into a thicket. And lost the scent. If Conor and Andi Craig were underground somewhere, a tracking dog might not pick that up.

Josue and I got hold of Tom immediately. He listened and heard me out; said they'd checked the area around the karst spring, but they'd go back. They'd need a different kind of dog. The kind of dog who could scent death underwater and underground. They'd need a cadaver dog.

'It doesn't mean she's dead,' I told him, my voice tight.

'No, but Forrest Strickler certainly is. And if she found him, and the dog found Forrest . . . then we'd find Elle.' And Tom, young as he was, had become the kind of man who faced things. 'Either way, Noah. We find her.'

FORTY-TWO

The cadaver dog was a German shepherd named Os, which was French for Bones. He was young, tan and slim with a black face and huge black ears, and when I saw him, he was soaking wet. He had trampled around the spring, and jumped in at one point, but he hadn't alerted yet. He kept moving, out of the water, nose to the ground, away from the spring, off leash with his handler, a woman in green khakis, walking with him at an angle, staying close but letting him concentrate on his work.

A thousand yards from the spring, he climbed up the hill then sat and buckled forward, nose to the ground.

They brought Elle out first, still alive, clutching a leather notebook that looked decayed, dirty, old. She'd found Forrest Strickler, the notebook he'd carried with him and what was left of his remains, which had washed up years ago into a passageway under the rock. And Elle had walked up the slope, gone off the path and somehow slid suddenly sideways, falling twelve feet into a sinkhole. You never see them and they happen fast, as if the earth opens up and swallows you down.

She'd cracked a vertebra in her back and was severely concussed, but there was no skull fracture. She'd been lucky. Severely dehydrated, in shock, but conscious and sobbing. Tom was right beside her, holding her hand.

'I can't tell you,' she said, looking over his shoulder at me. Looking hard at me.

'Can't tell me what, sweetheart?' Tom said.

She was agitated. Hands fluttering. 'I can't think about it. I can't . . . I can't get my thoughts together. Where's my dad?'

Perry was right beside her, as was Chloe, but whatever it was Elle saw, it wasn't them. Her gaze was locked tight on me.

I moved in close. She grabbed my wrist – thrust the notebook into my hands.

'You're safe now, Elle,' I told her. Squeezing her hand. Her skin was hot, her grip was strong.

'None of us are safe.' Her face was red with fever and pain; slick with sweat. Her red dress muddy and bloody and torn. She turned her head, and I saw the layers of clotted blood.

'We'll talk when you're ready. Whatever happened, we'll handle it.'

She shook her head. Looked at Tom. 'Don't. Leave. Me.'

'Never. You couldn't make me if you tried.'

I moved out of the way. I wasn't the doctor they needed right now. The IV fluids had already been started. They'd given her something to ease her anxiety and her pain, and her eyelids were already beginning to flutter.

I'd never seen Perry so shaken, his face white, and he held tight to a sobbing Chloe.

Elle opened her eyes and held out a hand. 'You're OK, both of you. I was so worried, so . . .' Her voice drifted off, and so did she.

Perry looked at me. 'She'll be OK?'

'She will. We found her in time.'

'Physically she'll be OK. But the other.'

'We'll handle it. You and me and Chloe. We'll figure it out, Perry – we always do.'

'We have to go,' Chloe told him. She blew me a kiss, her face tear streaked and chalk white.

Tom was with Elle in the ambulance, and it pulled away, siren pulsing. They would take her to the hospital in Marseille, and I'd catch up with them later.

Perry and Chloe got in their car, trailing behind the ambulance. I saw Os and his handler, off to one side. Os was sitting happily, alert, interested, feeling good about himself. Pleased with the beef jerky that had been his reward for a job well done, nosing his handler's pockets for more.

I headed her way, and Os watched me. He didn't seem alarmed, just aware, and his handler wisely had him a bit away from all the chaos and the noise, though it didn't seem to faze him.

'I know I'm not supposed to pet him, but I wanted to just say thanks to you and to Os.'

He stood up and looked at me when I said his name.

'You are a beautiful, big good boy,' I told him. I looked at the woman, who was smiling at me. 'He saved my niece's life. Both of you did.'

'I do not have much English,' she said kindly.

But Os did. He ran for me and jumped, paws on my chest, and I ran my hands up and down his sides, then scratched him under the chin, and he made a moaning sound just like Tash did. I knew I was breaking rules, but so long as the dog comes to you . . .

'Os,' she said.

He ran back to her and nudged the pocket of her jacket, and she laughed, digging out an orange-and-blue ball, like the ones Tash hoarded at home.

'*Récompense,*' she said, giving me another smile. '*Il négocie.*' She threw the ball, and he ran for it.

I found a place to sit – a flat rock a bit up the hill where I could watch and be out of the way. I would stay behind and wait. It seemed important. To witness and be present, for this man, Forrest Strickler. I didn't know what condition the remains would be in, but he'd been underground for some time, and he'd been in the water. I wondered how there could be much of anything left.

And while I waited, I read the notebook. I had to wait a little while for my hands to stop shaking, and to settle. I read slowly, but I was already familiar with the curl and curve of Forrest's handwriting, and the curious brown ink he liked to use. Evidently Forrest had not been in the water long. The notebook was damaged, and there were sections I could not read. But I got the gist.

On the first page were the familiar black and red dots, the geometrical drawings and the beginning of his obsession with caves. He called it *the code*, which made me think. Not symbols. Not unsophisticated cave-man drawings. Not cute little protective drawings that helped you sleep at night. But *the code*. He puzzled over it, copied sections precisely from a cave he would return to over and over again, and approached it with respect and the conviction that it was crucial. And Forrest Strickler was a highly intelligent man who had seen dark things in a war – and dark things in a village. I wondered if he'd seen dark things at home in Kentucky.

He didn't think the caves were haunted. He considered them sanctuaries.

He'd been exploring them. There was a small cave near that little stone house, and he had wondered if the missing people that lived there had wandered in and gotten lost. A cave was a dangerous place, and it was easy to lose your way. But as he explored, he began to think that maybe the boy, the mother and the grandmother had fallen into a karst hole – it could happen easily in regions of karst terrain; it happened at home in Kentucky. A place where the rock beneath the surface was soluble – limestone, gypsum – any kind of carbonite rock that could be dissolved by the groundwater that flowed naturally beneath the surface. This was how caves were formed. This was the reason for sinkholes, when the ground opened up and swallowed anything in its grasp.

But why, he wondered, did they all run from the house and disappear? Why did the grandmother, an ill woman who rarely left her bed, get up and go out in the night? Why did the mother leave in the middle of the night?

It was the same pattern. Like Andi Craig and Conor Walsh. Going under the house to the crawl space was not a casual act. Why had they done that? Why had they left fast – scuff marks from Conor's boots; Andi's flashlight left behind?

Forrest spent his free time in the cave, exploring carefully. There had been small earthquakes that you would barely notice if you noticed at all, but they had made the cave more dangerous. Some of the sections had shifted; passageways sealed off. He'd grown up around the limestone caves in Kentucky, and he knew the dangers. Like falling into deep water you didn't know was there in the dark – so deep it seemed like it went to the center of the earth. And it was easy to get lost and not find your way back. He would make notches on the walls, to mark his path. That was how he'd run across the curious symbols in the first place, a small section he might not have noticed otherwise – red and black dots, triangles, hexagons.

After the earthquakes, he found a new wall of symbols. Carved into the walls. Very old. He'd been copying them carefully before he died. The cave had been a spiritual place, according to the locals. Just like the caves in Kentucky. A place for people to go for sanctuary, for worship, to bury their dead, before there were village priests. And after.

But Forrest thought maybe the caves were a place to hide. To be hidden. To get lost.

Where else could you disappear without a trace and not be able to find your way home? And where else might you go following a primal instinct for survival, when you needed protection and a place to hide?

Caves have been protection from the beginning of time, and cave systems threaded the underworld with connections in rock, water, and pathways that moved and shifted with the mysterious and ongoing life deep inside the earth.

And I remembered a small comment at the end of one of his letters, that had seemed random to me when I read it.

> *We knew almost nothing about caves, Anna. But you can figure out a lot when you go inside and see what people left behind.*

It took quite some time before the remains of Forrest Strickler were brought out; there was nothing left but his belt buckle, his pen and bits of clothing that threaded his bones. Os was called back. There were signs of other remains. Other bodies. All from the same family, as it turned out. It took days to get them all out, but eventually they found a boy of around eight, a woman in her thirties and a woman in her fifties with advanced osteosarcoma, her bones so weakened with cancer there had already been two breaks. Yet she had struggled up out of her bed and disappeared into the night.

And then, on the next-to-last page of the notebook, folded at the corner to mark the place, Forrest Strickler had figured it out.

> *I found Madame Faure in the cave today. Crumpled in a corner, dead for a while. And I knew then exactly what happened. The only thing that would bring her out of her bed at night – she had been suffering so much, had been in so much pain. It was the same thing that brought me here.*
>
> *The cries of that baby, an infant, so young and in distress. It could not have been Cerise – I had checked my little granddaughter when I first heard the cry. But there was a baby in trouble. That isn't something you can ignore, and all my usual caution went sideways because I ran right to the baby. I knew it was there. I could hear it. And then I fell, and the cries stopped. It has been torturing me, but now I understand. There was never a baby. I had been lured to this place, this trap, by something I don't understand, just like Madame Faure, and her daughter and her grandson. And how many others, I wonder.*

It was a duck call. The way my daddy lured the waterfowl when he went out with his gun and his dogs.

We are being hunted.

The exact same thing Rory Hennessy had told Em, before he hanged himself in the office of his beloved school. *Hello, neighbor.*

And everything fell into place.

Conor Walsh and Andi Craig had been frantic, responding to the cries of an infant, as any human would. An infant they couldn't find. Cries that lured them under the house then out into the darkness, leading them into a trap.

You can call it compassion, you can call it decency and you can call it love, and all of that would be true. The cry of a baby in distress is impossible to ignore, activating an alarm in the brain circuit called the thalamocingulate pathway. Next, dopamine hits in the midbrain, pinging the neuro pathways of empathy and emotion. This is not a reaction of gender – to be human is to respond. They've tested the reactions in both men and women, and both sexes have similar scores.

No other sound elicits this response. The heart rate goes up, along with blood pressure and hand grip strength. The beautiful practical tapestry of the body, the mind, and the spirit working in sync.

FORTY-THREE

Tom had called a friend at the Kentucky Search Dog Association and liaised with the Osage police, and they'd agreed to send a dog who specialized in remains detection and live air scent. Another German shepherd. A K9 named Harley.

Forty-seven hours later, Tom got a call from the Osage police, and I got a call from Pammie.

They'd started Harley up in the crawl space under the house, and he'd bolted back out the door and led them through the backyard and into the tall grass of farmland a quarter mile from the house. His handler had been puzzled at first, to see Harley alerting in the middle of a stretch of glorious pasture, but she knew to be cautious, and even then, she got too close for comfort to the sinkhole that was hidden and covered over with tall grass, impossible to see in the sunlight or the darkness – until you were right on top of it. They measured it at thirty feet deep.

Andi Craig had smashed her skull, dying upon impact. Conor Walsh, who'd fallen first, had a broken back, a fractured hip and was suffering from prolonged starvation that had caused permanent damage to his kidneys. He'd been able to crawl to a drip pool for water, which was why he was still alive.

Pammie called me from the hallway outside his hospital room. I knew she was going to tell me that Conor had followed the cries of an infant, and she did tell me that, saying that they'd heard all kinds of voices in that house but never the cry of a baby before. But she had other news. Big news.

The middle school in Osage was gone. Disappeared into a massive sinkhole that hit in the dead of night. It had happened before, years ago, when the Corvette Museum in Bowling Green had a sinkhole open up that was forty feet wide by sixty feet long and thirty-five feet deep. The pictures of Corvettes that had crashed down into the sinkhole had made the news around the world.

'They've got video footage,' Pammie told me, talking so fast she was hard to understand. 'There were cameras all over that school, and you can see it happening in real time. It's all over the news.'

I asked her how everyone was doing. She and Patrick and the baby. Her husband Conor.

'He's hurt bad,' she said, a catch in her voice. 'He might not ever be able to work with horses again.'

'Just wait and see. Take it slow and see where it goes.'

'*And we're leaving*,' she said, sounding happy. 'We're going to Ireland. We're getting married there over Christmas anyway, so we're just going now, as soon as Conor can make the flight. I've shut down my business. Grammie said she doesn't want to live in a place where the ground opens up and swallows you down, so she's going with us.' Pammie laughed. 'I mean, she does have a point. And Conor owns part interest in the family business, a little artisan food shop and tearoom, in Galway, and I'm going to run it with his sister, and let him take time to get better, to get back on his feet. To tell you the truth, we can't get out of here fast enough. Thank you for finding my husband. The Osage police told us they found him because of you and Tom. That somehow you knew what to do. Thank you, Dr Archer, for all of your help.'

She was crying when she hung up, but I could tell she was happy. All of them going to Conor's home in Ireland. All of them getting the hell out.

FORTY-FOUR

That night I had dinner at Josue's place. Tom was a permanent fixture outside Elle's hospital room, and Perry and Chloe had checked out of the hotel in St Remy and taken rooms in Marseille. I would fly out late tomorrow. I had patients to see.

But tonight, all of us – Cerise, Josue and his wife, who was small, dark and shy of me – we all gathered together around their kitchen table, which was conveniently located in the living room, to eat artichokes fried and simmered with bacon and garlic, and *boeuf à la Gordienne*, and we watched the footage, over and over, of the middle school in Osage, Kentucky getting swallowed up. It felt more like a disaster movie than real life.

Cerise was tucked on to the couch, deep asleep and peaceful, as all of us milled around her. Eating, drinking, talking and watching TV. Josue had told her about finding Forrest and she had touched his cheek fondly, like he was telling her something she already knew.

Josue drove me back to my hotel very late, and between the wine and the beef and the relief of finding Elle, and the ease of being I had found in Provence, I slept very well – and very hard.

Sometime around four a.m., Cerise slipped quietly away, in the still-dark moments before the sun comes up, the time my patients most often take their leave. Josue called me as I was having breakfast. He was shaken hard and frozen in disbelief, something I'd seen often in my practice when the families faced the expected but always shocking death of the people they loved. The house was in turmoil with friends and relatives, his mother's body had already been removed, but he had something to show me – could he come by?

FORTY-FIVE

Josue and I shared breakfast together at the hotel, sitting inside, at a little corner table, near the bar. He wasn't hungry, but he had coffee. I had coffee, orange juice, croissants, fruit, eggs and ham.

'I know it is good for my mother to be at peace. But it's a strange thing. The caretaking has been hard, but I would give everything to have her back, sitting on that couch – just her presence in the room. You think when that happens, the *démence*, you have lost everything, but you haven't. No, because she was always still there.'

I listened. I'd heard this before. There are those who will tell you that the death of a loved one who's been ill is a relief. There are articles by therapists who tell you not to feel guilty for these emotions. Maybe it happens. There would be nothing wrong with that. But it was something I had not once seen.

Josue stared at the table and wouldn't meet my eyes. 'A thing has happened that is very strange. This morning, I found a letter from my mother, sitting in an envelope, addressed to me. I don't see how such a thing can be possible. But here it is, and it is real.'

He handed me the envelope – soft blue – and page after page of stationery.

Josue paused and cleared his throat. Took a minute. Frowned then looked up with a smile. 'My mother's handwriting is beautiful to me.'

'I'm astounded she was able to write at that stage of her illness. And this is puzzling because this isn't the handwriting of a woman with advanced dementia.' But it was dated one week ago, written on a Tuesday, at two fifteen in the afternoon. Noted, recorded, at the top of the page.

'She *couldn't* write. She hasn't been able to write by hand for . . . three years, so me too – I find this . . . unfathomable. *Parce que* – this is without question the handwriting of my mother. Which is very distinctive. Also very pretty, and always hard to read. And the things she says . . . I may read this to you? To translate the French?'

I drained the last of my coffee. 'Of course.'

'And after I read you this letter and show you what she enclosed, and after you get home, and when you have some time because I know you are a busy man, you will go to this place she mentions in Frankfort, Kentucky. And you will tell me what you see.'

He put his napkin on the table and began to read.

Josue – my dear son. I have extraordinary things to tell you.

I listen to you talk, you and Marina, and sometimes you cry, because you see me sitting so silent, so lost. Talking to people you cannot see. As if I was somewhere you could not find me.

But, my son, I was not lost. I cannot begin to explain the thrill of moving through the timeline of this life I have had as your mother. It is as easy as walking through a door. You wonder if I suffer – I can hear you whisper this to your wife. And yes, it is hard for me right now, too hard to find my way forward because there is no future left for me to have. And so I drift backward through the dream of this life and wander through the times that are precious to me.

Mostly, I am with your father. I know from your whispered conversations that you've heard he and I talking. That once in a while you've caught a murmur that reminds you of him. I know you have caught that flash of light, that blur of energy and heat, which is the only way you can see him now. He and I are in the early part of the dream. The life we had before you were born, the days I was pregnant, then you in your little high chair eating milk and bread.

Think of me as having one foot in both worlds.

And so, my son, one day I went back and back and found my grandfather Forêt. Young after the war and so deeply shocked and lost.

And you know I always looked for him, as I grew up; all my life, I looked for him. I never believed that he left us; I always felt he died and no one came to help in time. I always hoped to find him one day, gather his bones together with love and bury him next to my grandmother, Noémie.

See me moving backward – I am holding you again as a baby. I am in the kitchen cooking again with you and your father, and we go for a walk around the farm after dinner like we did before he died and the farm was sold. And then I go back further. I go to my time as a very little girl. I go to the night my grandfather disappeared.

I sat with King on the porch waiting, but I knew he would not come. So I moved back earlier to the afternoon when my grandfather came home for lunch. I watched him walk away that last time. But this time King and I followed.

My grandfather had gone to the cave, where I wasn't allowed to go, because little girls can get so lost.

This was the time of the dark things around us, in the village, and my grandfather had been exploring in the cave. And he was worried because I had followed him, and could have been lost, but he was not unkind. He said this cave had been a place of wisdom, and he showed me the paintings and drawings on the wall all in black and red, and the geometric patterns that intrigued him. He had a feeling about them. He thought it was a code. He had a notebook, and he was copying all of them down.

I told him we must go, that something bad was going to happen, and he must come home. And King was growling and whimpering, and my grandfather, unlike so many others, he would listen to a child, and mainly I think . . . he trusted King. A wise man trusts his dog, he always told me.

And as we came out of the cave, there was a big noise and the rush of water. And later, my grandfather went back with some of the men he knew and with my grandmother, and saw that water had rushed in and flooded, then seeped away again, down a channel under the ground. And my grandfather said to me – how did you know? He told me King and I saved his life. Because the water would have washed him down the hole and he would have drowned. His body carried away and lost to time.

And I stayed in this life that I had walked through like a ghost, making changes as if I had created it from scratch. And my grandfather Forêt was there as I grew up, and my grandmother was happy, and after I was newly married to your father and before you were born, Forêt and my grandmother went back to his home in the American city of Frankfort, Kentucky. They built a new house on the family farm, at the foot of a hill my grandfather called his mountain, and he had peacocks everywhere that sounded like cats calling at dusk. He would go out at supper time and feed them by hand. And there was an old mare he liked to ride – her name was Empress. And a little dog called Zip. And he and my grandmother, Noémie, they were so quiet and happy.

And King had died as dogs do, and my grandfather had been very sad. So after you were born, your father and I went to America to visit, to take you to see your great-grandfather, and to bring with us a puppy, born of King's puppies. And my grandfather and the puppy, they seemed to know each other somehow. The puppy cuddled into his arms, and it was the only time I saw my grandfather cry. And of course he named this little puppy King, because my grandfather said he was royalty, like all of the Berger Allemand. And my grandmother said this must be why they were so outrageous these dogs. Because royalty does not always behave.

And because we were there in Kentucky, your father did not die in a fall putting hay up in the loft of the barn. I had timed this so very carefully, a happy ghost walking through, part woman, part memory, as all of us are. This will be hard for you to believe I understand, so look, my son, and see that I have brought you a newspaper article from the local paper in Frankfort, where they wrote all about our visit from France. So you will know this is real. A gift to you of a memory you will not have, and a knowing you may not understand. With much love for you, Maman.

And then he handed me the clipping. It wasn't worn or fragile, but fresh and new. Like last week's paper. From a time when you could hold a newspaper in your hands.

The Frankfort *State Journal – First In Local News Since 1902* . . . May 5, 1983

FORREST AND NOÉMIE STRICKLER WELCOME FAMILY FROM FRANCE

It was a happy Sunday afternoon at the small farm in the countryside about six miles from the Frankfort state capital, where Forrest Strickler and his wife pose with their granddaughter, Cerise; her husband, Michel; and little great-grandson Josue, who have come for a family visit, all the way from their home in Provence, in the south of France.

Forrest Strickler was an infantry soldier in WWI, and that is where he met and fell in love with his beautiful French wife, Noémie. They left their home in Pente Douce, Provence, and returned to the family farm in Kentucky in 1980, after the death of Forrest's sister, Anna.

Noémie says the things she loves the most about Kentucky are the friendly people and the barbecue.

Pictured center is little Josue, age four and a half, with a German shepherd puppy brought all the way from France. Forrest has named the puppy King, after the very first shepherd he had.

Bienvenue, *Strickler family!*

I studied the picture; read the newspaper article through again. Forrest and Noémie looked to be in their eighties – Forrest thin and very tall, hair gone gray and carefully combed to one side, his arm round Noémie, who was wearing a simple cotton dress, her hair tucked into a tidy bun, reading glasses in a chain around her neck.

Cerise was a young mother – glorious hair rippling down to her waist, wearing blue jeans and farm boots, and wrapped in the arms of her husband, who was dark-haired and stocky. He looked very strong. Cerise looked so happy in the picture. It was hard to tell, but I thought I saw something knowing in her eyes. And her stance was that of a happy but determined woman.

Josue's fine dark hair was blowing in the wind. The puppy in his lap couldn't have been more than ten weeks old, still blue-eyed, with ears folded over and tipped down, because he was just a baby shepherd, who was giving Josue kisses, which made him laugh.

I looked up at Josue; tapped the little boy in the picture. 'And this is you.'

'Without question. Do you know where this is?' he asked me, pointing to the address on the mailbox.

'I'll find it.'

FORTY-SIX

Perry and Chloe and I went to Osage, Kentucky on a weekend – Perry to do another exorcism of many ongoing exorcisms, Chloe to measure the effect and me to just look at the sinkholes.

I met Chloe and Perry in the parking lot of the school. I had been out close to the house, out in the grassy farmland, to look at the sinkhole that had taken Conor and Andi Craig. It wasn't roped off or marked, and if I hadn't known the history, I might have stepped right in it. A roundish impression in the dirt, covered over with grass. You had to look hard to know it was there.

The one that took the middle school was something else. There's a reason Kentucky is called a karst state and is number seven in the nation for sinkholes. In Mammoth Cave State Park, you can walk the Cedar Sink Trail to go inside a seven-acre sinkhole. This one was fifty feet deep, sixty yards wide and ninety yards long. The school had been crushed and was a total loss.

It was hard to wrap your mind around. The ground gave way to a wide, open gap with dirt and rock and . . . a shattered school. The area was barricaded, roped off.

Em was there as she often was. She always seemed to know when we were coming. She and her grandson arrived in the yellow 'Vette, and he helped her out, waved at us and stood beside her, letting her lean against him, steady with her cane, and we all just gazed down into the sinkhole, which was mesmerizing.

Most of the kids were back home now, and Dr Bianchi had returned to Louisville, still following up with the last few. The history teacher had survived his cardiac event and was back teaching already, Mrs Garcia took her little dog Vernon to the classroom every day and didn't care what anybody else thought, and the math teacher had come out of her coma with no memory of what had happened the night she'd been alone with the dark things in the middle school. But she quit teaching. Something inside her could not bear to go back.

'Kids still going to class inside the old carburetor factory?' I asked.

Em nodded. 'But I have good news. We're getting a brand-new school, courtesy of Dr Silas Holtzer, whose malpractice insurance policy is footing the bill in a mediated settlement that was signed late last night. The attorneys are very happy to be leaving that old motel in Osage, and they booked it out of town as soon as the sun came up. We had to agree not to talk to the media about any of this anymore, which suits most of us just fine. Unfortunately for Dr Holtzer, his malpractice insurance has been terminated, and he won't be able to find a company that will take him on.'

I didn't tell her that hospital gossip had it that he was now under investigation as a reporter had found a Medicaid complaint against him that had been ignored. The state medical board had yet to pull his medical license, but without insurance, it was a moot point.

'You think we could shore that sinkhole up and rebuild right here?' Em said.

'Hell no. Beyond the issue of this being a geological nightmare location for a school, it's still not safe.'

'Oh, you mean that other stuff?'

'Yes, I mean that other stuff.'

'Then I guess it's a good thing it's all roped off.'

'May it stay that way,' I muttered.

'Are you coming to the pumpkin festival and the corn maze next week?'

'I'm bringing the wife and kids. Is there going to be a parade?'

'There's *always* a parade. My grandson is going to drive me in the 'Vette with flowers on the hood.'

He laughed. 'I sure am not.'

It was lighter now, the feeling in this town. Pammie and her family were gone. The house in the country sat empty again. Not a single reporter had been able to track down the owner, and plenty of them had tried.

Even if an uncomfortable feeling still hung in the air around the remains of the school, people were back to the ups and downs of their normal lives. The memories would be there, but so would the October Pumpkin Festival and Parade.

Em kissed my cheek when I left, like she always did. I didn't look back. The school lying smashed in the sinkhole made me uneasy, and I headed back to the car. There were already reports of some of the camera feeds coming back on, picked up by the school Wi-Fi account, which kept coming back up even though it had been shut down. These were things I did not like thinking about.

According to Chloe, the chemical signal that paired with the stone house in Provence, the karst hole that had swallowed up Elle, the school and the house in Kentucky was 1.8 million years old. This darkness had been watching and aware for a very long time.

And she'd been analyzing Patrick's rock, the code and the symbols, and realized they were a language, written in math. It was only part of the whole, but there was enough to be clear. It was an exorcism.

Quantum spirituality, she called it.

Whalers hunt orcas by harpooning their babies and dragging them to shallow water so they can kill the mother who comes when she hears their cries of distress. The dark entity at 1.8 million years has had plenty of time to learn to hunt humans. Likely they learned it from us.

And just for a moment, I had a flash of understanding, of how everything in the world connects.

FORTY-SEVEN

I was headed back to the hospital to do a final late round with my patients. There were two in particular I was worried about. But I took a detour on the way. I'd found the address on the mailbox that showed up in the picture Josue had shown me. That mysterious newspaper article from another life, where Forrest Strickler, Noémie, Cerise and her husband, a baby Josue and a new puppy named King had all posed, smiling, wind blowing their hair, in front of a wide, stone two-story house.

The address was off a two-lane road. A new subdivision was going up one street over.

The metal gate was there, swinging open, the fence sagging and unloved, and the mailbox had been painted hot pink. The house was empty and up for sale. I latched the metal gate, got an angle that didn't include the hot-pink mailbox and took a few pictures to send to Josue. So he could see Forrest's mountain, which rose from the gentle slope of the land.

And just as I opened the door of the car, I stumbled. Fell down on my knees, holding tight to the car door.

Tired, I told myself. Just tired. I needed to get through one more week of heavy work then I would ease back a little. Take a day or two off.

It was a longish forty-minute drive back from Frankfort to the hospital, even driving the backroads of Old Frankfort Pike and Leestown Road to avoid the afternoon traffic. And thundering down the corridor like I always did, I rounded a corner and ran quite literally into Hilde. I put a hand to the wall to stay on my feet. Hilde didn't seem to notice.

We stood not two feet away from each other. We hadn't spoken in months. Usually she ran away when she saw me. But not tonight.

'I, um . . . Noah, I don't know what to say. That stuff with the kids in the town and the media . . . it all turned out pretty bad.'

'I know who you talked to, I know what you said and I know who to blame.' I gave her a steady look.

She lifted her chin. Laughed just a little. 'Things did get carried away.'

'*Things* did not get carried away, Dr Sweetwater. *Things* did not slander me in the press.'

'*Dr Sweetwater* is it? I don't – I don't believe in . . .'

She trailed off. Fiddled with her hair. A tiny pink pearl earring popped out of place and rolled across the floor, almost touching my foot. She looked at me, waiting. In times past, I would always pick up the earrings that fell, the pens that dropped, steal half her muffins, listen to her ongoing issues with the latest man who'd asked her out.

Those days were over, as was our friendship. There was no saving it – I knew her too well. I moved to the other side of the hall and walked away.

It felt good to leave all that behind. It felt free.

FORTY-EIGHT

It was Tom who came to me. Again. For Elle.

I heard the car. It was early – four a.m. The time of day that belongs to me on any weekend days I have off, the rest of the world asleep.

I was sitting outside with Tash. Even Mr Timothy was sound asleep. Lately, he'd taken to stretching out on Vaughn's pillow, just above his head.

I had coffee.

Tom moved quietly and came to the French doors that led to my kingdom by the fireplace. He wore loose, battered jeans and a worn-out sweater the rusty color of autumn.

'Aren't you cold?' he said, sliding the doors open and giving me that trademark lopsided smile.

I wore thick white socks, boxer shorts and a tee shirt, and one of my old sweaters that Moira had somehow missed.

'A little.'

'The old man sits by the fire. You want me to actually build you a fire?'

'Nah, do that and the kids will be down four seconds later. There's coffee.'

He showed me his cup then settled in his favorite chair. I liked that he had a favorite chair. A bedroom he hadn't used in a while.

It struck me as odd sometimes, how families spread out and away. My mother and her husband were getting older. Were they OK? Would they tell me if they weren't? And Tom and Elle, falling hard for each other, living in Perry's condo downtown. All of them close, but sometimes I wanted to gather everybody up and have them here in my compound. Just to hang out and to keep them safe.

I set my empty coffee cup down. Time to make another pot, but not yet. Tom was not the kind of man who talked much or confided easily. One wrong move would shut him down.

He stared over my shoulder into the darkness. 'I've been thinking a lot lately. About Candice.'

This wasn't what I'd expected. But neither was I surprised.

He took a gulp of coffee. He'd be drinking it black. 'You knew her pretty well. From work. From taking care of her dad.'

I was curious how her father was doing. Fielding – a man who had experienced the dark and the light of the first Enlightenment Project. When it was new and raw and before it became a refined protocol. It was safer now than it had been then.

I would feel guilty about Fielding and Candice for the rest of my life.

'You're the one who got us together,' he said. 'With a little help from Moira.'

'Tom, I—'

He put up a hand. 'I still love Candice. I'm glad for loving her, even if we didn't have long. And I don't want to talk about any of that other stuff.'

I nodded. 'Understood.'

'But Candice, you know . . . She was dealing with those dark things you know all about before she got— before she died. And I didn't know how to help her. And now – now Elle is dealing with the same kind of things. And I don't know how to help her either. But you would know. This is your wheelhouse, right?'

He was matter-of-fact and quiet in his voice and his words. But I knew very well Elle going missing, almost dying, though hard on all of us had been agony for him. Tom was a private person, but you could hear it in his voice; see it shadowing him.

I thought about Elle and Conor and Andi Craig. Deep down in a sinkhole, alone in the dark. Alone *with* the dark.

'She says she doesn't remember anything. Elle. But she's not OK.'

'She may well not remember, Tom.'

'You get what I mean. It was really bad, and it haunts her, so much she can't think about it, but she feels it. Or maybe it's so bad she won't tell me. But she wakes up at night *screaming*. Crying. She doesn't like to be alone. And she takes Chewie with her everywhere and says she needs him with her no matter what.'

'She probably does need him. And if she has no conscious memories, that's normal. But her body remembers, even though her brain blocks things out of her conscious memory. And while that's good for survival in the moment, it's a problem later. Because your intuition and instinct are informed by these kinds of traumas. Sometimes I think not remembering is harder. It's hard to deal with your fears and face them if your mind locks them away.'

'It's not like Elle not to face things.'

'It's not Elle's fault – she has no choice in this. Look, you knew she was in trouble, that she would die if you didn't find her, and even though you did find her, that's hard to come back from. But if all you knew was that something terrible happened with glimpses of memories—'

'God. That would drive me nuts.'

'So she needs help with this. Professional help.'

'She won't get it. Not after what happened with Holtzer. This stuff is dark, Noah, and nobody else is going to believe her, except you and her mom and her dad, and she refuses to talk to either one of them. But you – you lived it. So you're going to have to be the one who helps her.'

'I've tried, Tom. She won't return my calls. Or texts. Or emails. And I have to respect her wishes on this.'

'Have you asked her to meet you at Graeters for ice cream?'

'Didn't think of that.'

'Ask her, Noah. And if she doesn't answer, keep asking and don't give up. I don't want to lose another woman I love.'

FORTY-NINE

After two texts suggesting a hot fudge sundae, I stuck to emojis. Ice cream emojis. One text, every single day. It was pushier than I liked to be. But I sent a stop sign and a question mark and didn't get a response, so I kept on sending.

Then I got creative. I sent a video of dogs eating ice cream.

And then I sent an emoji of an ice cream cone and an invitation to Graeters addressed to Chewie.

And that got an immediate response. We were on. I should have been texting the dog from the get-go.

Elle was almost the same – picking up the weight she'd lost after five days starving down in that hole; hands steady. But there was an air of having her guard up. Something knowing in her eyes. And I knew she'd never be the same, and knowing that crushed my heart. I knew what it was like to never be the same. And I knew that was how life worked.

Ice cream at Graeters was serious business as usual, and mostly Elle and I watched Chewie eating ice cream, and ate our own. I wish I'd brought Tash.

Elle had a triple-scoop hot fudge sundae with the usual three cherries and held a pup cup of ice cream for Chewie between her feet, where he stood under the table and licked it all up. When he started in on the paper cup, Elle laughed. I took the cup away from him and threw it away; handed Elle a wad of napkins.

She cleaned chocolate off her tee shirt. 'You're such a dad.'

'You say that like it's a bad thing.'

She gave me a little smile.

'Tom says you don't remember anything.'

'*I remember everything*. I just don't know who to tell.'

'I'm the guy.'

'Yeah. I figured that's why we were here.' She looked around. There were people meandering up and down the street. A couple with a baby eyeing our table. 'Can we go to the arboretum and sit on a bench at the top of the hill, and talk there?'

FIFTY

The parking lot at the arboretum was slowly clearing out. It was past dinner time and the after-work runners had gone home. Families had rounded up their kids and were on their way to an early supper and bath time.

The bench at the top of the hill was empty, and we settled there. Chewie jumped up and nestled between us. Elle shut her eyes tight and stroked his head.

'I'm different now.'

'I know.'

'It's like . . . being aware. I don't like it. I don't get how you do it. How you live with this; do all the things you do and oh by the way come and rescue me in France from things that *piss me off*. Things that are . . . unfathomable.'

'The rescue was a joint effort, Elle.'

'Yeah, but you. They couldn't find me until *you* came. You knew to listen to Cerise.'

'I did, but I still didn't get it until afterward.' And I thought of Cerise. Rocking a baby, shaking her head *no*, turning away in frustration when we didn't understand.

'You got it enough to find me.'

'It is true that I'm awesome – and a hero in this world.'

'What's fun about you, Uncle Noah, is that when you say things like that, I know you believe it. Even I believe it.'

I waited her out. And finally . . .

'I'm not sure how to talk about this.'

'Tell me what you *want* to tell me. And understand that you can come back from this – and navigate it. Not just survive. Thrive.'

She thought about that. 'I wish I believed you. I'm in a hard place. Because it feels like there's a part of me that's still buried underground in that . . . that darkness, that cave. Falling down through the sinkhole. It happened so fast. One minute I was running—' She stopped. 'It's terrifying to think it just happened like that, and now I have to be aware, like I always have to hold it out in front of me and not let it go, otherwise I let my guard down and think I'm safe when I'm not.' She gave me a sideways look. 'Who helped you? My dad?'

'Your dad.'

'Would you have been OK without him? Dealing with this on your own?'

'No.'

'Do you think I can deal with this on my own?'

'No.'

''Kay. So this is survival for me. Talking to you.'

'Yes.' I wanted to tell her about my patients. How they came to me with MS, tumors in their brains, fibromyalgia, because we live in a world that obstructs the basic things every human needs. It's not rocket science. And it's not their fault. 'Elle, everybody needs help in their life. Don't turn it down when it's offered.'

'I'm going to be much better at my job now, that's for sure.'

'It's called life experience.'

She gave me a sideways smile. 'The best thing about all of this . . . *Tom*. That connection I had to Cerise. Finding my cousins in France. Did you go to Josue's flower shop?'

'Didn't have time.'

'If ever I decide to ditch the psychiatry business, I'm going to open a florist. I loved how Josue and Martina's house was filled with flowers. In the sink, in the bathtub . . . is it weird to want flowers everywhere?'

'You brought lavender back from France, didn't you?'

'When I was in that lucid dream with Cerise? Yeah. I did.'

'So just do it the traditional way. Go to a garden center or something.'

She pulled Chewie's ears, and he licked her hand. A couple walked by with the serious pace of people who were striding for their health. Then she began to talk.

She hadn't been smart enough to be afraid while she was in Pente Douce. She was running away from Holtzer and taking time to meet her cousin, Josue. She was compelled to go and sit with Cerise, not just dream about her. Meeting her family in Provence – that alone was worth the trip. *And Tom was coming*. The two of them would be together in France.

And she thought she would be delving into the *history* of something awful. Something from the past that would give us insights into what was going on right now in Kentucky. She didn't understand that the dark things were *still there*. Her mom had explained that with entanglement, *still there* was only a construct of the brain, and things like dark-energy entities could be there or anywhere, just by being asked, pulled, imagined . . . or waiting for you.

And there was no way she could talk to her dad about this. Or even her mom, unless it was science stuff. Because it was too personal, because they would worry, because she needed a certain distance from them in her life.

And that made sense to me. But it was a lonely place to be.

She gave me a half-smile. 'Part of me just wanted to be on vacation in France. I don't do tourist things, but I was happy just walking, listening to people, sitting outside and having something to eat. I couldn't wait for Tom to get there.

'And I was in such a good place in my head that morning. I was worried – about Andi and Conor and little Patrick, that prick-face Holtzer. But that morning I pushed it all away. Took a bubble bath. Piled my hair on my head, put on this pretty red sundress I bought in a shop. It was incredibly expensive, so I put it on Mom's credit card. Because I wanted Tom to see me in that dress, and I thought about us going out to dinner and me wearing that dress.

'I had breakfast, and only ate one of the croissants, and I can't tell you how many times I thought of that basket of croissants with my eyes shut tight in that cave. I was so hungry. I promised myself that if I ever got out of there, I would go back to the hotel and sit outside and eat as many as I wanted. And that if they ran out, I'd just go from one place to another and eat croissants until I couldn't eat them anymore. I thought about food a lot. Even when I was scared. Which was pretty much always.

'My head hurt so bad. I passed out twice just crawling to the— Tom said it was a karst spring. An underground spring, like we have in Kentucky. Sometimes I'd just let my hand trail in the water, but I had to be careful. If I fell in . . . it looked deep. I didn't think I could get back out.

'And there was always something there, just out of sight, a presence that was *aware* of me. And I knew it watched me. And that sooner or later . . . it would get closer. But I slept a lot, deep and hard; I couldn't stay awake.'

'You had a bad concussion, Elle.'

'But then . . . it did come closer. Sometimes slow, creeping up on me. Like it was trying to seep into me. Or it would move fast and sudden. I don't know which was worse.

'Sometimes I couldn't wake up but . . . *it would be there*. Close to me, pressing in. I could smell it – and sense it. I would try so hard to stay awake, because I knew it was dangerous. And sometimes even now I'll just be . . . I don't know what triggers it, but just for a flash, I'm back down in that cave, and it's pressing close, and I want to scream and run into traffic and get hit by a car to make it all go away.'

She looked up. 'I'm sorry, Uncle Noah – I didn't mean to upset you.'

'It just means you want to escape. Keep Chewie with you, Elle.'

'I will. He knows when it happens. He pulls me out.' She frowned. 'It's odd, how sometimes I feel like I'm *there* but *not there*. And I see myself. Like I'm outside my body, watching. Tom showed me that picture of me on the Instagram account. Wearing that pretty red sundress. It's so odd to look at that and remember.

'I was going to that abandoned stone house, and it was so pretty, and it was so sad. Not dark, like that place where Pammie lived. Just sad. Like it had lost something. And I was walking toward it, and thinking I wanted to live in that little house and then I heard . . . well you know what I heard.'

'A baby crying.'

She nodded. 'It sounded so young and so sweet. Like a newborn baby cries. And I knew that surely the mother or the dad or somebody was there with the baby; it wouldn't be out in a field alone. But the baby kept on crying. It sounded like it was coming from inside the house, so I went in. And it was dusty and dirty and nobody had been in there for a long time. But I liked the way it looked inside. Simple. Mainly an old kitchen, and open space, and another room in the back. And there were stairs, but they didn't look safe. And the baby was settling into a whimper, but I couldn't place where it was. I was getting ready to go up the stairs, and then the baby stared wailing, and I knew it was in trouble, but the cries weren't coming from the house but from up the hill, so I ran outside, and I caught my dress on the doorway and it ripped, and I was running, running up that hill. And I didn't even see it. One minute I was running, and then I stumbled, and the ground was uneven, and then *I fell*.'

She took a breath. 'Cerise would come sometimes and sit beside me. She showed me the water – I was too messed up to find it on my own. And when she came, she had a sort of light she brought with her. And she showed me where her grandfather Forrest was. She showed me his bones, his jacket, his notebook. She put the notebook in my hands and said to hold on to it and to give it to *you*. Because you would find me. And I cried and said *when*. But she just said to trust her and to trust *you*. And that she would make things all right.

'She told me not to be afraid of Forrest's bones – he was long gone into another part of the timeline of his life, and he was OK and I would be OK too, and she was watching over me. She stroked my head and told me she would take me to a dream. And I went to a little farm, and she was there telling me who everyone was. I saw her grandfather when he was young. I saw him pick up a little girl and throw her up in the air and catch her, and give her a hug. And we went into a barn where there were lambs, and there were peacocks and feathers, and a big dog, and she said another big dog was coming to find me.'

Elle was crying hard now. She put her head on my shoulder and sobbed, and I knew she'd had enough for one day, and that there would be more dusky evenings on the bench in the arboretum.

I took her to a garden center and after that to a florist, and let her pick out everything she thought was pretty even though she told me she *only needed one flower*. But I didn't want to buy just one flower; I wanted to buy them all, and I got a bouquet of roses for Moira, and she got one for her mom, and one for her dad, and one for Tom, and she told me to buy flowers for my boys, and of course I did, wondering why I'd never thought of that before, and we bought so many flowers they were hard to fit into the car, so Chewie had to sit up front in her lap.

Elle had been in that cave five days. I would buy her every damn flower I could find.

FIFTY-ONE

When Perry and Chloe came to the house, hand in hand, they had a damped-down energy that put me on alert. Polite, smiling, a little bit off. I knew something was up.

They were expected. We had set up a Saturday night of drinks, talk, overall unwinding after all the shit we'd been through over the last few weeks. We'd sit outside on the pergola, in front of the fire that I'd been stoking gently for the last forty minutes, to create that perfect base of glowing red coals. I was good at fire building; good at keeping the fire going. It's an art.

The kids were upstairs – another hour of quiet time before they slept.

Moira and I were kind of buzzing. *Perry and Chloe as a couple.* Moira had made her famous spinach dip to spread on sweet brioche we had bakery bought. And I had made my holiday special: canned chestnuts, wrapped in bacon, liberally brushed with sweet chili sauce and baked on low heat until the bacon was chewy and the sauce became a caramelized glaze. Dude heaven on a baking sheet.

Perry kept a hand on Chloe's shoulder, and I liked their awareness of each other; the way they stayed close.

I had prepared three pitchers of margaritas, because sweet, sour and tequila on a Friday night after a long hard week was heaven on earth. Which is always where I want heaven to be.

As soon as Perry saw the tray of chestnuts, he picked one up and fed it to Chloe, who was spreading spinach dip on a chunk of brioche.

They were at the feeding-each-other stage, everything easy between them. Moira and I exchanged looks.

I filled the salt-rimmed glasses, and we all headed out to sit by the fire, plates of food in our laps. Moira was draped sideways, delicate, in a black cotton sundress that fastened around her neck and left her shoulders bare. Hair tied carelessly back in that way only Moira can pull off. Toenails painted deep blood red, silvery ankle bracelet glinting in the firelight. Shoes optional.

'Music,' I said.

I hadn't gone so far as to put out fake rock speakers, but the sound quality was pretty good – Chris Isaak covering 'Can't Help Falling in Love'.

Moira rolled her eyes at me, lips smeared with traces of red lipstick that was now mostly on the edge of her glass, mixed with salt.

Chloe frowned at Perry. 'You told him?'

'Certainly not.'

'It was Elle,' I said. 'The first night I met her she told me that she was conceived to this song. She told me a lot about the two of you while we drove out to that house.'

'I don't even want to know how she managed to get that into the conversation,' Chloe said, giving Perry a look. He didn't see because his hands were over his face.

But Perry was laughing. A little bit of outrage theater. Kind of . . . forced. Had Moira noticed? I didn't think so. She was enjoying her weekend off, making quick time with her margarita, so I refilled all their glasses and went inside for the second pitcher that was in the freezer – kind of crammed in sideways, but my luck had held and nothing had spilled.

As I hefted the ice-cold pitcher, I had a sense of watching myself as I walked through the kitchen, through the open French doors that led outside; a feeling of how much I loved this moment and a sense of dread. Something was off. Something life-changing.

They waited until everyone was well fed and tipsy. I had stopped drinking after the first margarita, but nobody seemed to notice. I watched them, all three of them, as if I wasn't really there. Just glad to be sitting with them, feeding them, filling their glasses, keeping the fire at a perfect pitch of crackling glow and flame.

And then Chloe and Perry exchanged looks.

As always, it was Chloe who jumped in.

'Noah, I've found some results we need to discuss.'

Moira froze. Put her glass down, changed her mind, picked it back up and drained it.

'Let's hear it,' I said.

'You know that I identified the chemical signature of several dark-energy threads – one that runs through that house and the school. That followed those children and is still out there. Perry has already done four exorcisms in both. It's not gone. It ebbs and flows.

But. These things are always out there; it's basic science. Like germs on the countertop.'

Not everyone would see it that way, but I nodded.

'There's another thread. Similar but not the same signature. Another dark-energy presence that is *scary strong.*'

I frowned. No wonder they looked worried. 'Where is it? What is it about this one that worries you?'

Chloe looked at Perry. He kneaded his thigh with a fist, a nervous habit I knew very well. 'It's Sasha. And it's very heavy around *you*, Noah.'

'Around me how?'

Chloe leaned forward. 'From within. It seems . . . it seems to be inside you.'

It hit me in the gut. I don't know what I was expecting, but it wasn't that.

'But you said you tested for this kind of thing. With the other signature. That you tried to find it inside the kids and the teachers, and you never found anything. Nothing from within, I mean. It was just always . . . around them.'

Chloe nodded.

'But you found some kind of thread of a dark entity *inside* me?'

'I did, yes. By accident really. I picked it up when I was testing at the school – the lockers, remember? When I slid in the water and fell on my ass? And when I picked up the traces in the locker . . . I also picked up traces within you.'

'*You didn't say anything*?'

'Noah, I was still trying to figure this shit out. I thought it might have been some kind of one-off. But it was on my radar. I thought it was some kind of anomaly, some kind of mistake. And while the other threads were all through the old section of the school . . . Sasha was mainly in Mrs Garcia's classroom. And . . . in you. And two other times I caught it when it registered on my gear. So I've been tracking three chemical signatures; two are very similar, but the Sasha one is strongest. The other two are distinct and different, so much so that I named them.'

'You fucking named them?'

'I did. The first one *Child Predator*, because it was in the school. And . . . *Beast*.'

'Naming them is horrifying,' I said. 'It gives them power.'

'Naming them is smart. Naming, organizing, researching. You

want to fight these things, you have to understand them with more than legends and whispers.'

'So when I was going after Sasha, it was going after me.'

'*Hunting* you,' Chloe said.

'It's inside me. A form of possession. That's what you're saying.'

'Yes.' Chloe nodded. 'Obviously, it hasn't been measured before. At first, I thought it might be just an after-effect of your possession as a child. Like a scar?'

I looked at Perry. 'What do you think?'

'I'm not done talking,' Chloe said. 'It's been escalating with a stronger and stronger presence.'

I sat back hard in my chair. 'Fuck.'

'It's growing. Every time you were exposed to any of the dark entities, *this one* grew. In very small increments. And then it would dip, then you'd have several exposures, and then it would grow again. Like your body is fighting it off. Look, I explained all this – you know this is some kind of entanglement on a molecular level. But the fact that it can be distinguished from you, I think that's good news.'

I sputtered; kind of a laugh. 'Good news *how*?'

'Because it's separate. Not . . . integrated. The problem is that it's growing.'

And I remembered what I'd told Tom about what was happening with Elle. I could hear my own voice echoing in my mind, explaining how her body remembered even though her brain had blocked things out of her conscious memory. And while that was good for survival in the moment, it was a problem later. That not remembering could be harder. It's hard to deal with your fears and face them if your mind locks them away. Hard to deal with possession if you don't know you're possessed. I'd thought I was talking about Elle. I'd also been talking about me.

Moira dragged her chair close to mine and held my hand. 'How do we get rid of it?' she asked.

'Moira, you don't just get rid of stuff like this.'

'Of course you do, Noah.' Perry's tone was bracing, which made me feel worse. 'Chloe just said your body is *fighting* this. You treat patients for infection all the time. Sometimes the infections keep a footprint and come back. So you've got an ongoing, dark-entity infection.'

'Virulent,' I said.

'I'm afraid so.'

Chloe's matter-of-fact look was something to hang on to. 'I think we can get rid of it. I have an idea; I've talked it over with Perry, and we've made a plan.'

'What's the plan?' Moira asked.

'A treatment. Like the ones you do. You invented this, Noah – you know how powerful it is. But I want to try something new – for the skull brain, the heart brain and the gut brain. ESWT – extra-corporeal shockwave therapy. They use it to break up kidney stones and gallstones. They use it for athletes to heal injuries; they use it for neuropathy.'

I nodded. 'I've had my eye on it for musculoskeletal and neuro issues. It's been around since the eighties; it's non-invasive and promising as hell.'

'Isn't that what we're using on Tash?' Moira asked. She squeezed my hand.

Chloe leaned forward with a smile. 'Exactly. And, Noah, you told me how well it was working for your dog, and it got me to thinking. Instead of the electric currents—'

'How does it actually work? Physically, what does it do?' Moira was looking at Chloe, who bent close, refilled Moira's margarita glass, and curled up sideways in her chair.

'It's transcutaneous,' I said. 'It goes through the skin. High-energy acoustic waves in either a diffused or a focused pattern. We talked about this before we went ahead with Tash, right?'

'Yeah,' she said. 'You researched the hell out of it.'

Chloe smiled at her. An encouraging smile. 'Think of it as a healing compass. Waking the body up; energizing it. It triggers mechano-transduction – *mechanical energy* – causing changes in the cellular skeleton, initiating a reaction of the cell core – like the release of mRNA. Nudging all of the cell structures – mitochondria, endoplasmic reticulum, intracellular vesicles . . . The enzymatic response initiates a revved-up healing process.'

Moira shut her eyes very tight then opened them. 'What's mRNA? I know I've heard of it. Why do you say it like it's some magical thing?'

Chloe laughed. 'Because it is some magical thing. It's an antigen – the cells know it, recognize it, and it stimulates an immune response. For healing. They use it to make vaccines. But this will be safer; it'll use the body's own cells, no foreign substances, no toxins. It just ignites what's already there.'

Moira bit her lip. 'So you're saying it could work like a non-invasive vaccine for possession?'

I gave my beautiful wife a sideways smile. 'Out of the mouth of hot babes.'

She frowned at me and gave Chloe a hard look. 'Intellectually I understand this, but you're talking about my husband, who is right here, who is OK as far as I can see. We've seen what can happen with the Enlightenment Protocol with electrical currents. *Magical things*. And terrible things.'

'Yeah, that's pretty much the definition of science,' Chloe said.

I kept hold of Moira's hand. 'So we use the shockwave treatment to hit all the neurons of my brain. Heal the mind, heal the body. And that third thing doctors and psychiatrists are afraid to name. Healing the spirit; healing the soul.'

'Exactly,' Chloe said. 'I think it's safer and stronger and smarter all around. Because it's regenerative medicine.'

I looked at my terrified wife. 'It's not scary, Moira. This is the endgame in healing. This is the goal. It's just a sound-wave treatment – they use it on dogs, horses, cats with injured joints or arthritis, yeah? Point it like a laser; fifteen minutes of pulses. One to three treatments. Two hundred and fifty bucks each if you're not getting ripped off. A thousand dollars each if you are. And the stimulation causes the body to actually heal and regenerate the joint. The bone. The tissue.'

'Do they use it on the human brain?'

I squeezed Moira's hand. 'They're using it for people with MS, Huntington's. ALS, stroke. Some of this is still very much in the research phase. The point is to heal the neural pathways in the brain that control muscle movement. Obviously, that's where I have the most hope for my own patients.'

'I want to do this in concert with all three of your brains,' Chloe said. 'Look at the incredible results you had with electric current in just the skull brain. Multiply the possibilities by three – using sound waves to target the neural connections that cradle all of these parts of the body and tie them together.'

'Which means side effects times three,' Moira said. She was losing the color in her cheeks, lines of worry around her mouth.

'*Regenerative medicine*,' Chloe said. '*Healing* to the power of three. There's nothing intrusive, no cutting, no toxic drugs. Just . . . energy.'

'Everything is energy,' Moira said. 'Good things and bad things – it's all energy.'

I frowned. 'The side effects I've studied seem to come from poor handling of the equipment.'

'What are they?'

'Rupture and fracture *rarely*; bleeding. Again, rare.'

'Rupture? Fracture? Your brain, Noah?'

I leaned back in my chair. 'Look, this is a great idea to up our game on the Enlightenment Protocol. It'll be the usual snarl of what's being done and regulations for what's going to be research, but that I can handle. But for me personally? No. Hell no. I'm too vulnerable for *any* kind of treatment. I've ruled it out. It *will* go wrong for me. And it won't be pretty.'

Perry and I exchanged looks. We'd been there together when it had gone bad.

Chloe waved it away. 'I've studied all your results and they're damn good. And you've learned a shitload since then, Noah – perfecting, fine-tuning, calibrating. Right?'

She looked at me. I stared at her.

'And I want to combine the radial, for large areas, and the focused, to target specific areas. I think we go broad and we go deep. Perry will be right there, and I'll run the protocol. We'll buy the machines; I've got them picked out. We'll slather you with gel and just point the laser.'

I stood up. Moved the screen away from the fire; added a log. All three of them watching me.

I stood behind Moira with my hands on her shoulders. She was trembling.

'You have to call it, Noah,' Perry said. 'We can just keep an eye on this. Not decide right now. You seem to be doing OK. But I like the idea of fighting it. And I don't like knowing that it's growing. Not treating it may be riskier than treating it.'

'I tend to go on the advice of *if it ain't broke, don't fix it.*' Moira caught my hand and looked up at me. 'You're fine like you are. I love you *exactly* the way you are.' She took a deep breath. 'Only *you* know if you need this, Noah,' Moira said. 'Base it on intuition. You're the fucking neurosurgeon.'

Those three words sounded right together. Like haiku. *The fucking neurosurgeon.*

And I knew what I wanted to do.

I headed to the kitchen; dug in a junk drawer where we kept loose change. Found a quarter and headed back outside. Flipped it.

It came up tails.

Moira looked at me. 'Seriously?'

'Seriously.'

'And?'

'Looks like I'm doing the treatment.'

'Do you want to flip that coin again?' Moira asked.

That pretty much broke the party up. 'Sleep on it and we'll talk,' Perry said.

'Bullshit,' Chloe told me. 'Let's get it done.'

Moira grabbed Chloe's arm. 'Why are you so damn sure of yourself?'

Chloe seemed to get very small. She gave Moira a gentle smile. 'Because as hard as it is to have this dark stuff entangled with me, all around me, I can't even imagine what it must be like to have it *inside*.'

I stopped Perry on his way out the door; motioned him into my office. 'What about you, Perry? Is Sasha inside you too?'

'No, but I didn't track him down and burn him up like you did.' He sat on the corner of my desk. I still couldn't get over seeing him in worn-out jeans. 'Chloe has tracked Sasha around me. As well as other entities. She's naming them; cataloging them – it's weirdly interesting.'

'So it's just me.' I took a breath.

'The kind of work we do, Noah, comes with consequences. We've always known that. And you've been exposed since you were a child. Exposed again and again. You've been waging an ongoing fight with this for years. But this kind of thing drains you. It comes with a cost. And I will remind you that I've had several Enlightenment treatments. They affected me profoundly. They strengthened me spiritually. And they strengthened me physically.'

'You've always watched out for me, Perry. Since I was eleven. Kept me away from this as much as you could, because you knew it was particularly dangerous *to me*. Do you really think it's safe for someone like me to have the treatment? Because clearly there's something wrong about me; something that makes me vulnerable to turning . . . turning dark.'

His look was grim. 'Yes. I think you should. But understand,

Noah, there's nothing *wrong* with you. There's something right with you, something powerful, something . . . extraordinary. *You've been targeted since you were a child.* That means you're dangerous to these entities, and it pulls them to you. That's what it has always meant.

'What's the real issue here, Noah? A fear that the treatment is going to strengthen dark things inside you? Or that you don't trust yourself?'

'Both, Perry. Both.'

FIFTY-TWO

Moira was clearing up in the kitchen, dropping things because she was watching me. 'This scares me, Noah. This scares me so bad. Our life is good now. I love you so much. I don't want you to change. I don't want some experimental treatment to fuck you up.'

'It's inside me, Moira. And if it's getting worse, things might not stay good. I might not be safe around you and the boys. You know that's something I've always worried about.'

She shook her head and wouldn't look at me.

I sighed. 'Maybe I'll take Tash for a walk. Or maybe . . . maybe I'll actually just—'

Moira put the dip in the fridge and turned around. 'Are you thinking of going to a hotel tonight, stepping away from the family, to sulk and keep us safe?'

'I don't know how to answer that.'

She dropped the dish towel into the sink and grabbed my arm. 'Sulk is a mean word. *I'm sorry* – that didn't come out the way I meant. Look, Noah, I know when you go off that way it's because you're worried that you are the problem, and you bring the threat. And that you need space to think and are feeling . . . protective. Of me and the boys.'

'Don't forget the dog and the cat,' I said softly, kissing the top her head. She was so little. The boys would be taller than she was in two years, three tops.

She put a hand on my chest. 'Thank you for including the cat.'

I took her hand. Kissed her palm.

She tilted her head sideways. 'I have a better idea, if you're up for it.'

'Which is?'

She leaned into me. 'Come to bed.'

She caught my look and smiled, then ran up the stairs. I was right behind her, hand on her ass. We locked the bedroom door. No cats. No dogs. No kids.

We slid into bed, and she wrapped her arms around me. Kissed me hard. Stripped me bare. And we had drunken, glorious sex.

Call it processing our feelings. Call it anything you want. If you want to think this was just our way of dealing with the issues life throws in your face, well, duh.

Works for me.

FIFTY-THREE

I had not had enough to drink the night before to have a hangover, which is more than you could say for Moira. I woke up early; let her sleep. Made coffee, omelets and muffins with the boys. Much as I missed Tom being around, I loved thinking of he and Elle together.

Bless Chloe for having a plan before she gave me the news.

I had, after all, created the Enlightenment Protocol to heal and to help people just like me. I'd created it for me.

I'd never understood before, the way that my patients felt. Intellectual knowledge and compassion don't get you there the way living it does. Something lethal and other inside. Cancer. Tumor. Emotions, cognition, everything going haywire with disease or injury; the horrible sense of having no control.

I wanted it fixed. I wanted it out. I didn't want it inside me like some malevolent ivy, creeping through my body, growing dark blooms. And hadn't I always felt it there? The ongoing tension had kept me in a chokehold since I was eleven years old.

And what had my protocol patients said? Over and over again. Like it's something inside them that wants to take them over. That wants to grow.

I wasn't going to be afraid of the treatment anymore. There was no room for that fear. It had been replaced by the terror of that other thing inside me, entangling and growing. And now I understood why some of my patients doubled down and endured every treatment out there, no matter how bad the pain, no matter how hopeless the odds.

And I wasn't going to sit on my sad-sack ass and let this have its way with me. I wanted it out.

FIFTY-FOUR

In order to survive and focus during the prep for this treatment, I had to let go of the roller coaster of hope. Hope is a jittery thing – it lacks practicality, it distracts, it offers soothing delusion. Letting go of it was a surprising relief. Instead, I opened myself to the steady wisdom and wise, measured energy of purpose.

And I thought about watching Tash go through her third and final treatment, watching her be sore for a day or two, then slowly and gradually stop limping, sleeping ever more peacefully without waking up in the night restless and panting, and I lost my fear.

Chloe rounded up the machinery with the same enthusiasm, she told me, that she had on the Chanel website, and wasn't life cool? I kept the brochures on my office desk at home. Acoustic energy – laser-targeted, concentrated sound waves. *Don't just heal the pain. Treat the condition.*

I kept my thoughts in the private red notebook in my desk.

The side effects that worried me were swelling, neuralgia, paresthesia. The biggest risk? Bleeding, blood clots and fucking stroke, which could destroy me. I knew I was pushing the limits. Both in the kinds of treatments and going for broke with the gut, heart and skull brains. But orchestrating all three of them was such a powerful idea, I couldn't turn away. Risky?

Hell yes.

Ready?

I was.

And in truth, my mind was racing ahead. Using this treatment for MS, healing stroke damage. Relieving pain without drugs. Parkinson's, Huntington's, dementia, muscular dystrophy. Autoimmune issues that I saw every week. All the fucked-up diseases that tortured my patients where there was not fuck all I could do to help. I could make their lives better. I could ease them through. I could explain what was going on. But heal them?

The possibilities were endless. That alone would be reason enough to have the treatment.

If dark matter wanted to own me, it was going to have a fight on its hands. And the whisper came out of nowhere all around me. The kind of whisper I tried not to hear but sometimes do.

We owns you already.

And if things went very bad, well, I'm a doctor, which comes with certain advantages. A vial and syringe locked away in the safe of my office, along with a letter of love to my wife and my sons. A humane death – I could easily inject myself.

I was ready.

FIFTY-FIVE

We'd located our NGO, The Enlightenment Project, Inc, in the Distillery District, a downtown-adjacent, up-and-coming part of the city that was moving from abandoned warehouses, railroad tracks, weedy lots and small businesses built out of cinder blocks, to up and coming chi-chi. It trended young. It trended university. And we had the entire top floor of a warehouse where bourbon used to age, sleeping quietly in wooden casks. Like vampires in a coffin.

Below us was a coffee shop, a cider mill and bar food restaurants that went in and out of business. Across the parking lot, a tiny and ridiculously popular bar, a pizza place and an upscale tavern. We'd had no idea when we'd rented the space how popular it was going to get. It was mobbed on the weekends; by late afternoon there would be nowhere to park. During the week, it was quiet and easy. Not far down the street on the other side of the road was the Manchester Hotel, where we hosted our 'guests' coming to town for the Enlightenment Protocol.

We used the hotel as a kind of hospitality oasis that relaxed them, spoiled them and got them in a quiet frame of mind, and that did make a difference. They were well fed – dinner if they liked at the Granddam restaurant, touted as an Appalachian dining hall, where they thanked you for being *mighty polite to plan ahead,* if you made a reservation, and we did, so our 'guests' could eat woodfired lamb chops or braised boar, though I liked the peach chicken for lunch. Perry and I were planning to check out their Lost Palm bar some night, because we couldn't resist the idea of a rooftop bar based on 1960s South Florida.

Much as I liked the idea, I didn't think we could hit the bar tonight after my treatment, in the way I'd taken Tash to Dairy Queen for a pup cup after hers. Mainly I was hoping to be steady on my feet without a brain bleed or stroke.

It was a Tuesday night. The bars were open but sluggish, the parking lot had multiple options and lights blazed on the top-floor location of our NGO into the dusky evening where it was already dark at seven fifteen p.m.

I got there early. Went through the MRI setup with Carl, the hospital tech I always worked with. He moonlighted for excellent pay as our MRI technician and had signed a confidentiality agreement. I think what he liked most was being close to the bourbon. I was always looking for bottles of rare, high-end bourbon that were sold on the black market to the wealthy – though most of them were fakes, which didn't bother him. It kept him happy and available at all hours.

I'd fondly set Horace aside – my beloved netting that fit my patients like a bathing cap, full of ceramic conductors for electrical currents. We had three brand-new toys for radial and focused shockwave treatment. Chloe and Carl and I had had a blast experimenting with them in the warehouse space, mastering the technique by watching training videos from the manufacturer's website.

The machines cost thirty thousand dollars each. One had ceramic elements with a concave surface for simultaneous, brief, high-voltage pulses that expanded to generate a pressure pulse, allowing us to create a precisely focused pulse with deep penetration. That one was for the gut brain. We'd use gel pads, instead of slicking me down with lube. The other two machines were used like a magic wand for diffuse shockwaves. Those were actually the ones that were painful. One to target my heart, the other my brain. The brochures promised minimal pain, and gentle and quiet machinery so as to reduce the flight instinct of horses, dogs, cats and neurosurgeons.

Three machines meant we could do all three treatments in concert, Carl and Chloe working side by side. Each machine sat on a wheeled stand, at chest level, with an iPad holder and a screen.

I would undergo the treatment while my head was inside the MRI machine. Tricky to maneuver, but we'd worked through the logistics and done dummy runs. Because I wanted to chart this. I wanted it on record. I wanted to see exactly how it affected my brain, and I wanted that mapped out for study later.

Or, worst case, it would be something concrete that Carl could show an ER physician so they'd know exactly where I was fucked up.

FIFTY-SIX

I focused on Perry, sitting beside me, bringing a sense of calm and ease into the top floor of the cavernous warehouse. Chloe and Carl had already begun, confident, busy with the machinery, as I lay on the gurney of the MRI and kept my attention on Perry. Because it hurt, the radial shockwaves that Carl handled. The targeted ones, Chloe's side of things, didn't. They'd offered to sedate me, but neither Perry nor I thought that was a good idea. And Chloe had her other equipment set up, recording chemical signatures and the presence of dark entities. Sasha.

'How dangerous do you think this treatment is?' I asked Perry, hiding a smile. I cocked my head to one side. 'On a scale of one to ten? I'd go with eleven.'

'You bastard,' Perry said softly. But then he smiled. And began. Quietly, steadily, and with confidence and gravitas. If I was prepped and ready, so was he.

'You understand, Noah, that this treatment is the physical part that ignites the thinking and knowledgeable neural pathways of your body, your gut brain, heart brain and skull brain . . . to regenerate and heal. But also to *cast out*.'

I shut my eyes for just a moment. Casting out sounded exactly right for the things that held me in a chokehold.

'Along with the brain and the body, there is of course the third thing, the elusive thing, the quantum spirituality, that wraps all of this together – that is *you*.'

The words *quantum spirituality* echoed in my head.

'It's time to harness your body to awareness and a fight. And as we ignite the mechanics of the body, we must also address the quantum consciousness, which goes hand and hand with your quantum spirituality, because you're not just mind and body; you are mind, body and conscious soul. So I will perform an exorcism, as your *spiritual* call to arms, and Chloe and Carl will conduct the ESWT, so that your brains can orchestrate a *physical* call to arms. This will be a concert of healing. Does that make sense?'

It did.

'I'll be using a new exorcism, with words I wrote myself, drawing on experience, the texts I love and intuition. You'll allow it?'

I gave him a sideways smile. 'Nothing better.'

'There are three parts to this, Noah. A prayer of protection. A prayer of transformation. A prayer of restoration. Let's begin.

'We are here with you, Noah, to address the primal injury and the primal trauma that you have suffered and are still suffering. It's time to bring this to a close, and free you from this spiritual attack and entanglement. And to light a match to this evil dark-energy entity that grows in a voracious fog around and inside you. It's time to burn away this envious possession and entanglement that burrows hard, hungry to consume you. Hungry to be you. We will end this dark and deadly trespass that has no place within you. We will show no mercy upon this entity of energy and matter that feeds and tries to consume the light of anything that is good. And we will cast it out and bring you home to the implicate order of consciousness and matter, to the memory that is a knowing, of your fully healed self.'

A prayer of disentanglement, I thought, as the words echoed inside me with a resonance that felt like something I'd always known.

Perry blew three soft breaths across my face. *Exsufflare* – cleansed. Then three more breaths – *insufflare*. In protection reborn.

That was my last conscious thought. And then I was gone. Into a dream. My first lucid dream, something I had researched, discussed with patients, but never really understood. I'd had no concept of how powerful they were. Until now.

A vision wrapped in a dream.

FIFTY-SEVEN

I was back in France, in the lavender field Elle had traipsed through in her pretty sundress before she disappeared just past the old stone house, and up the gentle slope of the rocky, grass-studded hillside. Where I'd sat on a rock and contemplated the slender mouth of the cave. The body of Chloe's Uncle Forrest, at rest for so long, and his notebook there for her to find.

I could feel the sun hot on my shoulders; smell the lavender that was heady and pungent and just a little sweet. And I felt shaky, overwhelmed with sensory overload. I crumpled to the ground, flat on my back. The sun was fading, darkness was falling and the moon was extraordinarily bright – full and round and way too big.

And then . . . *lightning*. It hit me full in the chest, and I gasped. I felt no pain; I felt . . . amazing. Like being hit by a bolt of pure energy, an energy my body welcomed. And then another hit, to my belly, and a pause, and I felt warm and peaceful but alert and aware, with an edgy *knowing* that made me eager for the next hit, which went right through my head, alighting my brain with an impossible-to-describe surge of wellbeing that flowed through me like a warm, salty wave.

I lay still, catching my breath. And I heard strange noises and got to my feet, because something was coming for me, out of the darkness, and I had a moment of pure terror until I saw that it was Tash, running straight toward me. I dropped to my knees and hugged her, and she gave me kisses and whimpers, and it was as if she'd been looking for me for so long and found me at last. I sat cross-legged on the ground, and she put her head in my lap, and it made sense to me that she would be here. She'd had three treatments already, and I was only just catching up. Had it been like this for her? This incredible feeling of everything being perfect in the world?

That and a pup cup from Dairy Queen must have made for a very good day.

And then it came again, a trio of lightning strikes, hitting both me and my dog, and I was thinking, *Incredible*, and just before things got dark again I could hear my own voice. *Jesus Christ, this could be addictive.* And somebody laughing from a long way away. It sounded a lot like Chloe.

And then the laughter faded as I lay back in the grass, dog at my side.

'Couldn't have done it without you, Tashie.'

I stroked her head and studied the improbable night sky, full of stars and moonlight, in this lavender field in Provence, thinking of Forrest Strickler, finding his way here to the love of his life.

Every detail was vivid: the ground beneath me, the soft wind, Tash settled close to me, warm and soft. And me, knowing that this moment was real and also a dream.

FIFTY-EIGHT

Two nights later we made it to the rooftop bar. My version of the pup cup. Because as it turned out . . . the shockwave therapy was a really good idea.

When the ESWT treatments ignited my defense system, and my body was on fire with healing, it saw the dark entangled matter as *other*, as *invader*. And cleared every bit of it away.

I didn't need Chloe's calibrations to tell me this, though she said it was gone, and of that chemical signature there was no trace. In truth, it was Mr Timothy who provided the final confirmation. That morning, he had curled up on my feet, purring loudly, while I drank my morning coffee. And I know now that he saw it, the dark-matter entity, and it wasn't me he was wary of but that. There is wisdom in paying attention to the opinions of cats.

FIFTY-NINE

I walked softly today, still a bit achy, but Tash, well into the second week after her third and final shockwave treatment, walked beside me with a spring in her step like a puppy. And as I'd shortened and slowed my steps to hers over the last few years, today she slowed her steps to mine. The lucid dream we'd shared in the field in Provence was a connection and a secret between us. It had stayed with me, bringing an acute awareness of brilliant illumination, a change in how I saw light. Colors were more vibrant, more alive; magnolia trees with waxy green leaves, red gardenias in pots. Colors the same and colors so different. Colors so *intense*.

For much of my professional life, I'd known and paid service to the integration of the physical body, the brain, the consciousness . . . the spirit. But now. Now I *knew*. I'd lived it. And pulling all of these things together had worked beyond my wildest dreams.

Sasha hadn't been able to penetrate my mind but had slowly entwined itself into my body. Holding me in its grip and killing me slowly. And when Perry had loosened that hold, and exorcized it, the tension that had been with me since I was eleven, that had become such a part of me I didn't even know it was there – that weight was off my shoulders too. The exorcism I'd endured as a child hadn't been enough. It had always kept a foothold inside me. I'd had no idea how heavy that was, how exhausting, how draining. Until now – now I was free of the chokehold, the sinuous snaking of dark matter that had lived like a literal weight upon my heart.

Like Tash, I looked younger. And both of us slept better at night.

Just as we rounded the corner and turned back toward the house, my phone pinged. A text.

Moira no doubt – letting me know she was home. It was Friday night, and we were taking the boys to the Lexington Diner for burgers. I would get a bacon bourbon burger, with tiny onion straws mashed between beef, bacon, pepper jack cheese and hot bourbon barbecue sauce. It would come with a wedge of dill pickle and a massive portion of fries glistening with salt. Moira and I would have the jalapeno margaritas; watch the boys hold giant hamburgers with both hands. I lived for nights like this.

Tash moved off the sidewalk to sniff something she found peculiar, while I fished the phone out of my pocket to read the text.

Looking forward.

Shit.

'Let's go, Tash.'

We ran.

SIXTY

Moira's car was in the driveway. On the porch was a giant cardboard box, torn open, chunks of Styrofoam packing and plastic wrapping jumbled in and out of the box. Addressed to Vaughn and Marcus Archer, care of Noah and Moira Archer, and Tash The Dog followed by three exclamation points.

Almost all of our names. They hadn't reckoned with the cat. I looked at the return address – the startup company in Texas that Mrs Garcia had told me about. I'd tracked it down to a virtual address service.

Sasha in my house. With my children. With my wife.

Rage-fueled adrenalin welled up inside me along with a sick nausea, and I was caught in the intense cycle of stress hormones and chemical reactions pouring through my body, fueled by my thoughts and fears. I told myself to control it. To bank it down. Funnel it into rescue so I didn't scare the kids.

The door was ajar, and Tash was barreling in ahead of me, barking, running in circles and losing her shit. I could relate.

Marcus and Vaughn were on the couch, wide-eyed and thrilled, and Moira had a bloody towel wrapped around the back of her hand.

Tash was barking hysterically at Sasha, who was strewn across the floor in plastic-wrapped parts. Mr Timothy, fur standing tall and swollen with rage, was emitting menacing growls. He'd captured Sasha and positioned himself between Sasha and Moira and the kids. I was really starting to like this cat.

I went to Moira and unwrapped the towel from her hand.

'I was trying to pick up that robot thing, and Mr Timothy bit me,' she said, sounding stunned.

'Vaughn, go get the first-aid kit out of the upstairs bathroom. Don't get between that robot and the cat.'

'What if he bites me too?'

'He won't.'

'Because he knows who's boss?'

'Because I know who's boss.'

I ran warm water in a bowl, added soap and swished it around, then led Moira into the kitchen, settling her on to a bar stool at the counter. I guided her hand into the water, and she watched it pool pink then red with blood.

I stroked Moira's cheek. 'I know your feelings are hurt, but don't be mad at Mr Timothy – he was keeping you safe.'

'And now we have Sasha in our living room.' Her voice was tight.

'I'll take care of it.'

'Are we still going out for burgers?' Marcus asked.

'Yes,' I said. 'Run upstairs and get ready.'

Marcus thundered up the stairs.

I grabbed a pair of reading glasses off the counter, picked Moira's hand up, took a look and winced. 'That's a nasty bite. When was your last tetanus shot?'

'Four months ago.'

'Right. The garden shears.' I pressed her hand gently back into the water. 'Keep it soaking.'

'It hurts like *hell*.'

'Lidocaine with antibiotics.' I was thinking out loud.

'That box was addressed to our kids. It listed all of our names. Except Mr Timothy.'

'Think of him as our secret weapon.'

'We're going to have to talk to the boys about this.'

'We tell them the truth with an upbeat protective spin.'

She nodded. 'This is so old school. Usually this stuff comes over the internet. What do we do with that thing?'

'I'll take care of it.'

'How?'

'First I'm going to bandage up your hand, then I'm going to grab Sasha by the throat and get rid of him. Give me an hour and a half, maybe two. It'll be a late dinner, but that's OK. And while I do that, I want you to put a plastic bag around your hand to keep the bandage dry and take a long, hot bubble bath. Have a glass of wine, then get ready to go. Special request: wear that new black sweater. I'll come back as soon as I can, and we'll pile in the car and go out for late-night burgers, and you and I will have margaritas. One for me and two for you. Tomorrow morning you'll sleep late and I'll make breakfast with the boys. But before all that, give Mr Timothy a surprise can of tuna to reward him for taking care of business.'

'He can split it with Tash.'

'Tash is going with me.'

'God, Noah. This thing scares me. My hands are shaking. It makes me crazy with anxiety.'

'Anxiety isn't a psychological problem; it's a survival reaction. You're doing fine.'

Moira rested her head on my chest, and I pulled her close. 'Thank you for being you,' she whispered.

SIXTY-ONE

Once again, I gathered up premium long matches and fire-starter sticks, while contemplating the future purchase of a blowtorch. I triple wrapped Sasha in large black garbage bags. I crammed all the packing material back into the cardboard box and shoved everything into the trunk of my Audi. Tash was right there with me, and when I opened the door of the car, she jumped in ahead of me and settled in the passenger's seat.

'Good to have you along,' I said.

I turned the music up loud and headed out to Jacobson Park.

It was full dark by the time I had Sasha in a melting blaze. The firepit was circled by four Adirondack chairs painted Mediterranean blue. They were new. I was settled in one of the chairs, legs crossed broadly, feeling the warmth of the fire on my face, Tash curled up, resting her head on my feet. We watched the flames leap and settle.

I told myself I was safe now, but I knew the fear would always be with me, the *knowing* of how dark entities could infiltrate and entangle. Fear was survival and resilience a hard job. I was the healer, the researcher and the one who wrestled with the dark. A scientist with no religion, but a spiritual side I'd been forced to accept, no matter how much it scared me.

And I was content, sitting side by side with Tash, in this moment that felt so very sweet.

Some things you have to live with. Some things will not let you go. But if these dark-matter entities were aware of me . . . I was aware of them. And as far as I was concerned, it was *game on.*

Fuck all y'all, I thought.

I stroked Tash's head, staring into the fire, contemplating caves with symbols and the language of mathematics that called up a powerful exorcism.

Milton Keynes UK
Ingram Content Group UK Ltd.
UKHW032316161024
449721UK00006B/73